BULL RUNNING FOR GIRLS

By
ALLYSON BIRD

SECOND PAPERBACK EDITION – 2013

JournalStone
San Francisco

JOURNALSTONE
YOUR LINK TO ARTISTIC TALENT

FIRST PAPERBACK EDITION – 2008

Screaming Dreams
13 Warn's Terrace, Abertysswg, Rhymney Gwent, NP22 5AG, South
Wales, UK

Copyright © Allyson Bird 2008

JournalStone books may be ordered through booksellers or by contacting:

JournalStone
www.journalstone.com
www.journal-store.com

Original Cover illustration Copyright © Vincent Chong 2008

ISBN: *978-1-940161-14-3*   *(sc)*
ISBN: *978-1-940161-15-0*   *(ebook)*

JournalStone rev. date: December 13, 2013

Library of Congress Control Number: 2013952622

Printed in the United States of America

Cover Design: *Denise Daniel*
Cover Art: *Vincent Chong*

Edited by: *Joel Kirkpatrick*

To the memory of my mother Laura Shakespeare. And my sister Sylvia Insley. I miss you.

"To live is to war with trolls In the holds of the heart and mind; To write is to hold Judgement Day over the self." Henrik Ibsen.

Acknowledgements

I'd like to thank Steve Upham for first publishing *Bull Running for Girls* and for his encouragement and enthusiasm. Thank you to Vincent Chong for the wonderful original cover and support from the beginning.

To the other editors who have all introduced my prose to the world, Sarah Dobbs and Lee Harris—amongst others. Thank you to Andrew Hook in the discussion of The Silk Road.

Almost all the stories in the collection are original except for: "Blood in Madness Ran" published in Hunger 2006. "Wings of Night" first appeared in Hub 2007. "Shadow upon Shadow" appeared in Black Petals 2008. "Dissolution" was published in *The Third BHF Book of Horror Stories* 2008. "The Silk Road" appeared in The British Fantasy Society publication—*New Horizons* 2008.

Contents

The Caul Bearer

"They were alive with a teeming horde of shapes swimming inward towards the town: and even at my vast distance and in my single moment of perception I could tell that the bobbing heads and flailing arms were alien and aberrant in a way scarcely to be expressed or consciously formulated." The Shadow over Innsmouth by H. P. Lovecraft.

Like the webfoot cockle women trudging out of a Dylan Thomas black, bandaged night, the flither girls made their way across Robin Hood's bay (or Baytown as the locals called it) to find limpets to use for bait on long lines. This wasn't a fishing village in Wales but it could have been, with the small fisher houses and the narrow, cobbled lanes in between. There were nets to be mended, lying strewn around the cottage entrances as if to capture land animals as they entered and left. Nets, stretched like cauls over the windows and on the front of the walls. A strong odour hung in the air from the fish that had been left to dry. Part of the wild village had already fallen into the sea, demolished by the northeasterly winter storms. Brid's mother had told her of the houses on King Street that had leaned over the cliff and tumbled into the sea a few decades ago.

Bridgette Moorsom was a caul bearer. She had been born with a caul over her face and the midwife had pressed a piece of paper over the membrane so that the caul stuck to it, and then it had been given to Brid's mother as an heirloom. The possession of a caul was said to protect the bearer from death by drowning. Brid now had it in a small box on her dressing table; she had never given it away. Why should she? A few sailors had offered a fortune for its protection but she had never parted with it. She had meant to give it to her fiancée on their wedding day. Oh, why hadn't she given it to him before?

A marriage had been arranged and then put to one side, like the wedding dress that hung in her mother's closet. Brid had no need of it anymore. She had promised to marry Benjamin Eskell but he had been lost to the sea a few months earlier. Brid's mother had been muttering on that Brid should have married Tom—Ben's brother—except that Tom was unhelpfully married already.

A cold, grey mist crept in from the sea towards the huddled houses of the small village and then wound its way up each street; first to the right along the one terrace, then after the length of it to the left and along again. Turning at each bend, like a sea dragon searching for a lair, or a lost soul reaching for a forgotten memory. Brid followed its trail to top of the hill, to the little cottage she shared with her mother. All the way along she was thinking about her lost lover and how she longed to be reunited with him again. Even death held no fear for her; she only wanted reunion. What could be wrong with that?

Once inside the cottage she nodded to her mother, who sat by the fire knitting a jumper. Each jumper served a twofold purpose: the first was obviously for warmth, the second in that each village had a unique pattern—it was how they identified and claimed their dead from the sea. Wives even put mistakes in the garment so that it was particular to their family. When they found Brid's fiancée, his face had been bitten away by fish and the pattern had proven that he was of their village of Bay Town. Brid could not look at that jumper.

"I'm off to bed."

"That's all you seem to want to do these days, Brid. You go to your room and you never talk to me."

"There's nothing much to talk about, Mother."

"You're young. There will be plenty for you to do in the future. Sit down here with me, Brid. I've hardly talked to anyone all day."

"I need to change out of these wet clothes."

"I suppose," responded her mother. "They look dry enough to me already—where have you been?"

"To the Bay Hotel."

Helen gave her an honest stare that was full of reproach. "We can't afford to squander our money, Brid."

Brid felt so wound up, so wanting to let go of her anger.

"Afford? We can't afford anything, Mother. I'm sick of the work, sick of the poverty. I couldn't afford to lose a man—but I did—and I know you want me to find another one to replace him, so we can *afford* things."

"It's not my fault that the men in this family either go away or die in the sea."

"No, it's not your fault at all—but if you hadn't driven father to work harder all the time and moaned at him whenever he gave you any kindness perhaps he wouldn't have left."

"He might come back!"

"We both know that will never happen, just as my Ben won't be coming back either!"

Brid's mother was knitting furiously at this point, as if every stab of the needle would make a hole in her worries. "There's some fried fish on the table," she muttered in a begrudging tone.

Brid gave her mother a disdainful look, took one of the candles from the shelf next to the fireplace, lit it from the main candle near her mother and left the room. She was tired of fighting; fighting her mother, the cold winter, and her grief.

Her room smelt of the sea; Brid had found some old bits of fishing nets and hung them from the beams. Faded ribbons and cradled mementos, love notes and tokens from the previous year, all hung in mid air as if waiting on the unseen hand of her lover to present them once more. That would never happen again...Brid knew. She wondered if she would ever find anything interesting to hang in the nets again.

She noticed dark pools of water over in the centre of the wooden boards and the curtain billowed unexpectedly despite the window being closed.

The cold had gotten into her bones and she started to shiver. Under the window was a small chest of drawers. Brid rummaged around in the bottom of one and pulled out a half-empty bottle of gin. She took out the stopper with some difficulty. She always felt guilty when she drank, and when she had enough she always drove the stopper home with the intention of making it more difficult to get at the next time. It never was that difficult, for she always managed in the end.

Brid slept badly that night. It wasn't a sweet repose, more a dream with the dead.

The wind was howling around the outer buildings, screeching around the rooftops and chimneys like a scavenging, northern wraith. Even the fishermen and their families slept fitfully in their cots. Brid fumbled at her bedclothes and cried out in her sleep. In her dreams she floated beneath the viridian sea, fighting off the levellers of the deep and losing.

She was unaware of the green phosphorescence in her room that clung to the floor, wove its way along the boards and then stretched its tendril fingers towards the crumpled sheets—then beneath.

In the morning there was blood on her nightgown. She made excuses that it was badly soiled because it was a heavy month and her mother let it be when Brid helped with the washing.

Each hour of her existence was an agony of delusion and nightmare. The future was something Brid rarely thought about now—only working and sleeping, and barely being bothered to eat. She could simply walk into the sea and never come out. What was the point of living if it was this hard?

Families helped one another out in Baytown. The Moorsoms and the Eskells (originally an old Scandinavian family) had married each other for generations and Brid's marriage was one more, intended to strengthen the bond between them. She gathered bait and helped with the fish, and the Eskells helped Brid and her mother in little ways. Tom would have been her brother–in–law and he still felt an obligation. He lived three doors along with his pregnant wife.

The cold, wintry morning called for as many layers of clothing as Brid could find, to wrap around her and still work in without being too restricted. And then it was down to the shoreline, and across to Boggle Hole and beyond, to get the limpets at low tide. As she made her way past Eskell cottage she caught sight of Jenna, Tom's wife, through the small dark window. There was no mistaking that it was Jenna due to the size of her swollen stomach—she was due to give birth any day now. Brid bit down hard on her bottom lip, trying to push aside her jealousy; she might have had been with child now if the sea hadn't taken her Benjamin.

Unlike the rest of the flither girls, Brid preferred to gather the bait on her own and on that particular day she lingered around Boggle Hole rather than follow the rest of the girls over the hills. They travelled away from the sea-beaten cottages and down to the other bays. Also, she was tired of their incessant gossip. Her heart wasn't in anything—she could only think of Ben. She caught glimpses of his scowling face, framed by the brown seaweed, in the rock pools, and imagined she felt the light touch of a hand on the back of hers as she prised the limpets off the rock.

Brid stabbed at the limpets, venting all her anger on them, until she caught her left hand with one lunge and her blood splashed the dark shells. Ignoring the pain, she stood up, threw a handful of the limpets into a basket, arched her aching back and looked out at the black sea.

The sea was almost as dark as night and the sky was only a shade lighter—just enough to work by. Out there was where the fishermen came to grief, near landmarks called Farside's Out and Ower Robin a Trum, and she wondered if it were possible for dead fishermen and sailors to return from the sea.

The wind whipped up and the ocean began to get rougher, flinging spray in her face as the tide came in. She imagined herself cut off by the tide—part of her wished it would—freeing her of her drudgery. The rain pelted her arms and legs and she pushed her black hair out of her eyes with the back of her hand. Salt had dried her lips and made them bleed. Just as she was turning to go back along the shoreline, just to her left a little of the soft, clay cliff face fell away. Brid looked up to see if more would follow but nothing else looked as if it was going to slip. There was just a small channel of mud and water sluicing down.

Something solid caught her eye. Most of it was sticking out of the cliff face and, at first, she just thought it was one of the rocks. Taking care not to slip on the sea-worn boulders, she went to investigate. The rain fell harder and the cold sting of it on her face made her curse under her breath. She reached up on tiptoe for the small, wooden casket and gave it a pull. It didn't budge with the first tug and she almost slipped. However, with the second pull the soft wet clay came away, and she caught the box as it fell. It was less than her arm's-length long but quite light, so she placed it in her large flither basket and made her way back across the foreshore before the tide cut her off from the Wayfoot, just below the Bay Hotel.

When the tide was out you could walk all the way across Stoupe Beck Sands to Ravenscar; she'd done that often enough, but not today. Many a wreck lay off the Ravenscar headland, hundreds of years of them. Sailors and fishermen had been washed up on that shore; their bodies harvested by the scavengers of the deep. Men in their pale mottled skin with slivers of flesh hanging from them. They were so rotten you could peel out the spine of the fishermen as easily as with fish.

The flither basket with its tiny cargo began to feel heavy. Brid slipped on the stones as she hurried to beat the tide, but she managed it well enough across the water's edge and up the cobble causeway to the Bay Hotel. The sea had more than once pounded the hotel in the terrible winter storms and hurled the tiny coble boats against the windows of the inn. But not today, although the sea was getting rougher. It was at the hotel that Brid sought shelter. Once through the door, which banged loudly behind her, she moved silently over to the fire and sat down beside it. She took off her wet shawl and her black jacket, and placed them over the basket to hide the contents.

The Bay Hotel was empty; there was no one behind the old, oak wood bar. For a time she sat alone. Either the bad weather had kept the rest of the flither girls down the coast or they had made their sodden way back to their homes. None of the locals were around. None had come down to the Wayfoot to see that their boats were still tied up. It was a while before the landlord came into the bar.

"Well Brid, there's not many out today. Do you want a drink to warm you up?"

"I haven't got any money, nothing for now."

Josh Brannislaw, a man of extraordinary height for a local and a widower of two winters, laid out two glasses and poured himself and Brid some brandy from a jug. She knew that it was from the fine cask, from one of the ones the excise men never found. The excise never found anything in Bay Town—there being too many secret hiding places. Brid made to get up from the fire.

"Stay there, Brid. I'll bring the drink over. I've got some bread and cheese in the back too?" he enquired with a raised eyebrow.

"Thank you. That's most kind of you."

He was not long out of the bar and seemed in a hurry to bring back the food for her. As he placed the bread and cheese down on the table his hand moved as if to touch her arm—but he seemed to think twice of it. She looked at him with watery, grey eyes and then past him to another table—where Benjamin sat looking out to sea with a caul over his white face. *If only I had given him the caul,* she thought.

Ben, with his old navy jumper, shabby through years of use. Ben, with his hair washed back by the sea and the caul stretched thin over his face—not the tiny dried thing that lay in the small box, but this made of a harsher material—its edges now twisted into hooks that seemed to dig into his skin, piercing it but with no show of blood. Brid had seen him in this state twice now, as if mocking her because she hadn't given him the caul. She glanced at Josh to see if he had seen Ben. He had not.

Brid ate the bread and cheese slowly and sipped at the brandy.

Josh methodically carried out his work behind the bar, spoke little and just raised his head from time to time as if expecting a customer to burst through the door at any minute.

The proximity of the fire did little to take away the chill, and as Brid put up her hands to draw in the warmth her eyes fell upon the covered box in the flither basket. Thanking Josh for his kindness she got up wearily, picked up the basket and left the inn.

Once at the cottage she placed the basket outside the door. Later that afternoon her mother would take the limpets out of their shells and bait the lines. Brid took the small casket, wrapped it deeper into her shawl, and crept into the dwelling. The main-room door was firmly shut against the cold weather so it was easy for Brid to climb the stairs unseen, although one step creaked under her weight—"Is that you, Brid?"

Brid greeted the call with silence.

"Brid, is that you?"

"I'm just going to change my wet clothes, Mother. I've left the flithers outside."

"Fine, Brid. So long as I know it's you."

Brid realized she wasn't the only member of the household who was more than a little jittery at the moment.

At the threshold of her room, Brid hesitated. The candle flame flickered as she passed over. Once inside, candlelight caught the profile of an old woman, and then rendered her into the darkness. She saw the rest of them, too; phantoms in the mirror, in the patterns of the old faded red curtains, on the grey bed throw, even in the pattern of water damage on the ceiling. The worn bedposts bore a resemblance to worm-ridden, charnel house heads.

Each night the phantasmagoria left their lair, where they waited for her during the day, and then they crept towards her, pressing their deformities closer to her so that she could hardly breathe in that room—lest they followed the intake of her quickening breath. She had told no one about them and even though they were driving her into madness (if she were not entirely mad already) she would keep their secret.

There was one face that would terrify her more than the others, and that was the one in the wooden lid of the old sea chest in the corner. It looked like the face of a drowned sailor bloated by death and days in the sea, with no eyes: just gnarls were those should be. Whilst Brid lay frozen in horror, the diabolical faces crept out of the shadows and hovered close by her pillow. An hour before dawn the last vestiges of mist would swirl to nothing beneath her bed and patterns became fixed on the surface of things.

There was a dead baby in the casket.

That is what she realised it was, bound in some foul green bandage. Its withered form could still be recognised, and within its mouldy shawl were charms and black tokens made of jet for the older, half-forgotten deities of the sea. Perhaps someone as grief-stricken as Brid had cast it to the ocean years before. The sea, through countless storms had cast it back up long after the spell had been fulfilled, and driven the offering into the soft cliff face. It wasn't the only baby in the row of small cottages that night because Brid could hear the first cries of a newborn, not far away.

That infant gave a plaintive mewling, a weak cry of alarm, and Brid stared at the dead one cradled in her arms. She snatched the charms from between the rotten bandages then put back the swaddled, mummified *thing* in the tiny casket and replaced the lid. Reaching above her head she put the small treasure with her other tokens in the large fisher net, and dressed quickly. As she left the room, she remembered to take one of her best woollen shawls from the bottom drawer. Brid hurried downstairs and lit an oil lantern with a taper from the dying fire.

The fisherman families rarely locked their front doors. There had never been any need, theft being such a rare occurrence. And Brid had no trouble entering the Eskell household. Once upstairs she could hear Tom's gentle snoring in the shadows and by the candlelight Jenna lay face-away from her baby, with her arm around Tom. The baby opened its eyes and looked at Brid. Even a newborn might cry at a stranger's touch. But the infant didn't make a sound when Brid placed one hand under its neck, the other under the body, and lifted it gently out of the cradle. She made it down the dark stairs with the assurance of one who knew she was guided, and slipped quietly over the threshold with the baby firmly bound in the green shawl. She clutched the child to her breast with one hand and picked up the heavy lantern with the other.

In her attempt to climb the pathway to the clifftop Brid only slipped once. The baby did not fall from her grasp, but the stumble caused the infant to cry momentarily.

"It's fine, little one. I won't fall again."

At the top of the hill she placed the baby on the damp grass with the lantern by its side, illuminating its frightened face. Brid could not know its name, for it bore none; it was too young and hadn't been christened. She tried to remember if Tom had mentioned anything about naming, but all she could hear was the swell of the sea crashing into the cliff face below her—and, far off—the scream of a woman in the night.

Brid knelt down over the child and pushed the charms under the folds of the shawl. She bound it; swaddling the tiny form and trapping its arms tight to its body. The baby let out a small cry of surprise when Brid held it high above her head. She spun round three times—her long grey skirt swirling in the strange, green mist that crept across the cliff face—and then, with the name of her fiancée on her lips, she threw the baby to the sea.

As the villagers hurried up the pathway towards the light of the lantern, Brid took the track that trailed off in the other direction down to the beach, and then she waded out into the sea. She felt something rough and icy make a grab for her thigh and then a cold hand on her leg that pulled her down.

Once summoned, there is no denying the deities of the sea. They know that you will deliver yourself up to them—sooner or later. It is only a matter of time.

Bull Running

Dedicated to all the crazy, wonderful mozos of the Fiesta of St. Fermin, to Ernest Hemingway and Orson Welles.

Something had happened that caused one Spanish family great cause for concern. A boy named Lorenzo called upon sixteen-year-old Elise at the small house she shared with her Aunt Pilar, in the little village of Alqueria. Only for a moment did the aunt leave them alone in the room. Elise was standing in front of a large mirror that showed her from head to waist. Her long, brown hair spread round the upper part of the frame. A look askance from her hazel eyes, a strange reflection—and a hint of something otherworldly and rather demonic—had made the boy afraid.

He made his apologies and left, troubled by what he had seen. The only other person he told was his cousin, Bonita Mendoza, who thought that she would curry favour with Elise by giving her a gold bracelet, which had been meant for Bonita's sister-in-law. It had not been enough. For, less than a week later, Lorenzo was found dead in the olive grove at the back of his home, with a bull's horn through his heart. The horn had been driven in so deeply, and with such force, that it had nailed him to an olive tree. After the postmortem, and when the horn had been removed, it was marvelled that it had not been sawn from a bull but wrenched from its head, and black, bloody flaps of hide still clung to it. The funeral was a quiet affair, with only immediate relatives in attendance. Soon after, the Mendoza family left the area.

Elise was prone to blackouts, for which the doctor could give no explanation. She had one just about the time of Lorenzo's death.

Five years later in 2003, during the hottest summer for decades (the final count would be four thousand dead in Spain and over eighteen thousand in Italy by the end of the summer), Elise Moreno decided to give up her job as a tour guide in Barcelona, prepare to don the dour clothes of a pilgrim, and set out on the road from Pamplona to Santiago de Compostella. She wore the sign of the pilgrim: a small cockleshell badge pinned to the green scarf she wrapped around her neck to keep off the hot sun. Elise had no idea why she was going—as she wasn't religious—feeling simply a desire to go; compelled to make the journey. She packed a rucksack with a change of shorts, three T-shirts, several pairs of panties, and a bra. The idea was to travel light as a pilgrim and that appealed to her. She caught a taxi to the airport and thought about how she liked the idea of leaving material things behind.

The flight from Barcelona to Pamplona was short, but there was enough time to read. For amusement she took along *The Canterbury Tales*, whose characters had undertaken another pilgrimage, many hundreds of years before.

On the plane, Elise sat next to an English woman who recognised the title of the book.

"*The Canterbury Tales*—are you a student?"

"No, just interested." Elise half-smiled at the woman.

"It's unusual for a young woman to be seen reading Chaucer, unless made to do so."

"Really?"

"Are you going to Pamplona for the festival?"

"No, the Camino." Elise pointed to the shell badge.

"Ah, I see—a pilgrim."

"Not exactly."

The last remark seemed to close all lines of communication, as Elise stared harder into the book, not reading so much as letting the characters drift off the page and make up a modern-day story in her head. She began to daydream her way along the Camino, not the pilgrim way to Canterbury. The present-day counterparts of the old stories jostled and jibed with one another to get in the front of the queue and attract her attention. This may have seemed a strange game to any ordinary person, but, Elise was used to the strange—it happened to her all the time.

Less than twenty-four hours later Elise had registered for the Camino and was on her way from her accommodation---a shabby hostel in Pamplona.

Pamplona; famous for the bull running which took place in July each year; a good golf club; a fine incorporation of immigrants from South America; and the Volkswagen factory. It was now late June. The usual tide of students and devoted faithful diminished in number as the summer heat threatened to boil people alive. Everyone setting out with the expectation of reaching their destination. For most, the first accomplishment was to complete the three-and-a-half week hike—seven-hundred kilometers—through parched days and uncomfortable nights. Another goal was to validate and celebrate belief. And a third, for some, was to find something to believe in. On this trip, not all would finish the journey; some would lose their beliefs, and more would find something that they had not bargained for.

A few pilgrims had come on organised tours, sending their baggage ahead by bus, staying in the best places, which, to Elise, undermined the whole concept of humility and the leaving behind of worldly goods. She had briefly met one tour operator as he shunted his pilgrims on to the tour bus in Pamplona. Those pilgrims called him Marcus, and he reminded her of the pardoner in *The Canterbury Tales* who sold false relics to believers. Marcus jangled his tips in his pocket and wore a perpetual smile.

Elise rose early and left Pamplona in the last week of June, taking with her a map, plenty of water, bread, cheese, and biscuits. She left before the morning progressed and the horrendous summer heat began to sear the valley. She walked up the ridge of Sierra de Perdon and looked across a countryside that had suffered much from the heat of the summer—the grass, tinder dry, ready to combust spontaneously. After the walk, she found a newly built hostel for the night, which was unusually quiet for the time of year. The heat had kept more than a few people away from the Camino. She travelled twenty-three kilometres that day, carried three litres of water, drank it all, refilled twice and felt as if she could have still walked further. Elise had no idea where her strength was coming from.

The next day she travelled twenty kilometres to Estella, spoke to no one and avoided a big, black, bad-tempered dog that snarled at her. Elise snarled back, stamped her foot and the dog slouched away whimpering, its tail between its legs. Estella was a pleasant town, and the hostel had a shaded courtyard where she ate pizza and thought of nothing interesting.

For six days Elise lived a solitary life, and if she met a fellow pilgrim she simply waved hello and went quickly on her way with no real comprehension of why she was there. The hostel was not too full and she kept to herself. One hot night, she opted to sleep upon an old table outside because a German girl, delirious with a fever, had been crawling around on the floor inside. The next day Elise was told that the girl had malaria and she was taken to a nearby convent hospital to be looked after by nuns.

On the seventh day Elise took the easy pathway surrounded by forest on each side and met up with an English boy called Michael, and his German friend, Frantz. Elise felt awkward, shy even, and was happy to hide behind her sunglasses and floppy hat, even though the sun hung low in the sky. She wore a vivid red thin-strapped top and beige shorts. With a forced smile she dumped her small rucksack in the dust and sat on a nearby rock, whilst the boys chatted to her.

"Have you been on the Camino before?" Michael asked her.

"No, but I believe that I can do it, even though the days are hotter than I thought they'd be," Elise replied.

"It's been too hot for me," he stated. "What brings you on the Camino—travelling alone?"

Elise looked thoughtful for a moment. "I can look after myself. Besides, it is rare to hear about robbery, or worse, on the pilgrimage."

"Sure, but that doesn't mean it couldn't happen."

Elise merely smiled.

"You still haven't said why you are doing it?"

"Why does anyone? I'm here looking for something."

"You'll find it on the Camino—everyone finds what they are looking for on the Camino," Frantz added.

"Even sinners like you, Frantz?" Michael gave him a friendly nudge on the arm and then took a swig from a water bottle.

"But why are you going in this direction? You are supposed to finish in Santiago, aren't you?" asked Elise.

"We were, but now we are going to get a bus to Pamplona."

"Why?"

"To run with the bulls. We've been thinking about it after reading Hemingway and, well, it seems like fun."

Michael rummaged about in his rucksack, pulled a book out and passed it to Elise. She noted that his brown hair was too long over his blue eyes. He kept sweeping it away with a shake of his head.

"Ah right—*The Sun Also Rises*. I've read it," said Elise. "It's about desire."

"It's about bull fighting and sex," replied Michael.

"Both dangerous."

"We're young. We're meant to face danger occasionally."

"Putting aside the camaraderie, bravado, and Hemingway's book, bull running *is* dangerous," she repeated.

"And fun," he replied. "Why don't you come with us?"

"To watch?"

"Of course to watch. As you say, it would be far too dangerous...." Michael hesitated.

"...for a girl, you meant to say," she finished.

"Well, yes."

"No—I won't go to watch." With total conviction, Elise suddenly knew what she wanted to do. "I will run with the bulls too."

She took off her sunglasses and for a moment a ray of evening sunlight broke through the trees and Michael caught sight of some strange reflection in her eyes. He blinked, and then there was nothing there, just the beautiful, hazel eyes of a stunning Spanish girl.

That night, whilst the boys slept in their tent (they had offered it to Elise but she had refused), Elise lay on top of her sleeping bag, thankful for the slight breeze, and gazed heavenwards. She marvelled at the brightness of the nearest stars and wondered about the strong compulsion she now had—to go to Pamplona. She wasn't entirely unhappy that she seemed to be guided by impulse and not determination. It wasn't long before Michael joined her. But soon all she could think about, amid the fumbling, was how beautiful the stars were and that there were so many constellations out there, though most of them she could never quite identify. Taurus would be visible to someone tonight.

It was the kind of sex that young men do, when they sense the girl isn't really interested. After he was finished he mumbled an apology, which—in her distraction—she didn't hear. She said nothing. He went back inside the tent. Later she heard Michael swearing in his sleep, fighting off creatures in his nightmares, and she supposed one of them might be her.

In the morning nothing was said. Michael smiled sheepishly as she packed her rucksack and she smiled warmly in return—the incident filed under impulse, opportunity, and youth.

They chose a hostel on the outskirts of Pamplona, the other hostels being full of eager, young people there for the next day's bull running, and they ate outside at a café. Elise enjoyed the evening, in the company of the two young men who flirted in turn for her attention.

As she raised her wine glass to her lips she could hear the blunt sound of something chipping on stone. The noise grew louder and a woman screamed. The people at the table in front of hers were closer to the cobbled street; they flung their chairs to one side and almost clambered over her to get into the cafe. Red wine spilled down her blouse as Michael grabbed her hand and dragged her into the entrance. Frantz followed close behind.

"Get inside. Quick," shouted Michael.

The sound became louder, thunderous.

Something horrid was thrown into the entranceway of the café.

Outside, a sweat-soaked bull scrambled and slipped on the wet cobblestones, fell to its knees in front of the occupants and glowered at them. They fell back in panic into the dubious safety of the premises. The bull managed to get to its feet and then, with an indignant bellow, was gone. Another scream and Elise craned her neck to see what else was causing the commotion. A few people ran off in the opposite direction that the bull had taken—away from the blood-soaked body on the pavement. Others stood over the man, staring and pointing him out to their fellow onlookers.

"Look—his hands and feet have been tied together," cried out one person.

Elise managed to break through the circle around the body. She looked down.

The face was unrecognisable; the nose torn away as it had been dragged along the cobblestones. The rope around his wrists was still secure, his hands a mockery of common prayer. The man had been tied to the bull and the beast had dragged its grisly burden through the streets of Pamplona long after he was dead. He was naked from the waist down, a torn bloody shirt covering the upper part of him. The most horrifying thing of all, even though most of the body was grazed and covered in blood, was that the man had been castrated.

The police and a priest were called. The police took statements and cordoned off the area. Finally, after Elise and the boys had told them all they knew the police told them they could go.

"Shall we go back to the hostel?" Michael asked.

"No, not yet," said Elise. "I need another glass of wine."

As they left the café the three continued to speculate over the grim incident that had taken place. Elise tried to avoid the trail of blood, which could quite clearly be seen on the street.

"What on earth had that man done?" added Michael. "Perhaps he fell afoul of some woman's husband?"

Frantz shrugged, "I'd rather not talk about it. There's a bar in the next street. Come on."

"Don't *you* want to talk about it Elise? Frantz is always like that, avoiding things."

"Yes, Michael—I do but let's find that bar first."

The Txoko bar was full of locals, but quiet. The three found a corner where they could discuss what had happened. The unusually silent people in the bar were staring at them, and in a city of a thousand tourists there for the bull running, it made them feel quite vulnerable. Elise wanted more wine and ordered two bottles. She drank a full glass quickly, poured herself another and one each for her friends. A withered old woman sat in a chair opposite her and seemed to challenge Elise to stare at her. Elise wasn't entirely sure that this was a woman; her legs below the knee-length skirt seemed mannish despite their age, and lipstick didn't sit well on her lips. Her black wig was slightly askew and Elise thought that she looked like a very poor imitation of Edith Piaf. The woman smiled—strangely—at Elise and shuffled off into the night with a brief glance over her shoulder.

The next day was the first day of the festival in honour of Saint Fermin. It was the seventh of July. At 8 a.m. a rocket signalled that the corral doors had been opened and a second rocket heralded the entrance of the twelve bulls in the uphill stretch called Santa

Domingo. Many of the young men wore white shirts and trousers with the traditional red sash around the waist, but many just wore what they felt they could easily run in. Elise wore a simple white blouse and shorts. She tied a red ribbon in her brown hair as a nod to tradition. The air smelt of sangria and sweat.

The bulls thundered down to Ayntamiento Square, down Mercaderes and into a street called Estafeta. Elise could smell the bulls long before she saw them. By stretching her neck and pushing the boys to one side, she could just about see between their bobbing heads. Two of the bulls looked tired as if they had been running for days and wanted to give up, but the other two looked lean and excited, like they had a mean streak that stretched back generations.

Some young men pointed and shouted, "Toro, Toro, Toro."

Elise could see four bulls; one turned on the spot, slipped on the cobbles, regained its footing—and came after her and the boys. The other runners shouted at them to run—to get out of the way. Michael and Frantz pulled at her arms, but somehow she got away from them. One of the animals was the largest bull she had ever seen—a giant of a black bull—and it had thundered around the corner with blood on its horns from the last runner who had come across its path. As the other bulls rushed past Elise, this huge bull stopped some distance away, stamped its feet and bellowed. She felt the blood rush to her face as she prepared to run again. From behind the wooden barrier the crowds offered her their hands, to pull her over and to safety. Elise waved her hand, shook her head and prepared to run. The crowd held their breath.

Elise ran *towards* the bull as it bellowed at her again. She sprinted the distance with ease despite the heat and with the elegant grace of a true bull-runner she jumped as high as she could over the horns of the bull. Her hands briefly touched its back as she vaulted off and into the dust. The crowd cheered and applauded. All was noise and laughter—a band struck up. As the bulls disappeared down the street Elise could hear the steady thump of the drum and it echoed the beat of her racing heart. She had never felt as alive as she did in that moment. The coursing blood ran as a river in her body, a river as dark as the Styx.

A few feet in front of Elise lay the body of Franz, covered in blood. She felt no emotion. Perhaps another bull had come along and attacked him whilst he was trying to attract the attention of the bull that charged her. She tried to get to him but the jubilant crowd swept her up as their sudden hero and placed her on the shoulders of two of the other runners. Frantz was forgotten as she felt the rush of excitement once more, giving herself over to the spontaneity and joy of the moment. She felt stronger than ever. Michael and Frantz were nothing to her now: too weak, all too malleable. Too human.

Elise was ready for anything and wasn't the slightest bit surprised when the withered woman came into her hostel room that night and asked her to get dressed. The woman then turned and left, expecting Elise to follow.

Elise did follow, down dark streets to even darker alleys, where young boys lay drunk and sleeping from the earlier celebrations. She saw the shadow of a church before her and was led down some steep, stone steps into The Taurobolium, her way illuminated by torchlight. Once within the underground temple she looked up to the ceiling. She was in a grotto. Shafts of light fell from holes in the wooden canopy, a hundred tiny stars. The walls were lined with stone benches and decorated with paintings and several carved reliefs. One statue was of Mithras killing the sacred bull; he knelt on the back of the animal, pulling its head back in submission. A stone serpent and a dog drank from the open wound.

The women were waiting for her. Two undressed Elise and gave her a soft full-length white gown to wear. She put it on in silence. When a glass of wine was given to her she took it and drank without hesitation. Within a minute she felt the effect, stronger than she had expected but not unpleasant, and she did not surprise herself when she took another willingly.

"Let us rejoice in the company of the Gods," said one woman wearing a similar gown.

"Let us rejoice," replied the women.

Without fear Elise took one step forwards and swayed a little. She felt giddy, her head full of images of the bull and the ritual—which she knew would soon take place. A bull was to be sacrificed; she knew enough about the cult of Mithras to know that. Elise was lowered into a pit. No woman had ever been an initiate, but she wasn't afraid. As the warm blood swilled over her face and dropped onto the cold stone she felt a surge of power within her and it was then that she understood. She wasn't to be a follower of Mithras.

Men, women and children could be heard calling incantations, and the chanting grew louder. Elise could hear flutes, drums, and cymbals, all building to a strange crescendo, then *some power* took full possession of her—she felt it surge through her body; she embraced new knowledge of every creature that had ever walked the earth and beyond, within the supernatural lands. She had become the manifestation of the goddess on earth—she who moved the universe—the goddess of judgement *in human, female form*. For years she had waited in doubt and fear for some feeling of purpose. Now Elise joined with the goddess in jubilation. As she looked up and cupped her hands to the slowing stream of blood, she stared without pity into the terrified—dying—eyes of Michael.

To her followers, who eagerly pushed forwards to anoint their foreheads with the blood of the boy, she spoke the words:

"I am Cybele, Damkina, Gaia, and Isis. I am the Magna Mater and you will all follow me. I accept this sacrifice, which will be one amongst many."

In The Hall of the Mountain King

"Just you wait, it won't be long.
The man in black will soon be here.
With his cleaver's blade so true.
He'll make mincemeat out of you."
German nursery rhyme.

Connie couldn't remember what age she was when she learnt that men could be bad to children. She was young enough not to know the sexual details but old enough to know to run when a male patient of Prestwich Asylum asked her to go into the bushes with him. There were a few such men. She always believed that she could run faster than them and had carried on with that expectation.

Connie lived on a small council estate called Clough Walks, of some twenty or fewer properties, at the end of the long stretch of Gardener Road in Prestwich, which was on the main northern route into Manchester. The beginning of Clough Walks was near Spion Kop where an enormous wooden cross had been placed to commemorate the dead of the Boer War. Not far from the gates to the war memorial lay a small, cobbled road that led to a tiny farm. It was called a farm but was really an old, detached Victorian house. Here, the owners grew quite a lot of their own food and kept a few chickens. Connie lived close by in a three-bed semi that backed onto the asylum fields, and unlike the Elysium fields they were not where the good and the great went to rest. The inmates of the large psychiatric hospital worked in the asylum fields, grew their own cabbages, turnips, and wheat in summer. Occasionally they would throw a few cabbages over the fence for Connie to give to her mother.

On one cold, frosty morning, when the windows were green-glaze frozen on the inside, Connie opened the curtains and started to scratch away. She scratched away at the frost, forming small stick figures on the pane and then she looked down on the asylum field, at the little men who mimicked her own tiny creations. The men in the field chipped painfully at the soil, with no chance whatsoever of getting to whatever was buried in the frozen ground. She got back into bed.

The night before, she had imagined the sharp features of Jack Frost at her window, tap-tapping on the glass, his cold, foul breath seeking small cracks to get to her. He was searching, probing and picking at the frame. Connie hid under the covers and sang to herself in an attempt to keep him out. But, she saw him in her mind—his crystal claws, harder than any diamond, and sharpened to needle points.

Realising that it was breakfast time, she got out of bed again but quickly withdrew her foot from the floor. The linoleum was cold to her bare feet. Her mother had promised her a new carpet in the spring, so Connie hopped around on each foot for a few seconds until she found her red slippers. She rubbed her feet against the back of each leg in turn; her long, lemon nightie with tiny orange paisley swirls on it, although usually warm, kept out little of the cold.

She tried to make more little patterns in the corners of her window, where the frost was thickest. As she did so Connie became aware of a long, pallid face staring up at her from the frozen field. The other patients had given up trying to harvest from the winter's graveyard, and sloped off—to the treatments that now awaited them. This one, pale figure stood alone, features nipped and gaunt, with hollow eyes. Connie jumped back from the window—but the man had seen her. He removed his hat and tipped his head a little, the bony peak of his bald dome looked unusual to her, as if it had borne the brunt of an unnatural birth. Connie's sister, Penny, had told her all about birth and how a baby was squished to within an inch of its life, and back again. Connie thought that this man must have started with a disadvantage because of the shape of his head, but she knew enough not to feel too sorry for him.

The man fumbled at his trousers and pulled something white and thin from within. It was then that Connie pulled the edges of the red curtains closer together and backed quickly away from the window.

Wanting to dismiss the image from her head Connie ran down the stairs, swung around the banister, straight into her older brother.

"Clumsy clod—watch it!"

"Watch yourself you fat banana!"

Rog had the same brown hair as Connie but his was longer than hers. He had kept his Beatles hairstyle of a few years earlier and refused to give it up, along with narrow winklepicker shoes. He was a tall fifteen-year-old and hung out with three mates of the same age from Gardener Road.

The kitchen door opened and Aunt Doreen came into view. "Quit it you two. Connie, come and give your auntie a big kiss."

Connie's eyes widened in horror as she stared at the red lipstick and caught a whiff of secondhand Avon perfume. She dodged past her auntie to give her mother a good morning kiss; Mother never wore lipstick and she always smelt of chamomile soap and fresh washing.

"*Give* your auntie a kiss, Connie."

She looked warily at the red lips again but relented, remembering that her auntie had given her an enormous Easter egg, the box a colourful, cardboard gypsy caravan. She hoped that her mother wasn't going to spit on her handkerchief and wipe lipstick off Connie's face like she usually did.

She did.

"Eat your toast Connie."

Wiping her cheek, and very much annoyed with her mother, she parked herself on the white wooden kitchen chair. The seat was padded with a sort of plastic covering; on it there was a pattern of pale blue circles and red triangles with black lines darting through each shape. Her mother had said that the kitchen table and chairs were modern, the in-thing, and that it would be a welcome replacement to the old utility furniture that had been taken off to the dump.

Connie's auntie sometimes called in for a cup of tea after she had finished her night shift at the asylum. She never seemed tired and hardly paused for breath when she related her stories.

"Rotten trick it is—seen it done before. Some patient dies an hour before the end of the shift—the nurses put them in a warm bath for a bit, then dry them off and slip them back between the sheets to look like they had just died on shift change-over. Dirty trick and they think we don't know—won't tell on them though. You never know when you'll need a favour in return."

The toast became suddenly all too interesting and Connie thought about what she had learnt when in the presence of adults; that if a child was looking at something intently, adults tended to think the child wasn't listening and talked about all sorts of things in front of them. Her auntie and her mother were no different.

Connie took her time eating. That's what ten-year-olds did during the Christmas holidays when they couldn't get out of the house. Six days until Christmas Day and, hopefully, her new bicycle and some smaller presents. Connie had not found the hiding place for the latter and she had checked the usual places—bottoms of wardrobes, tops of wardrobes and under her mother's bed.

The previous summer, Connie had wandered the perimeter of the hospital grounds. The boundary of the hospital, or at least part of it, was at the back of her house and skirted the edge of the Clough. She used to try and find ways into the place—unlike the inmates who wanted to get out. Some had been there all their lives because they had a baby out of wedlock, as Connie's mum called it, and the baby put into care. Ways to get in. Connie wanted to see these women and perhaps get them out.

The day before her sister's wedding Connie left her house, number thirteen, and ran down the wide pathway into the woods. A little way along, set against overgrown rhododendrons and brambles, were the old toilets. The roof was completely missing and the old concrete framework stood stark against the greenery. Graffiti covered the exposed walls; there were crude drawings of big-breasted women, perched on massive cocks, whilst flat men with goggle eyes looked up. No one used those toilets anymore, the block being as rundown as the Clough with its overgrown pathways and dark, impenetrable bushes. The toilets were boarded up—except someone had prised off a few of the boards. From a distance she watched as a man, one of the hospital patients, ducked underneath the broken boards.

Connie knew that she shouldn't, but she couldn't help herself; she crept up to the toilets and climbed the tree that overhung the gent's side. The old man was crouched low on the ground, for the toilet bowls had been smashed ages ago, and he squatted amid last year's dead leaves and old newspapers. Connie suddenly felt ashamed and backed away slowly, quietly down the branch. A snap, a snarl, and instantly the same hollow-eyed man looked up at her, a sick smile on his wasted face.

"Do you want to see? Do you want to see?"

Connie didn't want to see. She scrambled down the tree, legged it up to number thirteen with her heart thumping to the sound of her feet.

"Connie! Connie! Is that you? Tea is ready."

"I'm not hungry, Mum."

"Not hungry? Of course you're hungry. I've never known you not to be."

May felt her daughter's face but couldn't decide whether she had a fever or not.

"Can I watch some telly before bed?"

"I suppose, but only a little, then bed."

The siren-sound of *Dr.Who* met her ears as she switched on the telly and Connie lost herself in another world of monsters. Only these monsters she could deal with; they were safely behind a glass screen, and—unlike the male patients of Prestwich Asylum—they couldn't get out. Connie couldn't believe that she was making plans to get *in*—but that would have to wait until after Penny's wedding, which was the very next day.

The wedding day, a Saturday, was a flurry of activity. Her sister was to be married at Jackson Row in Manchester, the ceremony to be conducted by a registrar, and then back to The Church Inn for the wedding breakfast. The Church Inn was an old seventeenth-century pub where Connie's family had been christened, married and buried for seventy years. Her granddad had rung the bells there at the end of the Second World War, and her mother had practically given birth there; she had gone into labour over half a pint of Guinness and then been rushed off to hospital to give birth to Connie. The present owner of The Church Inn had a glass display case full of tiny sculptures of animals and little dolls, and he said that Prestwich had something to do with actual witches. Connie knew this to be untrue because she had written about Prestwich at school, and it was named after a priest's dairy farm.

Not many people paid attention to Connie on the morning of the wedding. Her hair had been cut to a short, brown bob the day before. Connie's mini dress was a mass of psychedelic blue and lime-green swirls, to be slightly subdued by a pale-blue coat and blue shoes. Connie retreated to her bedroom, away from the palaver that her older sister and mother were making. They were frantically trying to alter her sister's Biba wedding dress. Everything had been left to the last minute. Connie's father, Raymond, had been sent off to take the wedding cake to The Church Inn.

The wedding ceremony itself was a hurried, ushered-in affair; the usual relatives whom Connie hardly knew and would not see until the next family occasion, wedding, christening, or funeral. The turnout was small because it was a winter wedding and a few had made their excuses that it was too cold to attend and stand about for photos, and suchlike.

After the brief ceremony, most got lifts or took a taxi to the pub where the real celebration started. Connie was small enough to dodge most of the relatives but the occasional one would catch sight of the swirl of blue and lime-green and ask her if she liked school or perhaps The Beatles. Connie didn't bother to tell them that she liked Pink Floyd instead, although she had tried to tell her auntie a few months earlier that she used to like The Beatles, only her auntie had changed the conversation to school again. Connie was beginning to think that school was all adults could talk to children about.

After the meagre buffet, and bored by the fact that she was the only child at the wedding (her sister, Penny, was pregnant but Connie wasn't interested in that), she looked about for something to do. She looked at the silent jukebox and thought about asking her mother if she could put it on but her mother was deep in discussion with two older women, and Connie knew better than to interrupt *those* family conversations. Penny's new husband, Jim, sat next to his young bride. He looked sheepish and was downing pints as if there was no tomorrow.

It grew dark early at that time of year. Connie stared out of The Church Inn window. If she was going to go across to the churchyard to see the gravestones she would have to do it before it was too dark to see anything. She still hadn't found the oldest one. Shifting quietly through her relatives and avoiding her father, who was leaning against the bar looking absently in the opposite direction, Connie scooted out of the main entrance across some cobbles, and into St. Mary's churchyard.

St. Mary the Virgin Parish Church was well off the main road and situated in a cul-de-sac. The graveyard had been her playground for most of the summer. The vicar had told her about one coat of arms that was high up inside the church. She had been attracted to it because on it was a carving of a mermaid and the vicar told her that the motto of the Prestwich family to which it belonged was "In God have I put my trust." Connie didn't know if she should really trust anyone, including God.

From her house in Clough Walks she could get straight onto the pathway, through the woodland and up to the graveyard. Her mum trusted her out in the Clough and Connie never worried her mother about the bad men.

The gravestones intrigued Connie. She once found what she had thought to be the oldest, but her brother teased her that it wasn't and so she was still determined to find it. She thought the oldest was 1665. The family of Thomas Collier had died in that plague year and the youngest child was only a few weeks old. Connie was peering closely at another upright stone for dates and causes of death, when a figure suddenly bobbed up before her.

"Boo!" Her brother's red face loomed in on her.

"Absolute bastard!" Connie shouted as she reached around the stone and tried to swipe at him.

"Mum won't be happy with that language—even if you got it from me." Rog smiled his most mischievous smile. "And that dress— you look a right lemon."

Rog had five years on her but she still chased him around the graves, slipping on the green moss that covered the stones, until she was exhausted. Pointing and laughing, Rog made his way out of the gate across to The Church Inn. Connie recovered her breath and walked down the slippery path to the far side of the Church, to carry on her search for the oldest date, before nightfall.

Totally absorbed in her task, Connie didn't notice the fading light until it was almost impossible to see the dates on the stones. She thought she saw a shadow, over near the rhododendron bushes that surrounded the churchyard, but she just assumed it was Rog pissing about again.

Connie gave up. She couldn't see the dates anymore and her neck was aching.

As she turned, she felt a hand grab her, and another fall across her mouth. With almost supernatural strength her attacker pulled her rapidly back into the bushes and threw her on her back. Some filthy cloth was thrust into her mouth. She gagged at the taste. Connie was terrified by a cold hand fumbling at her tights, and delving into her knickers.

He whispered in her ear. "You're *my* girl now."

His full weight fell upon her and suddenly she heard Rog's voice.

"You dirty bastard, get off my sister. GET OFF!"

There was a rustle of leaves and the man threw himself to one side, fending off the blows from her brother. The man clenched a fist and struck at Rog. It was enough to stun him momentarily and Connie could hear more rustling of leaves as the man managed to get away through the dense undergrowth. She then heard the thud of hard boots on cobblestone, as he made his escape.

Rog gently pulled Connie out from under the bushes.

"Are you okay? Did he—"

Connie's tights were half way down her thighs. With difficulty, and sobbing a little, she pulled them up as far as she could.

"Connie. Did he?" Rog's voice was more insistent.

It was hard to see her brother's face above her in the darkness, but she reached up and bent his ear down to her mouth.

"It's all right Connie, no one can hear."

"No." The answer came with the quietest of sobs.

"Come on Connie. Let's go and tell Dad. He'll want to ring for the police."

Connie pulled at his arm. "No Rog, I don't want them to know. It was my fault. I shouldn't have been out here alone, in the dark. I know better too. I don't want to let them down. They won't trust me anymore. They'll *never* let me out."

"But we can't let him get away with it. What if he does it to someone else?"

"Rog. Please. I don't want them to know. There must be another way."

They could both hear laughter and the jukebox was playing a familiar tune, The Beatles' "Not a Second Time."

"Okay Connie. For now I will not."

Connie was very quiet for the next few days. Rog kept looking at her in a funny way and her parents commented more than once about how silent the house had become. She tried to carry on as if nothing had happened; in her head, it hadn't. She was careful not to go into the garden. There were no cabbages left in the fields for the patients to gather now, so they wouldn't be back until spring. She might be safe until then and in spring she would be safe anyway as she would be more careful. Rog had taken to meeting her from school, skiving off after the lunch break for a few days, until the headmaster informed their parents. Anyway, she felt fine now. She was big enough to cope. Both their parents worked full time, so she was on her own until Rog hurried home from the comprehensive school.

She hadn't seen her assailant's face but she knew him all right.

Occasionally, May let her go to work with her at the hospital. Her mother cleaned the doctor's quarters with her Spanish friends, Mercedes, Valbina, and Maria. Connie always wondered where all the women with babies were. The doctors all spoke foreign languages and seemed strange to her. They had strange doctors for strange patients. They didn't like a child in the hospital. She could sense that.

Doctor Theodore once said to Connie's mother. "A child shouldn't be in here, it isn't right."

Connie had once walked past a locked ward and peeped through the little window, only to see a bulky man sitting bolt-upright in bed, with his hands under the bed covers. She had quickly backed away from the door, hoping he couldn't see her.

After a while, Connie's mum stopped taking her into the hospital.

Then came the day she *couldn't* run fast enough.

She was walking down Gardener Road, after school, when that same man found her again. She had been to Parson's corner shop, down a side street, almost opposite the uphill path that led to the war memorial. He had been watching her. The road was quiet and it was getting dark. Connie left the comparative safety of Gardener Road and walked into Clough Walks. The route lay between sparse trees, to the small estate on which she lived.

As he grabbed her she screamed. From out of nowhere, her brother and his friends emerged. Two were carrying knives.

Immediately the man let go of Connie and backed towards the iron railings.

Rog put a protective arm around her. "Connie, get off home now and not a word to anyone, right?"

She nodded obediently and ran off towards their house.

The wooden cross is associated with Christ and criminals. In the early morning light Connie got dressed quickly, ran up the hill to the war memorial and entered the high, green privet enclosure that surrounded the cross. She looked up into the hollow eyes of the pallid man and smiled. Rusty nails had been hammered through his wrists and the man's head lolled onto his chest. His blood stank.

Her brother knew how to look after her, and she liked that.

Hardly anyone went up to the war memorial in winter. It was two days later, when a woman discovered the crucifixion while looking for her dog. She found the animal sitting on the ground, hanging its head, and whimpering beneath the lifeless corpse.

Rog and his friends had made sure the pallid man was quite dead. They had made sure that what he did to Connie wouldn't happen to anyone else.

Hunter's Moon

"After the first glass, you see things as you wish they were. After the second, you see things as they are not. Finally, you see things as they really are, and that is the most horrible thing in the world." Oscar Wilde is first reported as saying this about absinthe, by Ada Leverson, in 1930.

Susan caught the TGV from Paris, a bottle of absinthe in her backpack. In her head, the plan of a novel that refused to be written, at least until she had settled into her friend's farmhouse near Saint Seurin Sur L'Isle, not far from the town of Montpon Menesterol, which itself was on the edge of Le Foret de la Mole, in the Dordogne. She walked from the small station, her rucksack heavy, the Stone Roses playing over and over again on her iPod. Typically, she had packed too many books. She had a couple of kilometres left to travel, on a windy October afternoon.

The woman who had been looking after the farmhouse left a bottle of Bordeaux on the doorstep, and a spray of late white wild roses and briar thorn, to welcome Susan on her arrival. That cheered Susan as she had just recovered from glandular fever (been kissing too many low-lifers—she suspected). Also, there had been the fire. Although almost six months had passed, the scene surrounding that terrible night was still too fresh in her mind—and she had left her Manchester house feeling some relief.

We were asked to leave the street as they brought the bodies out. Some other neighbours took us in. Whilst the paramedics worked hard, the fireman broke into our house next door to check the property. The cats got out, fleeing into the backwoods. They didn't want to watch either. We stared out

through cold glass, like stricken zombies, mesmerised by the flashing lights
of the paramedic's vehicle. "Why wasn't it rushing away?" I thought.

The kitchen was in true French style, with huge stone sink and a
vast cooking range. Le Creuset was everywhere in orange and the
name reminded her of a small, French general or a loaf of bread;
Susan could never make her mind up which. She took off her
rucksack, reached for the absinthe and thought better of it.
Determined to leave the bottle alone for awhile, she took the white
bedding from the downstairs bedroom, intending to sleep in the big
double bed in the converted loft. Susan buried her nose in the duvet,
which smelt of lavender, and struggled with the billowing mass up
the old wooden staircase to a large room, where a door (presumably
once used when winching something up for storage) opened up to
nothing but the foggy fields beyond. Susan left the door slightly
open, looking forward to the cold of the morning mist. She would
soon be in the warmth of the thick white mass and would not care. A
near-full moon hung low above the horizon and the blue-shuttered
dwelling of the farmhouse lay beneath it. Her friend was away in
America and the farmhouse was Susan's, and hers alone.

The next day, Susan hired a bicycle with an attached basket to get
provisions from the small village of Saint Seurin Sur L'Isle. She
wandered around, getting a feel for the place. The afternoon was
spent lost in *The Wine Dark Sea* by Robert Aickman; Susan wished
that she had a green ship to sail away on. In the evening she snacked
on cheese, meats, half a baguette, and drank wine. She still did not
open the absinthe.

Halfway through the bottle of wine she glanced out of the kitchen
window, into the misty evening. It was still reasonably light and the
hills beyond took on a blue hue. Against the brief streak of reddening
sky she could make out the shape of a horse and its rider, standing
stock still, staring right at her. On impulse Susan waved. The figure
waved back. A few minutes passed before the rider turned the horse
and descended into the blue-grey of the evening.

Next day, Susan found a dead fox on the doorstep. The head lay at
an odd angle. The neck looked to be snapped in half and a chicken,
all bloodied, was wedged inside its mouth. She was both appalled
and confused by the spectacle. Finding a spade in the barn, she dug a

hole behind a half-crooked tree and buried both of the creatures. Susan shivered. She returned to the main house and made a fire with the wood that was stacked up by the hearth.

All that time, a tiny figure had watched her from behind the bushes, a girl of no more than ten years old.

It was then that Susan locked the kitchen door and decided to open up the absinthe. She took a crystal glass down from the dresser and from her rucksack took out her own little silver spoon with patterned crosses on it, and a bag of sugar cubes. She had a jug of chilled water handy. She placed the spoon across the top of the glass, placed a sugar cube on the spoon and almost reverently poured the cooled water over it. As the sugar dissolved into the green liqueur she watched the swirl of white wind its way into the peridot green like a ghost trailing through a verdant forest.

Just as dawn was breaking the firemen led us back up the once-shared path into our house. It had been relatively untouched. The door had one broken window, which they had put through to get to the door catch. There was smoke damage but the rooms were still intact. My heart was not. The fire chief saw the fear in my eyes and he led me upstairs into the corner of the bedroom, where I could still imagine the mummer-black face of the smoke as it had tried to get to us. The smoke-damaged carpet had been pulled away and a few floorboards ripped up. The fire chief gently took my hand and I crouched next to him, my blackened bare feet picking up splinters which I did not feel. He had some sort of heat-sensor that he stuck down through the gap in the boards, and he showed me its reading. He had to do this three times before he saw the flicker of recognition on my face. He assured me that the house next door was cooling down now, and there was nothing left of the inferno that ravaged it. I shrugged, and simply offered, "Thank you."

It became colder in the farmhouse so Susan fed the fire, using kindling which caught easily. Fanned by the warmth of the blaze and the absinthe-haze in her head, she poured a second glass, then a third, and looked down at her feet in front of the fire. The flame— shades of red, orange, and yellow—combined into a confusion of gold that seemed to be grabbing for her ankles, but then yanking back as if gasping for air. One tongue flickered up and became an intense orange, the like of which she had never seen before. It spat and danced its way round the hearth: brighter, sharper, snake-like with its spits and snaps; teasing, tormenting before jerking towards her ankles again. Susan had no idea how much time went by.

She sat up, clutching at the arm of her chair, the fire forgotten. Her half-empty glass fell onto the blue rug, spilling its contents—it too forgotten. On the other side of the fireplace she saw a figure sitting in the rocking chair. The person was wearing brown buckskin; a rifle leant against one knee, and there was a bottle of whisky in their right hand.

"No sense in drinking alone," the figure said in a thick Texas drawl.

"Who the fuck are you?"

The figure was dressed in a man's clothes but with a bosom straining at the buttons, which suggested that Susan was talking to a woman.

"Purty color. What is it you're drinking?"

Susan blinked—but the figure was still there. "Absinthe," she replied, in disbelief.

"Never heard of it. Must have come after my time."

Susan bent down to pick up the glass, looked up again—and the phantom was gone. Thinking that the visitation had been brought on by the absinthe, she turned to put the bottle away in the cupboard of the dresser. The bottle wasn't there. The little silver spoon was there, the bag of sugar cubes, the jug of chilled water, but the beautiful bottle of absinthe was not. She looked everywhere, thinking that she'd had a lapse of memory. Unsteady, and equally uneasy, she decided against sleeping in the loft because of the steep stairs, and wandered into the front bedroom of the farmhouse. The evening moon had risen, heralding a restless night for her.

In the morning she lazed about in the kitchen and drank the last of the coffee. There was little food in the fridge. She thought about going again into the village of Saint Seurin Sur L'Isle but decided on venturing further afield, perhaps to the town of Montpon for lunch. As she opened the kitchen door she saw on the doorstep a bunch of weeds, with yellow flower heads, all tied up with string, and a note. On the note, scribbled in green crayon, were the words:

JAGO HURTS ME

Puzzled, Susan sat on the doorstep, looked at the yellow flower heads, and re-read the note. Jago—who is Jago? Obviously a girl had left the note, because of the flowers, though, perhaps not. Was this Jago some silly kid who was bullying her? Susan put the note on the large oak table, closed the kitchen door and went off on her bicycle in search of lunch, coffee, and a few basic food stuffs to keep her going, although she wasn't really in the mood now to eat.

The journey to Montpon, on the backroads, was an easy ride. The road surface was fine, with only a few potholes hindering her progress. It was a cold morning and Susan was wearing a herringbone jacket, zipped up to under her chin. She never wore a scarf on a bike. It reminded her of how the dancer Isadora Duncan died; her long silken scarf had got caught in a car wheel, and it snapped her neck in two.

Susan looked at the blue swirling mist, which lingered and clung to the trees, even though it was midmorning.

The road wound around a large forest that was a mixture of oak and chestnut, which seemed as if it hadn't been disturbed for hundreds of years. Susan glanced at the sky getting cloudier by the hour. It was going to rain.

The errands didn't take long. She bought coffee, bread, more croissants, a tin of cassoulet, brie, and some wine, all crammed into the grey rucksack on her back.

In the Café du Commerce, Susan seated herself by the window, ate a modest lunch and drank her beer. She listened to "London Calling" by The Clash on the old jukebox, followed by Bob Dylan's "Lay, Lady, Lay". The waiter with large brown eyes smiled at her. Susan smiled self-consciously and looked away. It was quiet in the café and she was happy just to sit and read. She always took a book to a foreign destination, that reflected the people and the country, or at the very least was set in it. This trip, it was *Madame Bovary* and even the English translation was hard going—on an afternoon when she was far more preoccupied by the attentions of the French waiter, who lingered longer to talk to her as he served her beer after beer.

With great reluctance she said goodbye to the waiter; he reminded her of Gerard Depardieu, although the waiter would have made a better-looking Cyrano de Bergerac.

As the first drops of rain splattered onto her trousers, ink-spotting the pale, grey material, the chain slipped on the old bike and Susan caught her trousers on the chain ring.

"Shit," she muttered while reattaching it, before pedalling on down the lane and around the edge of the forest.

The rain came crashing down onto the road with such a force that she sought shelter under the trees. She rested her bike against an oak and leant back against another, when a brightly-coloured poster nailed to a tree trunk caught her attention. It advertised the Cirque de Foret.

Above the sound of the rain she could hear the noise of something else, a buzzing, like that of a woodsman cutting through a tree. Susan followed the sound, making her way through the undergrowth, until she came to its source in a clearing.

A man was cutting a fallen tree into pieces and had a large wheelbarrow next to him. He was a tall man, in his late thirties she guessed, wearing old green cord trousers and a threadbare navy jumper. His long, brown hair was tied back in a scruffy ponytail. Susan had no reason to speak to him. She didn't want anything from him, and anyway, she was just passing time until the rain stopped. There was also another man, smaller and much thinner. Above the din they seemed to be arguing, shouting at each other. The tall man then moved a little so that she couldn't see the other. There was a scream and the tall man stepped to one side. The small man clutched his arm. The noise of the saw stopped and, unthinkingly, Susan ran into the clearing. She took off the rucksack and used her jacket to attempt to stem the flow of blood from the man's wound, which was on the side of his arm just above his right elbow. He was howling with pain and the tall man was just standing there—the saw in both his hands—doing nothing.

"Jago!" the small man called out. Susan recognised the name. It was the name on the note—*JAGO HURTS ME*

"Can't you help him? Put that damned thing down and do something."

Jago put the saw down, gave her a contemptuous look which surprised her, and then took off his jumper. He tugged her jacket off the arm and threw the blood-soaked thing to the ground. He bound his jumper around the wound, with one hand picked up the saw, as if it was made of plastic, and with the other hand dragged the small man off through the trees, deeper into the forest. The small man was weeping bitterly and all Susan could hear between his cries was what sounded like a prayer. "Father of all delight, and mother of all our longing, come to me—" Susan couldn't hear the rest of what he said but she was puzzled by the words.

The small man whimpered as he was dragged at speed between the trees. He stumbled once and cried out. Susan could see the green branches, lashing him and adding to his torment. Susan hung back, wondering if perhaps she should just cycle to the local gendarmerie and explain what she had seen, or go back to farmhouse to think about it some more. She did neither, but still followed through the thickest part of the forest where the damp moss clung to channels of water. The oak and chestnut forest had given way to pine and the needles cushioned the sound of her footsteps.

Eventually she lost sight of the pair in front of her and just aimed for the general direction she thought they had taken. After half an hour of negotiating tiny brooks and the stinging lashes of twigs against her arms and face, she came to the edge of the forest and crouched low in the thick hem of trees.

I thought about life after death a lot following the fire, and wondered, if you met a horrifying death, did the spirits on the other side have to treat you for shock when you crossed over? I went to the library to read about all beliefs and was drawn to the Gnostics, dualism and monism, radical dualism and mitigated dualism and qualified monism—and became confused—so I put them down and read William Blake's "The Tyger." I felt that I could cope with that. I decided not to bring any lambs into the slaughter; made sure I took the pill every day and took pleasure in nothing. I stayed at home and read stories about survival, and Sharper Knives by Christopher Fowler. I began to read and write more horror as the years passed.

From the forest edge, Susan could see a group of three caravans— a little small for a carnival, she thought. One was blue, one bleak-red, and another a faded green. She shuddered with cold and hunger. Then the sound of voices distracted her and there was the smell of something burning in the air. Susan pushed back into the trees a little so that she could get a better view of what was going on.

"I've heard a dog with a necklace of tin cans around his neck make less noise than you."

Susan, startled, turned around and sat promptly down in the mud and pine needles. She put her hand over her mouth to stop from crying out. A few feet away from her, seated on a log, was the buckskin woman; the woman she had attributed to her absinthe dream.

"Don't fret girl, just keep it down some."

"I didn't think you were real."

"Well I'm not, in a manner of speaking."

"And what do you want with me?"

"Well, now that you ain't drinking the green stuff, I want you to help a child of mine."

"Of yours?"

"Manner of speaking, yes. She is my great-great-granddaughter. The child's name is Bethany Canary Burke. I did a bad thing. When folk raised some money for my girl to go into a convent, I spent the money on booze and friends—a terrible thing."

"Your child?"

"No, dammit, *that* was years ago. Ain't you listening? This child is my great-great-grandbaby. My gal grew up and married her cousin Robert Burke, who was this girl's great-grandpa."

"Was?"

"All gone now. The child has no one left, just her old, decrepit great-great-grandma. You understand me now?"

"Well, no. What has this to do with me?"

"I want you to get her away from them people who run this freak show—take her and get as far away as you can. Got that?"

"Me?"

"Jeezus. Cain't ya get your head around this, girl?"

"No—I mean, why me?"

"Because she's taken a shine to you. Who do you think brought that fox to you? She's like a little kitty bringing you presents—ya know, like to her ma."

"Why can't you look after her, and where is her own mother?"

"Well, that would be a little difficult seeing as I'm dead 'n all. Her relatives are all gone bad—her mom too."

Susan looked her up and down; the buckskin shirt and trousers, her long brown hair streaked with grey and tied at the nape of her neck with a bit of string. On her head she wore a shabby, brown Stetson. Her eyes, cobalt blue—and a scar down her left cheek that looked to be almost healed.

"You seem pretty much alive to me."

"What surprises me is that I *feel* like I'm alive too—but I'm not. Here, take my hand."

To placate the woman Susan reached across to her and tried to touch her hand. She could see the colour of it. It belonged to a strong woman in the prime of her life, tanned by long afternoons in the sun. It looked solid enough but Susan couldn't catch hold of it. Startled, she tried to grasp the woman's hand again but batted thin air in her efforts to grab something substantial.

"See what I mean? I can talk to ya and you can see me, but that's the measure of it I'm afraid."

In an attempt to ground something of what had just happened Susan just kept staring about; at the pine trees, at the wet autumn landscape, the soaked flat grass, anything but at the buckskin woman. She could smell rotting ferns in the air and all her senses were in full working order. In fact, her extra sensory abilities seemed in full working order too—for now she could see dead people.

"And if I don't help you?"

"Then a poor, sweet girl will suffer even more and you will be stuck with me for an awful long time."

"Define long time."

"Your whole life. I'll be with ya when you eat 'n sleep. Alongside ya when you go out with a man, when you stay in with a man. I'll be everywhere. They'll be no privacy, none at all."

Susan sighed…looked to the darkening sky and thought about the fact that her breakdown, finally—after the fire—was now fucking total…and she nodded.

"Okay. Where do we start?"

"Why, with an introduction, Sue—where else?"

"Who exactly are you?"

"Well, most folks called me Jane. We can start there. Come on, let's go see Bethany."

Susan followed meekly behind, like one who had just found out that her reality was rapidly running out of choices. Jane, of course, moved soundlessly through the undergrowth. Every snap of a twig underfoot, every swish of a branch as Susan pushed through was met with a hard stare from her new companion.

"Why are you here now? Why not before?" Susan asked.

"I'm as sure—as a coyote's heart when he yips at the moon—that I have no idea why. Now hush."

As they skirted the caravans Susan kept low to the ground, occasionally dropping to one knee whilst Jane listened carefully and motioned with her hands to move on, closer to the campfire, from which arose the most horrendous smell of dead meat cooking. They could see the two men arguing and the small man becoming more agitated. Susan saw Jago punch the small man in the face, and he called for another man to see to the wound.

One woman in red was sitting on the caravan steps, oblivious to the cries of pain coming from the small man. There were no other women to be seen. She proffered Jago her cheek.

"Let me kiss your other cheeks," he laughed as he drew her into the red caravan.

Susan and Jane crept around to the far side where a child was playing with an Alsatian dog. The girl, wearing a faded blue dress, was throwing a ball to the edge of the clearing from where the dog kept bringing it back. It wasn't long before the girl noticed that someone was watching her from the undergrowth, and she ran up to them both with the dog in tow.

"Come on Roux, come on boy, and sit!" she said as she plonked herself down by Susan. The dog obeyed without hesitation.

"She speaks English," said Susan.

"She is English," Jane replied.

"But she's in France."

"So what, you are in France but do you speak the lingo?"

"Well I understand a little but speak it very badly."

"Enough, Sue. Listen to what Bethany has to say."

"Did you like the chicken, Miss Sue?" asked Bethany, eyes eager for attention. "I had to run fast to catch the fox that had it."

"Thank you, Bethany, but did you have to kill the fox?"

"Well, I had to. I wanted to get the chicken to you, Miss Sue. Sorry about that."

"That's okay, Bethany."

Jane was beginning to get fidgety. "Down to business. Bethany, I want you to go with Sue here."

"But I don't want to, Grandma."

"But yesterday you said you did, child."

"That was yesterday, Grandma, and now Billy has promised me—"

"Don't matter what Billy promised you. Remember what Jago did to you!"

The child's face darkened.

The tone of Jane's voice changed from irritation to anger. "Show Sue your back, child."

Bethany thought for a moment and asked Sue to undo the back buttons of her dress. As she did so Susan's fingers started to tremble. She thought she could see something on the girl's back. When the final button was undone Susan felt her stomach tighten and had to quell the need to be sick. In letters along the middle of Bethany's back had been carved a word. Scabs were beginning to fall off, but the new pink skin, where the knife had written, revealed the word:

MINE

Susan began to cry quietly as she fastened up the girl's dress. She could see now that old blood had stained the blue material, and it brought back the worst of memories.

The inquest went well until I gave evidence, and told them that I thought the family might have had a chance to escape. But the only means of escape had been narrow windows along the top, which in effect had signed their death warrants. Well, I didn't put it quite like that. This upset the relatives who had told the grandmother that the children had died in their sleep—but I knew better. The grandmother would always remember it as a house full of smoke and no flames.

"Tell me, Bethany. You trust me don't you?"

Bethany smiled thinly. "If my Grandma says to trust you, I will."

"Did Jago do anything else to hurt you?"

"After he did *that* he said that he would never hurt me again. He said that in a few days he'll give me a reward. There will be a party, and I will be the Queen of Hunter's Moon. The other circus people will join up before...or after that...I don't know. Billy says something is stopping them from coming but I don't know what."

Susan felt a cold hand on her shoulder and she turned around to see Jago's wild eyes staring at her. The small man, Billy, was standing by his side, holding his bandaged arm and wincing with pain.

"Let me go!" Susan shouted as Jago grabbed her by both arms.

She struggled frantically to escape. She broke free but mind-bending pain exploded at the back of her head.

When she came around she was tied up with rope that tightened as she moved to free her hands. She thought that she must be in one of the small caravans. Bethany was crying, holding her hand, and Jane was sitting on the floor next to her.

"I should have heard him. I should have heard him coming," whispered Jane.

With a groan Susan lifted her head and peered around in the near darkness. The place was filthy with screwed up paper and dirty clothes. She lay on a small bed in the corner, and a dismal lantern sat on a box across from her.

"Don't be sad." Bethany looked afraid but added in a calm voice. "It's the Hunter's Moon tomorrow. I'll be crowned Queen and you shall be free. They will have to do as I say."

"Child, we have to get you out of here before tomorrow. Sue here is hurt. We'll have to get her some help too."

Jago appeared then in the doorway.

Jane got up from the caravan floor and stood directly in front of Jago.

"Why, you half-breed animal, if you touch my granddaughter again I'll slit you from throat to prick and feed your insides to that dog over there."

"He can't see you Grandma, you know that. Only Sue and me can see you."

Jago gave the girl a funny look. "Get to bed, child."

Bethany reluctantly left the caravan with him.

The desperation within Susan began to rise until her breathing became ragged and her heartbeat could almost be heard. She looked up at Jane towering above her. "If you can be seen by me can't you go and get some help from someone else?"

"I tried. Somethin' to do with Bethany—she has some sort of special connection to you and so you can see me. The only other person, well animal, that can see me is that dog Roux. We don't have much time, Sue. It's the Hunter's Moon tomorrow night. I think that they have a sort of weird ceremony cooked up for it and Bethany—"

"Oh God," Susan thought about the word that had been cut into Bethany's back.

As day broke Susan could smell the foul cooking pot again and she wondered what had been added this time. It reminded her of the sickening, goose-grease that her own grandmother had made her swallow when she had a sore throat. Her other grandmother had placed camphor crystals in a little cloth bag on red ribbon and tied it around Susan's neck. She had preferred the latter.

All that day she remained tied up, although she felt the binding loosen when she fought to get free. Jago had placed a filthy, black and white chequered rag across her mouth, and when he left her alone she'd lost control of her bladder more than once out of desperation and fear.

It was well into the evening when Jago reappeared in the caravan doorway. He had cleaned himself up a bit; his brown hair had been washed, and it hung loose in waves down to his shoulders. He reminded Susan of an artist's self portrait she had seen once. He had the same long face and nose, with beard and moustache surrounding a full mouth. Jago was also wearing a fur trimmed, brown robe, as if about to go to a grand ceremony—the crowning ceremony for the Queen of the Hunter's Moon. Over his shoulder the blood-moon had already risen, a warning to the innocent and vulnerable.

By his side was Bethany, dressed in white with all the red, gold, and orange of the harvest flowers bound into a circlet on her head. Tiny ears of barley and corn stuck out like a crown of thorns and her bouquet of faded, autumn flowers was threaded with purple berries. Her lips had been smudged with the ripe juice of purple berries too, and she smiled up at Jago, expectant, waiting for her reward. Jago smiled at her in return and put a protective arm around her shoulder—just above his scrawled handiwork.

The dog, Roux, squeezed past them, and sat down close to Susan. He began to whine a little, occasionally glancing up at her to see if she would give him some comfort, and then at Jane in the corner who was constantly trying to get the dog to do something. Bethany walked further into the caravan and Jago seated her on the small bed. He moved the lantern and placed it on a hook next to Susan. She could feel the heat of it on her face, whilst he untied the rope around her feet.

The woman in red came into view in the doorway, wearing a long, gypsy skirt. Her hair was black and she wore a necklace that looked as if it had been made of a dozen dried snakes, oiled to bring a little of their golden colour back. Susan thought of the serpent-fire of her absinthe dream in the French farmhouse, and frantically pulled at the rope that bound her hands. Billy was just behind the gypsy woman and they both backed down the steps a little and then leant over them to get a better look.

With a sudden movement the dog leapt to its feet and started to lick Susan's face. He brushed against the small, hot lantern once and howled with pain. He bumped it again and it fell off the hook and onto the floor. A flash of fire shot across the caravan floor. Billy and the gypsy woman scrambled back as Susan struggled to get away from the flames, trying desperately to get to her feet. She shot a glance across at Jago, who did nothing but remain still, his arm around Bethany's tiny waist—a slow smile spreading across his face

Susan felt the rope binding finally give way from her wrists and she snatched up the lump of iron that held the caravan door open and smashed it against Jago's head. Pulling Bethany up from the bed, she tried to get her away from the flames that now blocked the door. Realizing there was no escape, they both retreated further into the tiny caravan whilst the smoke thickened, and the heat grew unbearable. The dog whimpered and clawed at the floor as Bethany screamed.

Beneath her feet Susan felt weakened wood and she brought the full force of her heel down on the splintering planks. With another mighty effort she brought her heel down again until she could feel the planks give way beneath her feet. With more stamping and pounding she broke a hole through the floor. Quickly, she lowered Bethany and then Roux through the gap. She continued to hammer at the rotten boards until there was room enough for her to get through too. She ran from the blazing caravan to Bethany and Jane, who were crouching at the edge of the trees. Susan stared once more at the inferno, and once more, saw the flames engulf the Manchester house, back in England.

The council had done a good job on the renovation and the estranged husband tried to rent the house after the fire. I blocked him. If it was one thing I could do, it was to make sure that he didn't get the house that joined onto mine. A single mother got it, who knew well what had happened there.

Each night, last thing she would do was, say goodnight to her own tiny sleeping daughter—and then calm the dead little boys who tried to speak

through burnt faces. The boys, refused to leave.

A look of pain flickered across her face as Susan remembered those boys. She looked down into the cobalt-blue eyes of Bethany, and then those of her great-great-grandmother. Jane—with a triumphant smile—began to fade away into the darkness.

The red caravan burned brightly in the night, attempting to outshine the blood-red moon. Billy and the gypsy woman were nowhere to be seen beyond the smoke, but Susan thought she heard cries of pain; Jago, writhing in the inferno, and in his own madness.

"Where's Grandma gone?" Tears fell down her pale cheeks, across the berry lips and onto the faded autumn flowers that she still held in her hands.

"To a safe place, Bethany." Susan stared into the flames. "We will find our own safe place, Bethany, I promise."

Susan was crying now too, but more with a sense of release, than from fear.

Author note: This story has brought back painful memories but had to be written. Distance and time have made that possible. In 1994 I raised the alarm when I heard strange noises and black smoke coming from the house next door to mine, in Manchester. One pathway led to both houses and one month later I removed the withered flowers and rain drenched toys that lined that path. Each day for a month I had walked past them and each day I had wanted to throw them away but couldn't because I was afraid someone would see.

Shadow Upon Shadow

"The inhumanly still face leaned over toward her, the shadows of its great horns drooping over its forehead. Within the staring sockets she could see no eyes at all." By kind permission, from "Dolls," in *Scared Stiff* by Ramsey Campbell. MacDonald & Co. Ltd. 1987.

It took a long time to push, with a struggling will, to that higher part of Alice's mind where she could not tell reality from insanity—between what was imagined and the supernatural. In her indecision she was suffering. That night she had tampered with doors that should not be opened, pushed the car over the cliff with herself in it, and unknowingly had unleashed something from deep within her subconscious, or another place—where dark things live, where creatures as old as time, formless but nonetheless still dangerous, dwelt.

Breakfast and taking the kids to school was a blur, something done by another self who was as equally confused as her. Alice kissed the boys, Ellis and Ben, goodbye. She then made her way down Malvern Avenue, and up the Old Town Hall steps to the oldest part of the library. Here, she was helping the librarian clean, document, and index the Vanderbilt Collection that had been bequeathed to the people of Lawson Town ten years ago, but was still gathering dust.

Alice couldn't shake off the feeling that she was being followed, causing her to constantly look back over her shoulder.

It was as if she could feel someone's acrid breath on her neck, and she could smell something that reminded her of the stinkhorn that grew in buried wood, with its odour of rotten meat. However, there was nothing or no one there. She hurried past Walter Maitland's door and settled herself down to the morning's work, cataloguing all the papers of Sanders Vanderbilt's travels to China. He had thrown nothing away and the nineteenth century papers belonging to the trading family were in a dozen brown boxes, stacked in random order, taking up half the small room in the library east wing.

Alice shivered and stared abstractly at the snow-chill landscape of the car park, trying to remember the images of the night before. She replied to a question from Jean, the senior archivist, but could only hear the words in a somewhat dull tone, as if she were trying to eavesdrop into someone else's conversation.

"Alice, are you listening? Take your lunch at anytime you want today—Alice?"

"Sorry, Jean. I'm really not feeling very well. Can I have the afternoon off and work late tomorrow?"

Jean fiddled with her glasses and pulled out a red book that had suddenly attracted her attention from a shelf close by. "What's that you said?" She set her eyes on Alice and then nodded.

"You look very pale. Yes, you can go home."

Pulling her coat collar up against the chill wind, Alice made her way through the cold, winding streets, her face bitten by the ghastly February wind. She went home to the house on Holland Avenue, which was usually a warm refuge against the staggering cold. She paused at the gate and looked up at the pale-blue curtain that framed her bedroom window. She thought she saw the curtain move to one side before convincing herself that she had imagined it. Something sinister had happened last night in the middle of that room, something that she couldn't quite remember. Until a few months ago her everyday life had been rooted in the real world. Now though, she seemed to be slipping into another.

Alice made herself some cinnamon coffee and gripped the mug tightly in an effort to get warmer. Once settled on the couch, she switched on the telly and began watching a programme about cable cars in San Francisco. Suddenly she sat bolt upright, nearly spilling her coffee. Her mouth dropped open in amazement as the camera focused on one passenger in particular. It was her grandmother, on her father's side, May Thomas—sitting there in her best, blue Sunday coat and a dark blue felt hat with the violet brooch that she always wore. May Thomas, who had been ten years dead and was giving her *that* look she used to save for when Alice, as a young child, had been careless in her grandmother's house.

"You're in deep water, Alice—far too deep for you."

Her grandmother's tone was abrupt and cold. Alice could smell the sweet fragrance of Lily of the Valley in the air and she knew, in a part of her, that she wanted her life to be simple again, and that her grandmother was right. The sharp, blue eyes of May Thomas held Alice in a solid chain of contact from which Alice could not break away, and then the camera drifted from her grandmother, to the other passengers who looked as though they actually did belong on the trolley. Alice was shocked. She held back the tears and shivered, telling herself she would have to resist whatever Maitland had in mind for her. She then convinced herself that her imagination had got the better of her, and that she had not seen or heard her grandmother.

The telly was in the far corner of the room. Alice got off the couch and stumbled over to it. She turned it off and swayed slightly, the nausea welling up from the pit of her stomach until she could taste the bitterness in her mouth. The room began to spin around her and she felt guilty about the secretive encounters with Walter Maitland, that she needed to end. Her husband, Geoff, was away on business, and Alice believed she had seen her guilt mirrored in his eyes before he left. He didn't suspect...did he? It was not just the guilt that was haunting her but fear as well.

Alice prepared to go out and her thoughts fell upon last Tuesday, when she had gone to Maitland's house to tell him she was ending the affair. He had been calm. But he frightened her when he pulled out a kitchen drawer, and started rattling the knives. He held one up and the cold sunshine streaming through the window struck the blade and dazzled her. Maitland slowly placed the knife back in the drawer and shut it with a loud bang. Alice jumped and panicked. She could feel the sweat on her palms and see the wry smile on his face. Was he going to try and make her stay?

Today was the day she had agreed to meet him one last time and Alice hurried to his car, when it drew up around the corner. She slipped on the icy pavement and felt herself about to fall. Recovering her footing she made for the car and opened the door—hesitated for an instant—trying to remember a warning that could not now be recalled, and got in. Once inside she turned to face his dark, hooded eyes that both attracted and repulsed her at the same time.

"Where this time? Not the house?" she asked with more than a hint of nervousness.

"Not the house," he replied.

"Then where?"

"You'll see." He smiled and patted her knee. She shuddered. There were very few words between them. The usual day-to-day stuff was of no interest to them at all. Maitland was a mysterious man thirty years her senior, and Alice had been attracted to an *otherness* about him. She was interested in the occult. Maitland was charismatic and reminded her of the sinister Alistair Crowley. She had been willing to risk her marriage—everything—to experience something of the dark side of magic.

February. Cold. But, Maitland took her to a broken down hut in the middle of Nairn's Wood. Through rotten bracken to a small place that smelt of musk and strange, odorous plants, the names of which she would never know. He had been to the hut before her. The floor was covered with thick, animal furs—enough to cover them too, and keep the cold out. He lit three black candles and indicated that she should remove her clothes. He placed a fur pelt around her waist, which he tied securely with scraps of skin, still attached to the fur. The fur felt good, sensual, and seemed familiar. Maitland picked up a dark-green bowl and bade her drink the mixture that smelt a little like mulled wine but had an underlying taste that was unknown to her.

"I can't, I can't do this anymore," she pleaded.

Before entering her, he smeared his penis with a strange, animal-smelling cream that heightened her orgasm and no doubt his. During copulation her head filled with vile faces of creatures hideously deformed, and yet she found the attraction of their evil irresistible—it lingered like a fugue. When they coupled she felt the evil flow into her and it fed deep within her soul. He had not done anything too foul to her, yet, but the evil started to grow, nurtured by lust and need.

Alice knew that she had to stop. Maitland was beginning to scare her. Each rendezvous, outside the house, was arranged in the remotest of places; occasionally on the cold damp ground in the darkest part of the woods. They lay beside fires in blue-brown clearings that smelt of sacrifice, of animal blood and bone, where no one would hear her scream. In her ecstasy she hardly felt his hands upon her throat.

That night her sons looked askance at her with troubled eyes and she knew she had gone too far. She had been afraid for some time about ending the affair with Maitland. Alice suspected that nothing was ever that simple but she had to end it.

The next morning Alice did not go to work but chose to go to the library; not the one in the Old Town Hall but the one on Raglan Street. It had always been a place of comfort and peace for her. The library was quiet for midmorning—even on a market day—and each of the two rooms close to the main counter were empty. Alice chose to go into the room where three schoolgirls were sitting, legs crossed, on the large table under the window. Each girl was about ten years of age and wore a school uniform, none of which matched the colours of the local school. Alice remembered that Maitland had chosen her because, "…she had something about her that was childlike."

If the librarian caught the girls sitting on the tables they'd be in for it, she thought. The girls suddenly started laughing and making faces. They poked one another and pulled one another's hair. The noise was overwhelming, and Alice watched in surprise as they began screaming even louder, jumping off the table and overturning the chairs.

The librarian came in to put a few books away and the girls jumped out at her, waving their arms in front of her face, trying to attract her attention—but to no avail. She did not see them. They laughed at Alice and pinched one another, generating more screams that would wake the dead.

Perhaps they are the dead, Alice thought.

The librarian did not see them but Alice did. Was she going mad? She hadn't slept for two nights, but, surely sleep deprivation couldn't produce this.

"You see them too, don't you?" A man had entered the room and stood by her side. He was around fifty, with a beard and moustache, looking like some English professor with his notebook and pen. Next to him was a man wearing a baseball cap, who peered over the older man's shoulder trying to see what he was writing.

The man in the cap became irritated and distracted. "I said my name was David Dobson not Hodgson."

"Quite," said the professor, crossing out Hodgson and writing Dobson. He then wrote *young woman and fledgling eye*, on his pad.

Alice was speechless. There was a sickly-sweet smell of burnt brown sugar in the air. The girls were pulling out books and stacking them behind the librarian, giggling and waiting for her to turn around and fall over them. The professor continued to write in his notebook and then paused—

"You will soon get used to it. I see them all the time."

"So do I," said David Dobson.

The librarian turned around, but by this time the books were back on the shelves and the girls were seated again on the table, swinging their legs and singing a song that Alice faintly recognised as a childhood nursery rhyme.

Alice fled from the building and into what she thought was the comparative safety of the shopping mall. She had the sudden desire to buy something in green, but had no idea why or what? She made for the first shop selling women's clothes and wandered along the rows, pausing to choose a green skirt and a pair of bottle-green army trousers. Then, she paid for both and left the shop to go…but where? She didn't know.

It was then that she saw them

At every one of the half-dozen shops along each side of the mall she saw a man standing by the doorway, like some bouncer at the entrance to a nightclub. But there was something strange about them. All the men were Caucasian and dressed in black. Dark men outside dark doorways, and suddenly the entrance to each shop had turned into some black abyss through which she was sure one could vanish forever.

"Is there nowhere safe?" Alice whimpered.

She made for home. Seeing her dead grandmother on TV was nothing compared to the kids in the library and the men at the mall. She could go to her sister's. No. Her sister was looking after Ellis and Ben that night, as Alice had told her she would be working late at the library. Besides, Alice didn't want them involved in this, whatever *this* was. The world seemed stable before she began the affair and now her life seemed to be in pieces. She was falling apart; Alice could barely count out the money when she bought a bottle of wine at the liqueur store.

Once outside her home she nervously glanced up at the bedroom curtains, unlocked the door and sat on her stairs clutching the shopping bags and the wine. Her head was exploding with images of people and things that should not be there. What was happening to her? Was Maitland behind it all? Or was she going mad? Seated on the stairs she started a steady rocking motion to comfort herself. Then she pulled the skirt and the trousers out of the bag, wondering which to wear for protection—green is good isn't it—the colour of life. That might help—will it?

Alice burst into tears. Was the whole of the ghost world trying to get her attention? She was terrified. She dared not look over her shoulder and that rotten smell was still there.

She went through the house, too terrified to sit still for long. Alice felt compelled to throw some of her most-valued possessions out in the trash can: the radio her mother had bought her; the porcelain figure of the little child she had treasured; the wedding cards that she said she would never throw away, until now.

"They all have to go," she said sadly. Was this a precursor to her departure, and if so to where?

She almost threw out the manuscript that she had written, based on the Lancashire Witch Trials in seventeenth century England, but in the end some stronger impulse saved that.

Once done with the cleansing she felt exhausted. She heard the phone ring—that would be her husband—but she ignored it. She would sort this out herself. Alice opened the wine, poured a large glass, took it upstairs with her and sat down upon the bed. She briefly closed her eyes and sensed the great rushing of Maitland's face coming towards hers at break-neck speed.

"Boo!"

With that simple, childish word coming out of nowhere Alice held her breath as she looked into the dressing table mirror. The weak sunlight of a February afternoon lit the room and in the mirror, for a brief second, she could see the form of a man dressed in black.

Once more she fled her house, leaving the door open behind her.

She had no fear of the living, just of the dead—or her own madness. She tried to cross Delaware Road but found it difficult to do so, on account of a man in a dark overcoat standing so close to her, whose proximity scared her half to death.

Halfway there, Alice thought; but to where?

She backed away from the edge of the road and jumped instinctively as someone tugged at her arm.

"Are you all right, Miss? You don't seem okay to me." A cop was staring hard at her. She could see in his eyes that he was wondering if she were in trouble or if she were simply unwell and needed help in crossing the road.

"Can't you see him, can't you see the man?" she started.

"What man, Miss?"

"The man standing right next to you."

The cop looked around behind him. "There's only you and me here."

Alice didn't say anything as the tears once more streamed down her face. She had done a lot of crying that day. The cop helped her to cross the road and she wandered aimlessly into the park, and sat down on a bench. As the snow gathered and settled on her green coat she shivered until her lips turned blue with the cold. Far across the park, children were coming out of school, and Alice thought she saw her sister pick up Ellis and Ben. They never came across the park and so they would not see her. She closed her eyes and whispered a silent prayer.

She saw Walter Maitland just one more time.

Ellis and Ben never saw their mother again.

A body was found just north of town—or what was left of it after the dogs had been at it.

In the spring Maitland found a new 'Alice', for he had become nostalgic and realised that he missed the old one. Her name was Anne and she was an assistant in a drug store. She invited him over for dinner and whilst he sipped his red wine he thought about the new games he would devise for her. Maitland heard the rattle of knives in a kitchen drawer, just before he fell into unconsciousness.

In the kitchen, Anne made cinnamon coffee and nodded in agreement with the other woman, who spoke to her earnestly and then faded away into the shadows.

The Bone Grinder

"She thought of Jeanie in her grave,
Who should have been a bride;
But who for joys brides hope to have,
Fell sick and died, In her gay prime,
In earliest winter-time,
With the first glazing rime,
With the first snow-fall of crisp winter-time."
"Goblin Market" by Christina Rossetti.

The British rarely go into detail about death and it came as a shock to Christy when she went to Blackstock's funeral parlour to pick up her mother's ashes, that they weren't ashes at all, just small bits of ground up bone—a light colour of brown—all that was left of the small, fragile old woman.

In her grief Christy couldn't make her mind up where to put her mother's bits of bone, until they were to be interred at St. Mary's Church in Prestwich, Manchester. The remains came in a brown plastic container with a screw-on lid. The container was larger than she thought it would be, half the size of an upended bread bin. Christy would unscrew it every day to look at her mother, being very careful not to spill any of her out on the kitchen floor. There was no smell of death; just her mother's leftover life.

Christy felt old at forty. Those two hours that she had stayed with her mother after she died had aged Christy, without doubt. As her mother took her last breath Christy was horrified to see the years rush into her mother's lovely face and her tongue start to turn black around the edge. Christy had felt Death brush by her cheek, making her feel defenseless and afraid.

For a time she kept the brown container on the bookshelf in the living room...then in the garage. But it was chilling and impersonal in there, and at one point she even had it in the car, until the day she had to say farewell forever. Christy had heard of relatives who never gave up their dead, who could not stand for them to be mixed up with everyone else in the garden of remembrance. Her mother would have her own special place in St. Mary's graveyard, under the oldest of oak trees which was bent and weather worn, its lower branches spread wide over its charges, as if gathering them together for safe keeping.

Macabre books and films had engrossed Christy after her mother's death. She had never actually been to see The Sedlec Ossuary, a Roman Catholic chapel, which was underneath the cemetery in the Czech Republic, but she had seen a programme about it on TV, and the memories had stayed with her.

In the nineteenth century an artist had been commissioned by the Schwarzenberg noble family to sort the bones out. He placed thousands of human bones in four neat mounds in each corner of the chapel, made a coat of arms for the family and hung in the centre of the nave a chandelier that contained every bone in the human skeleton.

After the programme that night Christy had the nightmare

She felt a heavy, shifting weight pressing her down. She could just about push her hand up between skulls and bones; the hideous mass of bones moved with a gravel sound when she did so. Once at the top she could see by the light of the grim, bone chandelier the avalanche of grisly remains that she had managed to free herself from. Christy struggled to hold back the bile in her throat. The compulsion to be sick was strong but her reverence for the dead was even stronger. She would not further defile the bones.

That nightmare was two years ago now.

Christy had since taken on the job of a Duty Manager at the Mortimer Hotel in Manchester, where a number of waitresses came and went from the Baltic states of Lithuania, Latvia, and Estonia, all working for minimum wage. Not all Eastern European women were sold into sex slavery it seemed, though Christy had read on the net about the impromptu slave market raided outside the coffee shop in Heathrow. Money had changed hands before the police had broken it up and they had taken the young girl away into protective custody. It seemed that the going rate was four thousand pounds per girl and the girls fell into it because of threats to their families. Passports were taken off some girls and given to others from non-EU countries like the Ukraine and Moldova.

Christy shivered and was relieved to think that her girls (the waitresses Janina, Marija, Ona, Gabriele, Evelina, and Auguste) were at least safe for the time being from prostitution. Others were not so lucky, and recently Kamile had left abruptly. Christy liked to believe that they went home—as some did—when they were homesick. Some girls left without giving notice but whilst they were there, they worked hard and complained little.

The Mortimer Hotel, with its sixty basic bedrooms, was mostly for businessmen and overnight visitors to Manchester—but not the sort of place to stay in for more than one night. For thirty quid one couldn't expect much. Apparently the hotel had been renovated recently and Christy had taken the job a week or so after. She wasn't crazy about the work but her husband, Paul, was pulling his weight and she wanted to get the credit cards down to a manageable level.

Occasionally the hotel was open to anyone off the street for *Soul Night,* or other such lacklustre event. Up until now Christy had only been working the day shift, where she'd heard some complaints about noise in the early hours on a Saturday morning. But her shift didn't start until Monday, and the people who complained at the weekend had usually left by then. Betty, one of the old cleaners, had said something about complaints concerning unusual noises, and recently some filthy, bloody bandages had been left in the sink of room thirty-two. It *was* a cheap hotel after all.

On Monday morning Gabriele, one of the more able girls, had cooked limp bacon and underdone eggs again.

"Gabriele, you need to leave it in the pan longer, get it crispy, and cook it longer—do you know what I mean?"

The pretty Lithuanian girl smiled her most *You-have-to-forgive-me-because-I'm-still-new-and-foreign* sort of smile and Christy left it at that for the time being. The minimum wage wasn't much to survive on, although the girls did live very cheaply up in the old attic bedrooms of the hotel. Unless Gabriele actually did cause an outbreak of food poisoning, Christy wasn't going to get too arsey about it.

"Cook it for longer, longeeer, okay Gabriele?"

Gabriele nodded enthusiastically, "Okay Christy,"—and proceeded to dish out the undercooked bacon again.

Perhaps that is the way they cook bacon in Lithuania, thought Christy.

She spun on the spot, recalling that she had come into the kitchen for another reason.

"Where is Marija this morning?" Gabriele's smile dropped quickly from her face and she shrugged.

"Have you seen her?"

"No Christy, perhaps she not wake-up."

With a last, disappointed look at the breakfast Gabriele was taking out to a soon-to-be-unsatisfied guest in the dining room, Christy took the lift up to the fifth floor of the hotel. Here were the dingy and neglected staff bedrooms; the staff who usually rose early in the mornings. That is, if they hadn't left for other jobs.

Perhaps that is what had happened to Marija, thought Christy.

Marija's room was number fifty-eight, at the end of the dismal corridor that had not benefited from the meagre renovation programme. The carpet was a dark grey, covered with equally dark brown stains, and one in particular reminded her of the silhouette of John Hurt in his grotesque role as *The Elephant Man*.

Christy rarely ventured into this part of the hotel.

Before her time as a manager a young girl had committed

suicide in one of the rooms. Christy didn't know the details, nor which room it was. Perhaps it was the room she now approached.

She knocked on number fifty-eight. No answer. She knocked again. Still no answer. She took the passkey out of her pocket and unlocked the door. There wasn't a particularly *bad* smell—just stale cigarette smoke mostly, and damp. Christy switched on the light.

A few posters adorned the walls. A cream-coloured lamp barely lit the travel posters, which offered paper promises of happiness in exotic destinations, such as Bali and the Maldives. An old wardrobe stood sentinel in the corner and a teak-coloured dressing table sat by one wall. On top of the dressing table was a three-panelled mirror—a trinity of three mirrors. Christy's mother used to have one. She could angle the side mirrors to see different parts of herself. Christy had used the mirror to look at her naked body when entering puberty, at the time when most youngsters explored the quickly developing parts of their body.

The bed had been stripped and an old mattress lay uncovered. Here, the memories of everything that had ever happened on it were traced within the cover and deep in the heart of the springs. No clothes, nothing personal left over, nothing to suggest that a human being had ever been content in that room. How could they be? It was a room without windows situated in the upper part of the hotel. A tiny attic room, in which a window would have been welcome, to at least let through one ray of sunshine and offer its occupant some hope.

As Christy stood in front of the three panelled mirror she smoothed out her work clothes and tidied her hair, noting that she would need to colour out the grey soon.

She became aware of movement in the mirror.

A figure slowly appeared behind her left shoulder, black hair floating around a pale visage. It lingered long enough for Christy to recognise the look of despair and pain on its shriven face, and then it was gone.

Christy had never in her life been more afraid as in that moment. She ran to the door, stumbled, regained her balance and attempted to open the door, fingers trembling. It wouldn't open and she could smell the cold, charnel house breath of something long dead and felt the icy touch of an insistent hand upon her shoulder. She fought to tell herself that it wasn't happening, that there wasn't anything there. She tried to block out the experience—*as it was happening.* For behind her, pulling her now by her waist as if it wanted to combine its icy death with her still warm life...was *something.*

"Stop this. Stop this." The words more hissed than spoken from some unseen thing.

Christy struggled to turn around and push whatever it was that was holding her by the waist. She saw nothing, but then felt the reluctant letting go of invisible hands and heard a low, soft moan, now over near the dressing table. Another attempt at the door and this time it gave. She ran without closing it behind her, through the tepid light, and into the partial darkness of the stairwell.

On the next floor down Christy steadied herself in the well-lit corridor where the guest rooms were. Tight lipped and telling herself that it never happened, for the last half an hour of her shift she busied herself with paperwork at the front desk, close to the main entrance and the street.

As Christy left the Mortimer Hotel that evening she put up her umbrella. Nervous and still in denial, she welcomed the cold air. It was already dark and raining. She pulled the collar of her coat up around her neck to keep out the cold and hurried along the pavement, careful to dodge the puddles and keep as dry as possible. The rain ferociously pounded the road and sidewalks, as if demanding immediate entrance to the concrete. In the distance, just a little way past the street where her old mini was parked, she could hear raised voices.

Through the pelting rain she saw two figures: a man pulling at a woman's arm and dragging her towards a car, where another man sat behind the steering wheel. The driver shouted something at the other man, which had the effect of heightening the tension between the three. The girl screamed and Christy started to dash forward, but held back as the girl was bundled into the car and driven off, away from Cooper Street. Christy was unable to get the number. She thought she could have been mistaken, but the girl looked like Kamile, the waitress who had left her job a few weeks earlier.

Christy fumbled in her pocket for her mobile phone and called the police, explaining what had happened. But they didn't seem interested, stating simply that they would send a spare car around the area when they had one, which she knew meant never.

The next morning another girl, Janina, didn't turn up for her shift and Christy nervously sent one of the maids to check her room. The maid found that most of Janina's clothes were still there. Christy phoned the police again. This time they came round straight away, took a few details, noted that the girl had not been in the country long, and went on their way.

Reluctantly, Christy phoned the agency for another girl. They agreed quickly but that didn't satisfy her. Girls couldn't go on disappearing day after day and just be replaced as if they were practically worthless. She would go and see if she could find Kamile and see if she wanted her old job back.

That evening Christy drove around the streets of Manchester trying to find Kamile, knowing it could be a useless effort and doubting that she would come back. The girls never came back. It was a bitter night and the rain of the previous evening had been replaced by a scattering of snow.

Not far from where she had seen her last time, Christy believed she saw Kamile again, talking to a man before getting into his car. Christy recognised him as one of the men who had hauled a girl into that same car the night before. This time Christy had a chance to follow. She tried to drive just far enough behind to keep up but not be too obvious. People, for all their evil acts, could be seen— and what you could see perhaps you could do something about. Christy liked Kamile and didn't want her in any kind of trouble.

After a few minutes or so the abductor's car pulled onto a road between two high gate posts. It was a familiar place to Christy, as the road led to the crematorium where they had burnt her mother's body. Leaving her car a little way down the road, away from the main entrance, she looked for another way in.

Christy remembered a little side door in the high perimeter wall and tried the latch. Surprisingly that door opened and she ventured towards the back of the crematorium, over the lawn and through the circular garden of remembrance. She was careful not to trip over the small memorial stones, visible in the moonlight. She worried about being seen, but Christy took a chance—she had to know what was going on. It was a cold night, the temperature had dropped and the snow was lying thick enough for her to see footprints at the back of the crematorium, where members of the public were normally prohibited.

It began to snow more heavily, the kind of snow that piled up quickly and could take days to thaw. It only needed a few hours of it. The fresh footprints that led up to the back door of the crematorium would soon be covered up. There were no windows at the back of the building, for obvious reasons. She glanced up and saw black smoke belching into the night sky from a tall chimney above the snow covered roof. She shivered, more from disgust than the cold. She supposed they must do some of the disposal of bodies at night; but what of Kamile? Why had the two men brought her there?

Christy dreaded that she already knew the answer to that question.

At this point she thought it best to ring the police and try to get them to investigate. She put her hand into her pocket for her mobile phone and then swore, realising that she had left it in her bag in the car. She would have to go back.

As she turned, she slipped on a patch of ice near the door and fell against it with a heavy thud. With a stifled cry of pain she fell onto her knees and tried to get back to her feet, but too late. The door opened to the outside and knocked her down again. This time it was her hand that scraped against the ice and stone. She cried out again. Rough hands dragged her to her feet and hauled her into the building. Terrified, she struggled against two bulky figures as they pulled her further into the bright light of the crematorium.

The first thing that she noticed was the smell. A mixture of formaldehyde and an odour equally unpleasant, that must be of burnt flesh and bone.

The room was quite large, crowded with large steel tables and an old cart. On the cart was an open coffin. The two men had wasted no time, for as the taller one dragged Christy past the coffin she saw the body of Kamile—but she was raised up, too high, as if something was underneath her. The heat from the furnace became overwhelming and beside it stood a third, small stringy man in a boiler suit, who looked rather nervous.

"Look here, you didn't say that you were bringin' two here tonight. I can't cope with a change of plan."

"You'll do as we say Bill. There isn't going to be a choice for you."

Christy tried to back out of the room, away from the coffin. "No, please—don't do this. I won't say anything."

"Yeah, right—course you won't," said one of the men.

"Like you could keep quiet about this."

"If my life depended on it, I could."

"It isn't up for discussion."

"Bill. Get on with getting rid of those two in that coffin." He pointed at the cart.

Christy stifled a sob as the crematorium attendant drew the cart closer to the furnace. She turned away in disgust as she heard the electronic conveyor start up and the sound of the coffin move into the fire. A loud bang signified that the furnace door had been closed. The cart pulled back and the process started.

Two bodies, in one coffin.

Christy struggled again and the man in a black overcoat shoved her across to the corner of the room and threw her down into an old high backed armchair. She winced when her arm banged against the wooden chair.

"Tie her feet and hands," he said to the other man in the doorway. That fellow took a plastic cord from his pocket, wrapped it around Christy's wrists and pulled hard, the plastic biting into her skin. He did the same thing to her feet. Just as he gave a last, painful tug a mobile phone went off in his pocket—

some ridiculous frog ringtone that Christy had never found funny. He fumbled and answered.

"Yes, okay. Dave…" He thrust the phone at his mate and bent down to see if the plastic ties were tight enough.

"I'm in the middle of—" Dave looked annoyed but he deferred to the voice on the other end of the line.

"Okay. I'll be straight over." He threw the phone across at the other man who clumsily caught it. "Sid. You wait with her. I won't be long."

"But, can't we get this over with first?"

"No."

"Can't I sort this out?"

"I wouldn't leave you to sort out your own shit let alone this."

Bill looked even more distressed as Dave left the building and stepped into the raging blizzard outside.

"Watch out for the icy roads!" called Sid after him, then he sheepishly bit his lower lip.

"Where's the can? You watch her. I'll pee myself if I don't go. And you fucking watch her well."

Bill pointed to a red door opposite the exit from the building and Sid rushed over to it.

The heat from the furnace was intense. Christy could hear the roar of the fire as it consumed its contents.

Bill shook his head, muttering away to himself in the corner. Christy looked on, her eyes open wide in terror, as she saw him take a pile of human bones from a cardboard box in the corner. He threw them into a funnel and started the bone grinding machine. It would have been the same machine that had reduced the remains of her mother to tiny bits of bone. The noise was unbearable. Something jarred and stuck and he swore under his breath as he turned the machine off.

"Fuckin' machine. Always jammin' and I can't do me job properly. It's supposed to grind into smaller stuff but it's useless—only renders to bits of bone. Ashes—that's a laugh. The damn council won't buy another machine."

Bill gave her a quizzical look, "What the fuck was you nosing around here for?"

"Some girls who worked for me disappeared."

"So you're scum too, just like those bastards. At least I do a real job and earn a decent wage doing what other people couldn't do. Never broke the law until now."

"No, you've got it wrong. The girls did work for me at the Mortimer Hotel."

"Ah that place, another dump."

Christy tried to pull her hands apart, but the plastic ties made that impossible.

"How can you do this?"

"Do what—the burnin' and such? It's me job."

"No, doing the dirty work for them." Christy nodded towards the red door.

"They'd kill me if I didn't."

"You could get caught."

"There isn't anyone that would squeal on them lads. They'd be dead within a day. Anyway, it's not like we're leavin' the bodies around for the police to trip over them, are we?" Bill smiled. "When they're done in the oven, I grind them and put a little of the extra girls in the legitimate containers. It makes them a little fuller than I'd like but I spread the rest in the remembrance garden, tidy like."

Christy felt as if she was going to be sick. The only thing that stopped her was the determination not to be. Then Bill started up the bone grinding machine again. This time she couldn't help herself, and threw up over the side of the armchair.

Bill stopped the machine again, collected the bits of bone in a brown container and brought it over to show Christy.

"Look. It ain't so bad now, better than being food for worms, eh?"

The container was almost full. Bill thrust it in front of her face and she turned away, trying not to be sick again.

"Perhaps there is one of your girls in here. The bastards called her Maria, though that is not how she said it. They had a bit of fun with her in this place before they did her in. Imagine. Fuckin' bastards. *In this place*. No respect those bastards have, none at all." Bill put the container by Christy's side and went back to the bone grinding machine.

Christy thought she heard a rustling sound coming from the container, as if the bone particles were settling. It was only when Bill turned his back that the particles seemed to rise out of the container and take on some sort of shape. It drifted close by Christy and she felt the plastic ties snap and fall away from her wrists and feet. She thought she saw the outline of a woman, the form shifting with some difficulty to retain its suspension in midair, bending over Bill, forcing the stricken attendant back— back towards the furnace.

The police had no alternative but to believe most of what Christy said when they did a thorough investigation at the crematorium. Christy had pulled some heavy boxes against the toilet door so that Sid couldn't escape and later the police found a whole gang of criminals who were involved with the exploitation and disposal of unwilling young women.

There was no trace of Bill. But as Christy went back to put flowers on her mother's memorial some days later, she passed by the back door of the crematorium. The snow was melting and as she placed her foot on the pathway leading out of the remembrance garden, she heard the sharp crunch of bone against the grey stone and she knew that Marija had put him in the best place possible.

The Conical Witch

"Once upon a time a number of children lived together in the Valley of Childish Things, playing all manner of delightful games, and studying the same lesson-books. But one day a little girl, one of their number, decided that it was time to see something of the world about which the lesson-books had taught her; and as none of the other children cared to leave their games, she set out alone to climb the pass which led out of the valley." The Valley of Childish Things and Other Emblems by Edith Wharton.

The bad reputation of stepmothers per se has been well documented. To bring one into the family less than a year after the death of a mother might be considered bad form. But Martin had insisted that he was doing it for the good of his young daughter, Lotte. And Lotte, considering that she was on the verge of puberty, needed a female to relate to. That the woman her father had chosen was a mail-order bride from Russia of all places (she spoke little English), *and* that he went to bed in the daytime with his new wife, had nothing to do with it. Daria was from Minsk, in Belarus, and had been a waitress in a café.

Within hours of Daria entering the house the new stepmother lived up to the reputation—and when her new husband's back was turned, she would make strange gestures with hands and eyes that would root Lotte to the spot until she released her and gestured once more for Lotte to get out of her sight.

"In my country, mothers are the heart and soul of the family," Daria said in a sharp tone that made Lotte's hair stand up on the back of her neck.

A ten-year-old child can still believe in magic—Lotte did. She knew all about witches from all parts of the world. She believed Daria to be a red witch (simply because of the colour of her hair), and that whatever happened from now on, they would be at war. Whoever had the strongest spells would win. And in order to win you had to know your enemy. Lotte had learnt that from her father, who owned a small company that shipped 'antiques' into Russia, and, apparently, women out. He was quite good at his job and told Lotte that he knew how to thrash the competition. Daria, to Lotte, *was* the competition. But it would take more than special offers and dodgy salesmanship to get rid of her—it would take magic.

Witches from around the world, wise women (perhaps even downright evil women), were needed to help—no white witches for Lotte. If it meant using blood and stuff in spells, so be it. And for that she would need some assistance.

Against the trend of the day, which demanded that a child never wander more than three metres from the perimeter fence for fear of abduction and, God forbid, a neighbour patting you on the head and getting mistaken for a pervert, Lotte was allowed to visit Mrs. Grimshaw, who lived on the rundown farm across Tanner's field. As Lotte lived in a small market town, there was not as much tension as there was in the city.

Mrs. Grimshaw had gone through two husbands, that most people knew about. She eventually told Lotte that she had been married five times in all, but only Lotte was entrusted with this information and sworn to secrecy. Lotte was allowed to do errands for her because Martin was so taken up with his new bargain bride he never seemed to notice that Lotte wasn't in the house. It was to Mrs. Grimshaw that Lotte now turned to complain.

From her name you would surmise that the woman had always lived in Yorkshire, and perhaps been married to Yorkshire men. She had travelled the world in the late Sixties and Seventies, and led a bohemian lifestyle. One husband had been the cousin of a shaman doctor of Kyzyl, which proclaims to be the exact centre of Asia. Mrs. Grimshaw had seen him sacrifice lambs to gain power from spirits. Another had been a waiter in Paris, a third a sailor who had died but not been buried at sea. Those were the ones she talked about often, but she never mentioned the other two, or any children she may have had.

Lotte could see Mrs. Grimshaw's farm from her own house. In the winter, when the cold weather wound round her like a rough shroud, Mrs. Grimshaw wore thicker skirts, always a few inches from the ground, with a black coat that ended at knee length. She had shoulder length, black hair and was quite youthful looking. Lotte said that she looked like a huge, black witch's hat drifting along the farm track and foggy fields. Mrs. Grimshaw had laughed at that and said that she wished that she had a conical hat but Lotte didn't quite understand that.

The inside of Mrs. Grimshaw's farmhouse was steeped in mystery.

The lower portion of two kitchen walls was set up like an old haberdashery shop. There were dozens of tiny drawers set in large frames, in which she kept the peculiar objects she'd picked up during her travels. Although the farmhouse from the outside appeared normal enough for an old seventeenth-century house, it was more like the design of a farmhouse you would see in Northumberland near Hadrian's Wall. The house had a small fortified tower on one corner and, along the side that faced the open moorland, the converted barn wall had three small slits. The same slits were above the old kitchen, and in the bedrooms. Mrs. Grimshaw said that part of the house was much older than seventeenth century. In Northumberland a house such as this was needed because of attacks from border reivers. But, on the South Yorkshire moors there hadn't been that sort of problem. The house also wrapped itself around numerous secret closets and passageways that she occasionally showed to Lotte, making her swear an oath to secrecy first.

Mrs. Grimshaw wasn't always a good person, but it didn't stop Lotte from liking her.

"Now remember, Lotte, if Mrs. *Grim*shaw is unhappy she gets out her grand *grimoiré* and is quite capable of nasty things. Learn to toughen up a little, Lotte. It is a hard and restless world and is getting more desperate by the year." There was always more than a hint of humour in her voice.

Lotte would ask for more clarification and sometimes it was like a classroom in the old kitchen, as Mrs. Grimshaw lectured her on how the world was going to hell in a handcart, and they might as well get a little ahead of the game. Mrs. Grimshaw was a twenty-first-century witch for a lost generation, who were all sold on technobabble. She used a computer herself, for her small advisory business and immediate gratification—in that she could instantly find out about anything she wanted. However, there were still some things that resisted the advances of technology. She wasn't entirely into black or white magic, but the many myriad shades of unfolding grey that Lotte found hard to understand. However, she listened and learned with interest.

After Lotte's mother died Mrs. Grimshaw gave Lotte a worry doll from Guatemala. She did a good trade in them by mail order, via the Internet.

"Here Lotte, put this under your pillow. Every night tell the doll your worries and it will worry for you."

Lotte looked down at the little thing made of card, wood, and cotton in her small hands.

"I don't think that its head is big enough to keep my worries in."

Mrs. Grimshaw smiled down at her.

"My stepmother is a witch too, you know," said Lotte.

"It used to be a serious accusation to be named as a witch, Lotte. These days—not so much. Just what makes you think she is one?"

"The cat is scared of her—won't come to her at all—and when Dad's at work, I hear strange sounds from her room."

"Well, that could be anything. Grown-ups get up to all sorts."

And with that Mrs. Grimshaw moved on.

"Is that all you have to go on, the cat doesn't like her and strange noises?"

"She spends a lot of time going through this huge box that she brought with her from Russia."

"So she's Baba Yaga now is she?"

"Who is Baba Yaga?"

"An old Russian witch, who according to folklore, lived in a house with chicken legs and a fence around it made out of human bones and skulls on poles. The gates are fastened with human arms for bolts. She has iron teeth that make a terrible noise when she snaps them together. The chicken legs are really tree stumps—these people built their huts upon tree stumps. The roots would be the splayed chicken feet, see?"

"Oh, right."

Lotte looked around the large farmhouse kitchen she was sitting in. It was dirty and small, dark-red splashes of something were on the lower cupboard doors and there was a strange smell that Lotte associated with animals. There were many shelves in the kitchen and jars of all shapes and sizes. Something in one of them was staring down at her but she wasn't afraid. There were jars with pink spongy stuff inside and some contained mushrooms and other more unusual woodland things. There were jars she could not put a name to, and a container with what looked like little boys' willies in it—they had a shrivelled look to them like old mushroom stalks.

Maybe that's just what they were.

She was beginning to learn that perhaps Mrs. Grimshaw could be a witch of the very worst kind; downright malevolent occasionally, and also, she could be gentle when it suited her. She despised modern technology but used it to further her aims. Lotte wasn't afraid of her.

"We'll talk whilst I work."

Lotte remained silent for a moment whilst Mrs. Grimshaw cut open a plucked goose.

"What are you doing?"

"Making something from goose grease."

"Making what?" asked Lotte, wide-eyed and genuinely interested.

"An old remedy. Goose grease—fat from around the kidneys used for many ailments. I use it for sore throats."

Lotte turned up her freckled nose.

"Now don't you make faces, Lotte. When people were poor and because they always had, folk used all sorts to get better."

"And did they?"

"Sometimes, but it was all most people had. It would get rid of things occasionally. There's a new demand for it now."

Lotte began to think about something that she wanted to get rid of and she didn't care how it was done.

"What sort of things have you got rid of in your time, Mrs. Grimshaw?"

"Many things, Lotte. And I'm not going to go into the ins and outs of them all. I'll teach you to make goose grease though."

Mrs. Grimshaw's offer to show her how to do that reminded her of her own mother, who had taught Lotte how to paint little houses and trees when she was little. She missed her mother and once more suppressed all thoughts of her; Lotte bit her lip until it bled. She always did that when she remembered the last time she had seen her mother—in the funeral parlour. Lotte had sneaked past her father when he was talking to his brother and gone to kiss her mother goodbye again. But she didn't kiss her mother goodbye. Her mother was all grey around the jaw, had bright red lipstick on (which she never wore when she was alive) and she smelt funny.

"Do you ever wish anyone away or to come back?" asked Lotte.

"Sometimes—why?"

"I want my mother to come back and my stepmother to go far, far away."

Mrs. Grimshaw looked at her sympathetically.

"Have you ever heard of a story called "The Monkey's Paw?"

"No."

"Never mind. There's no bringing your mother back, Lotte, but if you are so unhappy with your stepmother, I can think of a plan to send her far away."

"You'd do that? You don't mean to kill her do you?"

"No—nothing that extreme, but I can assure you that she will never cause you upset again."

"What about daddy?"

"We'll fix him up with a new wife, someone you will like."

"You?"

"No, not me, Lotte. You'll see. But first we have to think of a way to get rid of Daria."

"Without *killing* her."

"Without killing her," agreed Mrs. Grimshaw.

Mrs. Grimshaw made Lotte a drink that looked pretty awful: purple berry coloured, but tasted rather nice. They set to—to devise a plan to get rid of Lotte's not-exactly-wicked, but not-so-nice stepmother.

"We'll need hair from her brush and something else. You know the kind of thing, Lotte."

Lotte indeed knew the kind of thing that they would need, and she knew where she could get it from too.

That night the 'family' ate takeout ham and pineapple pizza. Daria was all over Lotte's father as usual, and Lotte saw the signs that they were both going to have an early night *again.*

"Dad—" began Lotte.

Daria was bent over Martin; she was whispering something into his ear. His eyes began to glaze over as they usually did when she did that. Daria's red hair kept brushing the side of his neck and Lotte reckoned she had a one, possibly a two-minute window of opportunity.

"Dad, can I have some money for the science school trip, please?"

Martin blinked briefly but otherwise didn't budge as his new wife continued to whisper in his ear. Her right hand was clutching at the table in her urgency and Lotte looked on as the red nails began to lightly scratch the surface of the wood. Martin was staring down at the hand and the nails with a faraway look on his face.

Too late—the moment had gone as Daria dragged Martin up from the table.

"What—what was that, Lotte—?" said her father.

Lotte was about to reply when she saw the look of sheer hatred on Daria's face, and Daria yanked him out through the kitchen door. That look chilled Lotte to her core.

Later, when her father was snoring in the armchair and Daria was having a bath (the kind that took hours), Lotte sneaked into her father's bedroom. She took the hair from her stepmother's hairbrush, together with a tiny golden earring from amongst the many earrings in Daria's jewellery box, and turned to leave the room. Then, Lotte noticed a large box which she had never seen before, just jutting out from under the bed. Carefully, she slid it out over the thick carpet and raised the lid. Within the box was a smaller box, which she took out. She placed the hair and the earring on the carpet, put the smaller box next to them and closed the lid of the larger box quietly, pushing it back under the bed. She took the box, hair, and earring back to her bedroom and pushed them under her bed. Lotte then went downstairs.

For a short time she picked at the pizza, poured herself a glass of milk and then finally went off to bed, eager to look inside Daria's box. She could still hear Daria singing in the bath, so Lotte thought that perhaps she could take a quick look in the box and put it back before anyone was any the wiser.

This box was dark brown in colour, with a few funny symbols on the lid which Lotte didn't recognise. It was also unlocked, which surprised her.

Nestling within six little compartments were the most beautiful

Russian dolls that Lotte had ever seen. When her father had gone off to Minsk she had hoped that he would bring one back for her. He never did. Each wooden doll was painted in a different manner: a peasant girl in green, a bride, a blue-green mermaid, an elderly wise woman and a princess.

She took the sixth and last one out of the box. It was exquisite—a lady in a long, gold gown and sleeves trimmed with white fur. She looked like the Snow Queen, with a crown made of icicles.

It took a few twists to get the wooden doll open, Lotte fully expected to find another identical doll inside, with yet another identical doll inside that. There could have been around six, but there were no more dolls inside the first. Lotte put it back and chose another of the six, the bride. With all her effort she felt the doll give a little and held it up to eye level so she could see more clearly as she opened it. One twist and the top was off, to reveal the strangest of sights inside. It *seemed* to be doll-like enough, but was curled up a little and had closed, sleepy eyes and a tiny cord sticking out from its middle. It was a dark tan colour, leathery in texture, smelled, and looked revolting—not a pretty doll at all.

Lotte carefully put it back, quickly screwed the top of the doll back on and looked at the remaining four. She found that three out of the six wooden dolls had the other kind of dolls inside. When the coast was clear, she put the small box back in the larger box, in her father's bedroom.

The next morning Lotte was up early and out, without seeing Daria. She wanted to speak to Mrs. Grimshaw as soon as possible. It was the May school holidays and Daria would sleep late, lounge around the house watching reality TV and read magazines with the latest celebrity gossip.

Lotte let herself in the back door of the farmhouse, where Mrs. Grimshaw was potting herbs. There was soil all over the table and spilling onto the floor as Mrs. Grimshaw enthusiastically continued her work whilst Lotte told her of what she had seen in the dark brown box.

"If I do something about her it won't be very pleasant, Lotte."

Lotte looked thoughtful for a few seconds. "Mrs. Grimshaw—"

"Yes, Lotte?"

"Remember when I said that I didn't want anything too terrible to happen to her?"

"Yes."

Eyes downcast, Lotte fidgeted a little with a drawer, opening it to survey the gruesome contents. "Well. I don't think that I mind at all now."

The plan was straightforward enough, though not as simple as Lotte thought it would be. Still, it was interesting in its procedure. They heated wax and formed it into the rough shape of the Russian woman.

There were a few things that Mrs. Grimshaw did that Lotte didn't like, but she never would dare say so. And although Mrs. Grimshaw was kind to Lotte, she could spin on a coin and be nasty. Lotte had seen her do so with people who called uninvited.

Mrs. Grimshaw took a dead sparrow, cut out its heart and placed it into the warm wax under the right arm of the effigy. She then cut out the bird's liver and tucked it into a small cavity under the left arm, sealing it in with her thumb. They both placed three sharp pins into the effigy. Next they wrapped the red hair around the neck, and for good measure, sealed the small earring into the back of the wax doll too.

"There—done. Take it home with you—and whatever you do, don't let Daria find it. If she thinks you've seen what is inside the Russian dolls she will hurt you before this can take effect. You don't have to go home just yet do you? No? Good. Come on, let's go feed the chickens."

When Lotte got home later that evening the effects of the spell were already evident. Daria looked pale. She was helping herself to a glass of red wine when Lotte entered the kitchen.

"So it is you. You will have to help yourself from the fridge. We will not be ordering anything in tonight as your father is away on business and I am ill."

After picking at leftovers in the fridge, Lotte went to bed and settled under the bedclothes with her favourite book, *A Hundred and One Ways to Experiment with the Elements*. She artfully conjured up a light breeze that blew the Egyptian cotton sheets into the air to form a tent over her head. She had just begun to make a more elaborate township out of the sheets, moulding them into individual houses, when she heard some strange sounds coming from downstairs.

She ran down in time to see Daria clutching her chest and grabbing the side of the kitchen table. "I must go upstairs, help me, Lotte!"

Lotte did as she was instructed, aware that the wax effigy was still lying in her bag in the hall. She hadn't found the time to hide it yet. As they crossed the hall Daria kept looking down at Lotte with a puzzled expression, in between taking deep breaths to ease the pain. As they passed the bag Daria muttered something in Russian and glanced furtively around the hall, but nevertheless insisted on getting up the stairs as quickly as possible.

Once outside the bedroom she seemed to breathe a little easier.

"Go away, Lotte—I don't want you near me. You are bad for me. I can feel it."

When Daria pushed the door closed behind her it didn't click shut and Lotte could see quite clearly through the gap. Daria was on her knees on the other side of the bed, fumbling for the box and mumbling to herself. Sweat was pouring off her face and she wiped it on the white damask bedcover. She paused to take a deep breath and when she did so she used the bedcover again to wipe her face. Each time she did, it was as if a whole layer of her face was coming away. There were bits of skin and blood lying like the thinnest of apple peelings upon the cover.

Daria finally got the large box open and removed the smaller strange box containing the Russian dolls. She placed it upon the bed. Lotte could see it clearly; she could also see Daria's face clearly too. It reminded her of her mother's dead face, as she had looked in the funeral parlour. But the flesh was pink and coming away as if it was being sliced with a razor blade. Whatever she had felt about her mother's face that day, her stepmother's face was far worse. It was as if she were being stripped alive by unseen hands, and she, with immense willpower, and a mumbling of spells, was trying to keep the pain away.

Lotte was terrified, but she couldn't stop watching. She wanted to know what Daria was going to do with the dolls. A thought partially formed in Lotte's mind—but she pushed it to one side.

The answer came all too soon as Daria twisted the top half of a Russian doll open and picked out the dead thing from within, lifting the tiny form to her face. Lotte could not bear to look. Daria's flayed face then seemed to soften and she whispered to the tiny form in a soothing voice. It was a voice that Lotte had never heard from her before. Daria began cooing to it, telling it something that Lotte didn't understand, something about goodbye. It reminded Lotte of what she did with her worry-doll made of wood. She could see tears falling from Daria's sunken eyes as she stroked the little object. This didn't seem to be the stepmother that Lotte was so afraid of, the one that had replaced her in her father's affections. Lotte pushed the door open slightly and stepped inside the room. It was getting dark outside and although she was still afraid of her stepmother, she was more afraid of not knowing what was happening. She had to know the truth.

Daria looked up. Thin ribbons of skin were still peeling off her face. She sobbed but continued the soft chanting and placed the tiny thing back into the Russian doll.

"I'm sorry. I thought that—that—" Lotte moved closer.

Daria blinked a snake-like blink that caused Lotte to falter in her steps.

"You thought that I—used these?"

Lotte nodded.

"No. No—I would never do such a thing. They are—" Daria tried to explain in English, and Russian, but Lotte was only ten years old and could not fully understand.

Daria—in her madness, had *kept* her dead offspring.

"But you *are* a witch?"

Daria nodded.

"These are yours, and don't belong to other people?"

Daria nodded again.

It was all beyond Lotte's comprehension. "We need to see a friend, a woman. Will you come with me?"

Between sobs of pain Daria answered, struggling to her feet. "I doubt if she will be able to help. She would have to be a very strong woman." Then Daria started the soft chanting again, to reduce the pain.

Lotte half smiled as she sealed the Russian dolls into the box, picked it up and turned to face Daria, whose torment from unseen hands had subsided, for the time being at least.

"Don't worry about that, she is."

Before they left the house Lotte got dressed and gently draped her own mother's silk scarf over Daria's head. They made their way through the garden, across the road and down the track towards Mrs. Grimshaw's farmhouse. Nobody saw them. Lotte didn't forget to take the bag containing the wax effigy. Out of sight of Daria, Lotte had removed the wax effigy from the bag, and pulled out the three pins. Daria seemed a little stronger then and was able, with Lotte's help, to make it to the farmhouse.

In The Wake of the Dead

"And thereupon we all entered the cave. It was a large, airy place, with a little spring and a pool of clear water, overhung with ferns. The floor was sand. Before a big fire lay Captain Smollett; and in a far corner, only duskily flickered over by the blaze, I beheld great heaps of coin and quadrilaterals built of bars of gold. That was Flint's treasure that we had come so far to seek and that had cost already the lives of seventeen men from the HISPANIOLA. How many it had cost in the amassing, what blood and sorrow, what good ships scuttled on the deep?" Treasure Island by Robert Louis Stevenson. Published 1883 Cassell and Company Ltd.

In silent halls and sheltered dells the air was thick with the fear of cholera. From the corrupted city of Sligo it had spread with leaden wings, bowed down with a history of a thousand corpses, to the very perimeter of Holland Park. It sought fresh victims. The iron gates of the park were locked and the lady of the house (who had just given birth to a tiny daughter) refused any person to enter or leave under any circumstances. Even the vicar was refused entry and all his letters returned unopened. The letters had never been placed into her ladyship's hands; such was her fear of contamination, and her ignorance in believing that cholera was contagious. No one person could convince Anne Halifax otherwise and, in accordance with the wishes of the Mistress of the house, the gates stayed firmly secure.

The father of the child, John Halifax, Captain of the 1st West India Regiment, had been killed in action and Anne Halifax had retreated, in her grief, to her private apartment to wait out the rest of her confinement.

The great house was made of blue-grey limestone and looked out at the flat-topped Ben Bulben. Lavender-edged pathways led to the most wondrous ships' figureheads: Ares, god of war; Boreas, god of the northern wind; a rampaging lion; and the once, most-beautiful mermaid—all beaten by the pounding waves of the Bay of Biscay, and the cruel winds of many storms.

Within the great house life carried on at its languid pace, slower even, due to the day being heavy with the heat and the fact that the new babe was born to a fatherless household.

No governess ruled the older Halifax children and the only movement about the place that afternoon was when the gardener gave white roses to the maid, to place on the mahogany table in the entrance hall. Sometimes, only the sound of the pollen bees could be heard as they lumbered from flower to flower. However, the sickness was an ever-present threat to the peace of the great house.

Tilda Florence, cook to the family for seven years, often wore the expression of one of the figureheads in the garden—that of the wooden sea-maiden, looking as though she didn't know in which direction to go. Tilda was wondering who would be the next to die from the cholera. She pulled apart the pages of the Sligo newspaper and scoured it for a familiar name and found one instantly.

"Look now, another one gone down." For a moment her lost look was displaced by an alarmed one. She pushed back a lock of black hair under her cap and glanced up at the gardener, Dewy, looking for a response. No one called him by his real name of Algernon Patrick Moran. He seemed to prefer Dewy.

"Who is it this time?"

"Of cholera, at his residence in Sligo, on Tuesday last, Thomas Little, Esq. Surgeon of the County Infirmary. For upwards of thirty years he enjoyed, deservedly, the highest position as physician and surgeon in this province."

"That's a sad loss to us all, Tilda. He was a well respected man."

Tilda moved on a little too quickly for Dewy's liking:

"Look, here's another cure for the cholera too: "Chalk mixture, six ounce; tincture of Catechu, four drachms; Glycerin of kino, four drachms; opium, one half drachm. One tablespoon of the above tincture to be taken after each discharge from the bowels. In case of the diarrhoea being obstinate, let the chalk mixture be made of decoction of logwood."

"Another cure. I'm real glad that your ma taught you to read."

"You wouldn't be so whippy with your tongue if you had cholera and we had to nurse you. I'm thinking I'd just put you on the other side of them iron gates and let you fend for yourself."

"Now you wouldn't do that to yer Dewy—would ye?"

"I might not, but the lady is convinced if we touch someone who has it we're done for."

Tilda and Dewy had always been close but had never become lovers. They were both in their late thirties, with unusually, no history of marriage, or even a hint of a romance with anyone else. With a sigh Tilda threw down the newspaper and carried on making the dinner. The house was filled with the smell of herbs and roast chicken, which made them both forget about cholera. After all, were they not safe from the cholera or anything else in the Halifax house?

The heat of the day turned into the heat of the night. Even for August it was unusually hot. Not that Sligo, settled between the coastland hills, suffered from heavy downpours, for the island off the bay caught most of the rain. They did suffer terrible storms in the winter though.

Now, the older children of the house were ten years of age. A boy named George, and a girl called Geraldine. Albino twins they were, pink-eyed with moon-white hair. Their looks made a few people wary of them but that didn't matter to the cook and the gardener. They simply had no liking for the children, as they thought them to be rude and churlish. George would pull up plants that had been tended with loving care by Dewy, and Tilda had caught Geraldine more than once sticking her grubby little fingers into pies, puddings and cakes in the pantry, spoiling them for the dinner table. George was far too fond of finding a hollow reed, catching a frog, sticking it in its backside and blowing it up to overwhelming proportions. Dewy, who would not harm any creature (unless ordered to by the mistress of the house), had often wondered if he could cure George of his zealous nature. He had been working on an idea for over a month now, but had yet to put a plan into action.

Unknown to all, the children had taken to midnight ramblings and had escaped Holland Park, bound for the house called Elsinore on Rosses Point where their cousin Alex lived. They had found a way out that even Dewy hadn't reckoned on. It was behind the laurel bushes where no gardening was ever done and there was a small hole in the stonework of the ten-foot-high wall. There was just enough room for a ten-year-old child to get through, and if Geraldine had picked at any more pastries in Tilda's pantry it would have been a tight squeeze.

The children had put a great deal of thought into their nighttime excursions. During the day they wore white cotton clothes to keep cool. But on these trips they toned down the colour and wore their winter greys and blacks. They made their way past the enormous, brooding gargoyle that had once adorned the prow of the *San Juan de Silicia*, wrecked at Streedagh on the coast close by.

Alex was to meet them on the beach below Rosses Point to play with the things that they had found there and had kept hidden for the last year in a cave. Again the entrance was only big enough for a child to enter.

Over the years many ships had run aground on Perch Rock, near Rosses Point, on their way past Coney Island and a formidable structure had been erected on the rock to warn the mariners. Upon a fifteen-foot limestone base stood a twelve-foot metal man, dressed in the garb of a Royal Navy sailor in a Petty Officer's uniform. The effect of moonlight on the statue created an eerie sight, reflecting off the metal man, as one arm pointed to the safest part of the channel to pass through.

Alex was sitting on a rock waiting for her cousins. She had, by nature, been given the *correct* colouring of the Halifax family, following the male line of descent, and had coppery hair and apple-green eyes. The twins ran across the silver sand to greet her.

"And about time too. I don't like sitting here with the metal man staring at me like that. He gives me the willies."

"Why would you be scared of that? I'd have thought you would have been more afraid of the fairy folk coming for to carry you off. You're always talking about them—you'll draw them to you, you will," said George.

"No, the fairy folk are gentle, kind in their ways." Alex smiled and then frowned as she looked out apprehensively at the metal man.

"It's all shite anyway." George had brought a lantern with him and was trying to light it.

"Says you who looks under the bed every night and checks the closets. Hey, don't light that yet, wait till we get to the entrance. We don't want anyone to see it," replied Geraldine.

"The only person to see this dim bugger would be the metal man. Come on, let's get in."

Once in through the narrow entrance, the children found some candles and lit them. They had quite a place there. Alex had, before the cholera, begged for the thrown away things that her parents were going to get rid of and between herself and her cousins had brought them down to the cave. George had to dismantle a large chair to get it through the entrance, but with a few nails and a hammer had done a reasonable job of putting it back together on the other side. Of course, no one except him was allowed to sit in it. There was a box of old wooden toys that Alex had rescued and an old, Indian rug, which the girls sat on to hear George tell his tall stories.

"What's it to be tonight, George? Pirates, ogres with great hammers, water spirits?"

"The only watery spirits we will have tonight are those that belong in that bottle," he laughed as he pointed to a bottle of rum he had taken from his father's cellar two weeks ago.

"For your enjoyment tonight, my audience, it shall be your very own tale, Alex, the one you have heard so very often but love so very much."

Alex raised her eyebrows and smiled.

"Get the skull," said George as he cocked one leg over the side of the chair, smoothed his white hair away from his pink eyes and tried to make himself comfortable, shifting about on the damp, blue cushion.

Both girls in unison chanted. "Oh no, not the skull—"

They scrambled over to the corner of the cave and came back with a round object wrapped in a green paisley shawl.

"You do it, Geraldine; you know how I don't like to touch it."

"Why should I?" asked Geraldine, edging away from the object that lay in between them, within the tattered shawl.

"Fannies," exclaimed George and tugged at the edge of the bundle.

The skull tumbled from it and barely touched the edge of Alex's dress. It was a recent skull, not yet stripped of the base gristle that clung to its chaps and mottled head.

Alex screamed and that made the twins laugh.

"I don't see what's funny. Get on with the story George." Alex took a deep breath and settled as far away from the skull as she could, but not too close to the dark corners of the cave with its half-shadows. The sea usually never came into the cave and only in the worst winter storms was the interior blasted by the driven sea.

"On—nay, *mostly* on the foggiest of nights when the cold sea lay dead off the point, the smugglers would come along the pathway that went up to Elsinore to store their ill-gotten gains far below the house. The previous owner had built passageways that tunnelled deep under the very house you live in, Alex. Underneath the very kitchen you eat your breakfast in. Underneath the very floor where you sleep in your warm, comfortable bed."

Alex moved closer to Geraldine and shivered. A shadow loomed upon the cave wall behind George. Alex shivered even more and Geraldine took hold of her hand.

"In those passageways, the pirates led by Rove Maloney, hid the spoils of their wrecking. Along with Pen Willy, Craven Blackstock and Gin McCarthy it is said that they brought with them more than treasure, but human prisoners whom they tortured and ate in some terrible ritual. All this happened in the very passageways that lie under these hills, perhaps in the very cave we're sitting in now."

Alex was staring into the flame of the lantern and then at the back of the wall behind George where the shadow seemed to be growing larger with each uttered word.

"Rove Maloney, Pen Willy, Craven Blackstock and Gin McCarthy."

The shadow seemed to grow larger and ripple slightly.

"Rove Maloney, Pen Willy, Craven Blackstock and Gin McCarthy. Rove Maloney, Pen Willy, Craven Blackstock and Gin McCarthy. "

With the names sounding like some incantation the shadow suddenly split into five distinct outlines, one being George and the others looking like grotesque shapes, shifting and lurching around the wall of the cave, seeking some prey to take down.

Alex screamed and tried to bolt out of the cave. Geraldine caught her and tried to hold her still. "Alex. It's only a story, don't scream, someone might hear."

Alex began to cry inconsolably. "No it isn't, they're here. With George saying their names and three times and all—they're here."

"Don't be silly. It's only George firing up your imagination, that's all."

Alex insisted on leaving and began to make her way up the side of the hill back to Elsinore. The twins mooched around for a while and then decided to go home, as the mood had been thoroughly spoilt by Alex going off.

Tilda heard the back door bolt and wondered what the children had been up to in the garden. Anne Halifax heard nothing but the cries of her little mewling daughter.

The next night the twins left with a lantern, with the shutter a little way open to guide the way, so that they would not be discovered. The looming, wormwood shapes of the ships' figureheads guarded each walkway, and more than once Geraldine looked over her shoulder to see if they would follow. Once a little way from the house and out of the walled garden, they opened the shutter of the lantern a little more and made their descent down to the shore.

Alex was once again waiting for them.

"I didn't think that you would show up tonight," said George.

"No thanks to you, George. I really think you shouldn't call names up like that, made up or otherwise."

"I didn't make them up; old Griff told the story to me. It's true—all of it."

The three of them sat on the shore with the lanterns carefully positioned so that the light shone inwards towards the land and not out to sea. They didn't want to confuse some foreign captain and cause a shipwreck. Many a ship in the past had fallen foul of pirate wreckers with lanterns, leading them astray and onto the rocks.

"What do you want to do now?"

"I never did finish the story."

"No thanks." Alex took a deep breath. "We could go up to Elsinore and play in the old shed. That would make a good den as no one goes there or into the cellar. There is a room off the main cellar corridor. I have a key to it."

The night was warm but an eerie green mist hung low to the ground, weaving its way around the rocks, searching with dead man's fingers into each slight crevice and swirling around the boulders. The pathway around the point and up the hill was rocky and a little unnerving in the darkness. The children had been told by so many adults never to let lantern light drift out to sea, so as cautious as ever, they kept the light shining inland. The path undulated and as they went over the next rise they were surprised to see the flames of a large bonfire on the beach. As they drew closer they could see quite clearly the figures of four men sitting by the fire, staring out to sea.

"What fools—light from this point would guide anyone into the shallows," said George. "The sailors will read everything wrong. The lights from here and the other two islands will confuse them," said George. He shouted at the men. "Hey, put that fire out!"

The figures turned slowly around to look at the children but did not call back. Their clothes seemed odd but the children were used to the foreign fashions of sailors so took no heed. The evening began to change around them and it grew suddenly cold, heralding the wind, which changed direction as if winter had fallen. The sea became rougher and the rain began to fall, cold with a bitter sting to it.

George made as if to go down the rough track that left the main pathway down towards the beach. Alex grabbed his arm.

"Don't, George—I don't like the look of them."

"The fire, they can't light a fire."

"I think that they know that, George. I really think that they do. The rain will put the fire out."

"What do you mean?"

"Pirates. They're the pirate wreckers, George."

George stepped back and turned to Geraldine.

"Where's the light from the metal man, the warning light should have been lit by now?"

And then the wreckers moved. Slowly at first they lumbered towards the children through the softer sand of the lower banking. By the light of the fire Alex could see their hollow, cadaverous faces and the limp way that they held their arms. She screamed and turned to run. The other two ran in front of her, scrambling up the banking towards Elsinore, away from the creatures that the incantation had brought forward. Once there, they banged on the front door and screamed for help.

Candles were lit and there came a crashing from within the house as master and servants stumbled into one another in the near darkness. Alex's father shouted and wanted to know just who was at the door.

"Let us in, let us in!" cried Alex. "Father—let us in!"

Through the darkness the children could see the fearful wreckers coming closer with muffled voices. Even in the darkness they could see their milky, filmed eyes. And yet still the large oak door would not yield.

Alex started to scream once more as she pounded on the door until her hands began to ache. All three of them were attacking the door now, kicking and crying out for refuge.

"Father! Father!" Alex put her back to the door and started to sob into her hands, knowing that the foul wreckers were almost on top of them.

Suddenly the door gave way. The children were hauled inside and the great door bolted behind them.

Alex hid behind her father, begged him to get the guns and to keep well away from the door.

It was Alex that jolted George out of the desperate state he was in.

"Say the names! Say the names again!" she screamed.

George was breathing heavily but started to mutter the incantation again. He said the names twice and then a third time.

"Rove Maloney, Pen Willy, Craven Blackstock and Gin McCarthy—be gone."

The dreadful wreckers turned away from the solid oak door and made their way clumsily back down to the shoreline to the tiny cave where the skull was lying half buried in the sand.

There was no sleep that night in Elsinore and there was a great commotion back at Holland Park after hearing the news about what the children had been up to. Anne Halifax had no qualms about sending the children to boarding school in England. Alex was left to live with her father in Elsinore, forever dreading a pounding at the door, her nightmares terrifying. In these nightmares she could smell rotting flesh and would wake in a fearful state.

All had thought that George had banished the wreckers but on wild stormy nights in winter, when the ships came too close to shore, they fell afoul of the dreadful creatures. The wreckers stood their ground and fed upon the poor sailors as they were washed ashore.

But the dead left the children alone—except in those nightmares.

Pirate wreckers—wreckers that George had brought back, in some foul form from beyond the grave.

Geraldine never went back to Sligo. She finished school, and before the decade was out, she was quickly married off to a master silk weaver in London. However, George did come back and whenever he was allowed to see Alex, at a wedding or other such family occasion, she was carefully chaperoned and was never far from her father's admonition.

Sometimes, there were a few years between sightings of the wreckers and then there would be reports from sailors, that strange, mysterious lights had almost led them aground on Rosses Point and, those that had not perished on the rocks as a result of them, told of how they had nearly come to grief. Burnt out fires were occasionally found on the beach at Rosses Point and no one ever found the culprits who made them. Fathers, sons and brothers were lost to the sea and local people, who at one time deep within their family history might have spawned a wrecker or two, knew that none of them were the cause of the calamities.

When Alex's father died and was buried at Drumcliffe there was no wake, and on returning home Alex shuttered Elsinore House and would not let anyone come close to her, except for Tilda Florence and Dewy, who had come across from Holland Park some years before. They had fallen out of favour with Anne Halifax on account of the fact that they had not kept an eye on the children when she was recovering from childbirth, on that awful night so many years ago. The only other person that Alex would see was George and they could often be found deep in conversation with furrowed brows and earnest exchanges.

George was the company agent for Donovan's shipping in Sligo. On the last day of October he was on his way home from business in Glasgow aboard the ship *The Iris*. A day or two later Alex and George planned to announce their engagement.

Alex stood at the drawing room window, watching the sun go down and the sky turn blue-black. The sky looked bruised that evening and as the cold, winter sun backed down Alex thought she could see streaks of blood on the shoreline, and began to think back to that terrible night all those years before. The sun disappeared and she was left apprehensive and in brooding spirits.

The wind started to howl around Elsinore and she sought out some comfort in the kitchen. There had always been little formality between them and Tilda called Alex by her Christian name, although

Alex was now mistress of the house. Tilda wouldn't dream of calling her anything else and Alex liked it that way. Tilda was baking and Alex was moving things about that didn't need to be moved and generally getting in the way.

"Alex! Wouldn't you rather be in the drawing room with yer books? He won't be seen until morning. The ship has to get into Sligo, and then he has to make sure the cargo is safely attended. Then he'll come to you."

"I know, Tilda. I know, but you know how I feel about him being out there tonight."

"Yes, I know accidents have happened, but they will not happen to George—they simply won't."

"Accidents?"

"Yes, accidents, nothing more—now be still."

"But Tilda you've heard the stories and you know what happened to me—to us!"

"I know that the night all those things happened to you, you had been drinking that awful rum and that you believed the stories told by Old Griff."

"And what about the skull?"

"What about it?"

Alex shrugged her shoulders. "Griff said that if the skull was buried in the graveyard—"

Tilda didn't let her finish. "The skull probably isn't there now anyway and what if it is? Do you really think that it will make any difference?"

Alex leaned across the table and would not leave it alone. "And can you say that you have never thought of those stories on a night such as this, when the remains of the sailing boats and bodies have been broken and washed up on the shore? The men and boys so pummelled by the rocks that they are beyond recognition?"

Tilda didn't say anything. She was speechless and had never seen Alex in such a state, not even on the day of her father's funeral—not ever.

Alex went back to the drawing room but could not be still. The wind howled even louder and she could feel its chill throughout the house in spite of the fire. She picked up half a dozen books or more but could not settle on any. She sat in the armchair next to the window and fancied that she could see a glow from a fire that had been stacked on the beach. In her frustration she could not sit down any longer and paced the room from hearth to window, from window to hearth. With each step, as she drew closer to the window, she thought she could see a fire on the shore.

"No, it can't be. Please, God, let this ship pass safely."

Then she could stand it no more. She reached for her cloak, pulled on some stout walking shoes and unbolted the front door. A shovel lay next to the door. She had planned to do this many times but in her fear she had never had the courage to do it. She was determined to find the skull. If she found it, after all these years, she would bury it in Drumcliffe graveyard. Perhaps if it lay on sacred ground the curse would be gone.

She needed no lantern to go down the pathway from Elsinore. She had travelled this way a hundred times before, in her nightmare, down to the wreckers on the beach. Alex descended with difficulty against the icy wind, which flailed a thousand sword-sharp points against her, but still she went on towards the bonfire that she could now see on the shoreline.

There were no wreckers on the beach, just the crashing of the waves against rocks and the stinging sand that had been whipped up by the wind. Alex thought that she could see the green mist shapes of the wreckers appearing. There was no light on the metal man, no lantern to guide any captain. There was no safe passage that night for ships, only the light from Rosses Point to bring the vessels to the rocks and the cannibal pirates.

Head bent against the fierce wind and clutching the shovel in one hand, she made her way down past the sand dunes, where lay the bones of the men from the Spanish Armada, wrecked in a tempest in 1588. Their bones turned to dust and whirling like dervishes also looking for a sacred place to rest.

The fire was too big for her to put out alone so she took a piece of burning wood from the outlying embers and headed to the small cave she had spent the last ten years trying to avoid.

Utterly terrified (but with George in mind), Alex made her way through the narrow gap into the cave. She thrust the torch before her and squeezed through the narrow entrance.

Alex frantically shone the torch this way and that, looking for any trace of the skull or remnants of the old green shawl. She found nothing but a memory of that awful night when George told his story, and the shadows on the wall heralded the forms that were becoming substance on the beach. She sunk to her knees in desperation as the storm heightened and the wind threatened to shatter stone.

"God help us from the wreckers!" she cried. "Forgive us for what we have done; we had no right, no right at all!"

The storm fell silent and then she could hear the sound of metal grinding against metal, as if something was moving that had not moved for many years. She could hear cries and the wailing from outside the cave, and the deep thud of something pounding the sand. Alex dropped the torch and placed her hands over her ears, so dreadful were the screams. At last they stopped.

She picked up the torch and left the small cave. On leaving she tripped and fell over something, finding herself a breath away from the face of a creature not entirely human—or alive—but which had not been entirely dead. She could smell the evil of it. Alex screamed and made a grab for the torch. As she stood up it became apparent that the wreckers had either been pulled limb from putrid limb, or had been pummelled against the rocks by something with great strength. A wrecker's head had been squashed to a pulp and was surrounded by giant footprints, which led off—back to the water's edge. The bonfire was no more than a column of smoke that vanished within seconds. Alex felt the bile rise in her throat and she was sick against the rock that she clutched to steady herself. She muttered another prayer and raised her head.

She looked up and out to sea. It was calm now and a vessel was making its way to Sligo harbour. The torch had been lit at the base of the metal man and he stood there defiantly, pointing at the safe passageway between the island and the point. It was then that she knew George would reach a safe harbour.

Author's Note: "Elsinore House now stands empty and is falling into ruin. It was once the home of the smuggler John Black. William Butler Yeats and his brother Jack, as boys, spent their summers there, in the home of their cousin Henry Middleton."

The Sly Boy Bar and Eatery

In November 1996 a group of divers looking for wrecks in Beaufort Inlet, North Carolina, U.S.A. came across an anchor and cannons. The wreckage is believed to belong to the Queen Anne's Revenge, the flag ship of Blackbeard. The ship was lost in the vicinity in 1718. Recovery of the wreckage is ongoing today.

The white house on Taylor's Creek had been converted into The Sly Boy Bar and Eatery. It had been open for just one year and was the fastest food place in town. It looked out onto the Atlantic at Beaufort, North Carolina, and was set amongst water oak and cedars. Tangled vine twisted around the columns like snakes trying to gain entry. Built around seventeen hundred, the property had a double front porch made out of Scottish-heart pine, pegged together by builders that were more accustomed to making ships; and the whole place shook badly when the wind howled in from the Atlantic. Two tall chimneys stood the assault of winter every year, threatening to shatter and hurl their bricks into the angry sea.

Pizzas from oven to table in ten minutes flat—delivered by the sauciest waitresses with enough sass to make sure the place was filled to overflowing with guys, six nights a week.

Wanda headed the team of women, all dressed in short red skirts with white tops that were screaming out for a wet T-shirt contest. Yes, six nights a week, twenty-three varieties of pizza, with extra toppings and the most incredible seafood, if you could wait for it. That was no hardship, with the dozen varieties of beer that the bar advertised. A circular bar stood in the middle of the deck, in the shadow of three rigged masts. Table linen the colour of aquamarine, small star lights set in a midnight blue ceiling, shipwrecked old brandy barrels stove into the sandbanks that edged the deck, and the boarded floor covered in gritty sand. The entire place was literally a shipwreck; a shipwreck from a bad theme park, all plastic and lifeless.

Blowfish and Peeble Danby were cold and hungry. They pulled off on the North Carolina coast road when they saw The Sly Boy.

"This will be fine. I'm, really, *really* hungry."

"You're always hungry Peeble—there's no filling you up."

"Well, let's see if this place can."

"Do you think the diving equipment will be all right in the truck?" Blow checked that the tarpaulin was well tied down, concealing the tanks.

"No one is going to run off with those full tanks in a hurry and why would they?" said Peeble.

Blow thought for a moment, looked out to sea at the setting sun, and then followed Peeble into The Sly Boy.

The interior was quite a surprise: the sea-green shimmer of the walls, the cannons on the deck, the shifting sand beneath their feet.

"What the—"

"Hi boys, come on in."

Wanda showed them to the alcove seating area that lay underneath the overhanging captain's cabin. She insisted on tablecloths even though the local boys usually ended up dancing on the tables. It was no excuse for poor etiquette on her behalf, she thought. The Sly Boy, unusually empty on Thursday evening, never closed until dawn each morning. And the food was considered to be wholesome and satisfying even though the clientelle were frequently too drunk to appreciate it.

"Here's the menu and on the board are the specials." Wanda pointed at the board positioned near the ship's bell which hung above the bar. Peeble checked it out, squinting to see the list.

SPECIALS

BLUEFISH WITH ALMONDS AND LEMON.
SALMON EN CROUTE—FRENCH STYLE.
SQUID IN INK—NOT FRENCH STYLE BUT SPANISH STYLE.
WE GOT SPECIAL PIZZA USING THE LEFTOVERS FROM THE
ABOVE.

WANDA—NOT ON THE MENU; IN CASE YOU ASK.

"Oh, and the rest of the waitresses are not on the menu—before you ask," Wanda sat on the edge of the table.

"Well, I'm glad we cleared that up," Peeble said.

"Would ya like to know a little about The Sly Boy?"

Blow shrugged, "Sure—why not."

"Good," said Wanda. "'Cuz I've got all night. This house once belonged to Blackbeard the pirate," she began and smiled, revealing something green sticking between her teeth. Blowfish pointed discreetly at his teeth, and then at hers.

"You got somethin' wrong with your teeth?" she asked, "or you trying to tell me you're hungry?"

"No, you have something between *your* teeth and in your hair too. Something, er—green."

Wanda fiddled in her red hair and yanked. She pulled out a strand of dry seaweed and finally used her little pinkie nail on her teeth.

Blow couldn't take his eyes off Wanda's thigh. It looked way too pale and had an odd mottled pattern on the surface of the skin.

"Where was I? Yes, the house—when it was high tide the pirates would have tied their boats to the columns at the front of the house and just stepped right in. Course, the tide came up higher in those days."

Peeble stared at Blowfish, which meant—*like why are we listening to this when we should be eating?* There was something else, though; something that was making him squirm uneasily in his seat.

Wanda caught the stare and moved herself along. "Well, I think that fact is interestin' — what d'ya want to order?"

"Can we have a minute?" asked Blow.

"Sure, take your time I'm not in a hurry, we're open all night. Would you like a beer?"

They chose from the twelve different beers and once her back was turned both of the brothers tried unsuccessfully to suppress their laughter.

"I'm kinda glad Wanda isn't on the menu," said Blow.

"Yeah, she ain't the kind of girl Mom would have approved of."

"Well, she ain't the kind of girl Mom would have approved of for you. She never cared who I shacked up with. You were always her favourite."

"That's not true Blow, she loved both of us and you know it."

"I know that when I became a diver she didn't think it was real work and when you became a diver too, she worried about you, but not about me."

"That's bullshit Blow, before she died —"

"Before she died she asked for you."

"I'm the oldest—I was around longer, and when are you going to put all this grieving behind you? It's time to move on."

Blow brought his fist down hard on the table. "Don't tell me what to do. I'll stop grieving when I'm good and ready."

"Suit yourself, but you ain't never going to get laid thinking about your mom all the time. It ain't natural."

At this point Wanda stepped in. "Seems to me you boys should be thinkin' about eatin' somethin' right about now."

Blow glared at her and then looked hard at the specials.

"What kinds of fresh fish do you have?"

"We have sea bass, amberjack, silver snapper, red snapper, trigger fish, and bluefish. The red snapper is brought in and we feed them up in tanks—like pets."

"Since when do you feed pets to customers?"

Wanda gave Blow a wry smile and took a deep breath.

"We'll take the bluefish and fries," said Peeble quickly.

They were both still arguing about the last days of their mother's life when Wanda brought the two fish dishes. What raced through Blow's mind, was that he wished his mother had loved him more. What raced through Peeble's mind, was that he wished he'd got laid more, and obviously not by his mother.

Served whole and staring up at him Peeble toyed with his fish. It did look good. Blow watched Peeble cut into it, as he began to pick at his.

"I've gone off it now, Peeb, I think,"

Peeble cut into the bluefish and then he thrust the plate over to his brother. "I think I have too—look at that!"

Blow turned the plate around and lifted up the side of the fish, expecting something none too wholesome inside. He found something none too wholesome inside all right. The fish hadn't been filleted.

"Whoa, what the hell is that doing there?"

A little blackened, but still identifiable by the nail (which actually did look a little like a sliced almond), was a finger. Even more macabre, the finger was still wearing a gold ring.

Blow backed his chair away and made for the men's room. Peeble shook his head and beckoned Wanda over. Speechless he pointed at the finger on his plate.

"Sorry about that. I keep tellin' Clara to fillet them, but she keeps on servin' them up like that. You can't go wrong with the pizza, though. Of course, the meal will be on the house. D'ya want another?"

Before he could think of a reply (and wondering what Clara could use instead of olives for a pizza, which didn't really bear thinking about) Wanda whisked the plate away, and returned with two more beers.

"I hear you goin' divin'?"

Peeble wondered how she knew that. Had Blow been shooting off his mouth again?

"Up the coast a little."

"There's somethin' I want you to do for me."

"What's that?"

Peeble quite liked the proximity of her mouth to his ear. He could smell sweet apple on her breath. Wanda whispered, "If you don't want your brother to end up all chewed up by blue crabs or somethin' else, I'd listen if I was you. In fact, perhaps I'd better take you to your brother."

Peeble looked about and was surprised to find all the waitresses staring at him. He stood up. There must have been about a dozen waitresses and he found it odd that he hadn't taken much notice of them before. Two waitresses came up behind him and gently pushed him forward. He had no idea what was going on but he needed to play along to find out what the hell they had done with Blow.

Wanda led him along the sandy decking over to the far side of the room and to a door half hidden by fishing nets. Next to the door was an enormous figurehead of a mermaid that had once adorned the prow of a far better ship than the lurid Sly Boy. The mermaid stared down on him with a smile akin to a poor copy of the *Mona Lisa's* smile. The door led down to a dimly lit cellar. Wanda picked up something that glinted in the half-light. She was holding a blunderbuss and, what's more, it was pointed in Peeble's direction.

He backed off but the two waitresses pushed him forwards after Wanda. She picked up a torch and led him down a long passageway that must have gone on for five hundred feet or more, before they came to the end. Peeble could see bright moonlight reflecting on water.

Wanda pointed the gun to one side of him. "Over there."

Peeble looked anxiously around for his brother. Wanda's torch fell upon Blow's face. He was chained to the rocks with the tide lapping up around his feet. Peeble could see the glistening backs of turtles in the water a few feet away and he knew that blue crabs would soon be all over the place.

"I'll take him down in a minute. But if you don't do what I ask, your brother will be out here tomorrow night, food for the turtles and the blue crabs."

"I could just call the cops."

"If you did, he would be dead before they could get to him. I'd see to that."

"What do you want?" Peeble asked.

"Somethin' no one else has succeeded in gettin'."

"And that is?"

"Why, Blackbeard's treasure—you could say it's ours anyway. He owes us."

"Why don't you get it?"

"Oh, we would, but it's too far out for us."

"But Blackbeard's treasure is supposed to be lost off Portsmouth, New Hampshire. What makes you think it's here in North Carolina?"

"It's here all right, just out of reach. But you can bring it to us. Other divers have almost succeeded."

Peeble saw the crazed look on Blow's face as a blue crab edged closer to his feet and stopped, hesitating as if waiting for reinforcements. It didn't have to wait long.

"Get him out of there. I'll get the treasure to you," Peeble gave in.

"Well—what are you waitin' for? Go and get your divin' gear." Wanda motioned with the blunderbuss once more.

"Just one thing. How come you haven't got your hands on it before now if it's so close?"

"You'll see," Wanda replied, her half smirk breaking into a full grin.

An hour later, after checking his diving gear, Peeble was on the bottom of the inlet staring at a partially buried sea chest. Wanda, who apparently had no problem breathing underwater, swam to some nearby rocks and showed no inclination to come any closer. Peeble had no trouble fastening the hook to the old chain already around the chest, and he couldn't help wondering why the other divers before him had failed to get the chest to a boat above. Or, at the very least, drag the chest across to where Wanda and the other women could get their hands on it. He looked across at her: she seemed eager to come and help him, but something was stopping her. She was undoubtedly a revenant—a supernatural creature— but seemed tied to the house, and no more than a little ways beyond it.

Peeble didn't have to wait long before he found out what had defeated the other divers. He felt the current move him forwards slightly. He turned and saw that the sandy bottom was being stirred up by something—something big.

Out of the murky water came a face so wild in its countenance it terrified him. Wild, black hair floated around milk white eyes— the eyes of Blackbeard himself. He brandished a sword menacingly close to Peeble, who instinctively drew back. The sword hit a rock then fell to the seabed. It had come to within an inch of Peeble's shoulder. He felt his feet sink into the sandy bottom as he tried to back away, but Blackbeard pinned him against the rock and was feeling for the knife that was tucked into his belt. Blackbeard was all fire and fury, the weight of the water hardly holding him back at all. Peeble looked frantically at Wanda, only a few feet away. She also had a knife in her hand and either could not, or would not come to his aid.

He felt himself weakening in the struggle and saw the dim glint of the knife coming up to his throat. Then he felt Blackbeard's body slump slightly towards him and Peeble managed to push him away. Blackbeard tried to reach over his shoulder. Peeble saw a harpoon in the pirate's back and looked around for the person who had fired it. He saw another diver swimming towards him and recognised the diving suit: it was his brother Blowfish.

Blackbeard was still struggling to get the harpoon out, when he stumbled backwards towards the waiting hands of Wanda. As she tore her knife across Blackbeard's throat Peeble saw a look of victory in her eyes. In a violent rage she brought the knife down again and again until she hacked his head off. No blood stained the water.

It didn't take long for Peebles and Blow to drag the treasure chest along the seabed to where the boat was positioned above them, to where Wanda was waiting with the other wives on the sandy sea bottom. The boys weren't going to cross a woman who was not only undead, but had just finished off one of the most notorious pirates that had ever plundered the high seas. Exhausted, they then dragged themselves to the safety of the small boat.

Once on board Peeble took off his mask and coughed. "How did you get away?"

Blow smiled at his brother. "Come on, Peeble. None of those women had been laid for over two hundred years. There had to be one who would—"

"You're kidding me—you didn't!"

"Relax. I didn't. I can't say it didn't cross my mind though, as they still look pretty good to me."

"You're one sick man, bro," Peeble said, shaking his head.

He briefly thought how goddamned hungry he was and dismissed it instantly, remembering the bluefish. He straightened his stiff back and stretched. It was no good—he had to know. Against their better instincts, they both jumped into the water one last time.

Peebles and Blow saw Wanda sitting on the huge chest half buried in the shifting sand. They attempted to get closer but she put her hand up in a warning gesture, the red hair flying in the sea around her like tortured snakes. Her jaw drop mouthed the words:

"Not for you."

There was a sudden movement of the chest and the jolt looked as if it would rock Wanda apart. She fell off. The lid slowly creaked open by itself. The two divers didn't follow the wives as they unloaded the chest, bar by bar. They saw what Wanda had done to Blackbeard, and although *his* head would remain for all eternity, detached from *his* body, they really, really did not want to lose theirs.

Fourteen wives made off with the silver bars. Wanda, originally known as Mary Ormond of Bath, North Carolina, made sure the treasure was delivered to the descendants of the forty children of Blackbeard the pirate. After the many generations there wouldn't be much to go around, but it was the principle of the thing that mattered.

Oh, and as an afterthought, Wanda placed Blackbeard's severed head up in the rigging in The Sly Boy. No one ever knew it was real and people often commented on how grisly it looked. As for the smell, it was amazing what she could do with a little sweet apple and preservatives.

The Celestial Dragon

"The silence of pure innocence
Persuades when speaking fails."
The Winter's Tale by William Shakespeare.

It was the wonderful taste of tiny, mouthwatering egg custard tarts that Lian remembered most about a trip she had made with her father. Her father, Victor Lee, had taken them on the 11 a.m. hydrofoil to Macau, and Lian had been disappointed that it didn't travel fast due to a low fog that hung on the Pearl River Delta.

Once in Macau they sought out one of the little bakeries and Lian ate three egg custard tarts in a row—and her father just laughed at her and took the box away. Lian was tall for her age, a head taller than most girls of ten. Her teacher, Mr. Yimou, had often called her a dreamy girl, but Lian knew her father was proud of her. It showed in his brown eyes and his smile when he gently chided her.

Victor Lee had taken his daughter to Macau to buy an antique wardrobe. The trip had been two months before her father's death and the wardrobe had been delivered the day after her father's funeral. Lian's mother had cried when it arrived. Three weeks had passed since the funeral and now the memory of the custard tarts made her feel sick and unhappy.

Victor Lee's head, upon hitting the ground after falling from the roof thirty-seven floors up, had split open like a melon and a brown eye lay a few metres from the body. Lian knew this because she had returned from school and been about to enter the building at the time. And it was she who used her jacket to cover up what remained of her broken father.

Lian's mother had been out shopping at the time of her husband's death and Lian's sister, Suki, hadn't been seen for a week. Lian had no idea where she was. There had been a letter demanding a ransom of twenty-five thousand Hong Kong dollars that her mother and father had already paid, but Suki had not been returned to them. The police had no success in finding her and Lian and her mother were overwhelmed by the loss of half their family. The verdict on her father's death had been suicide, through the grief of losing his daughter. But Lian knew her father would not have left them. Would he?

The New Year was only a day away and the apartment would usually be filled with bright gold and red banners. Last year, as a family, they had gone down to the Wan Chai harbour front and watched the colourful performers and floats. The air had been filled with the smell of the polluted harbour, only occasionally cut through with the faint aroma of cooked meat.

Lian looked up to the mountain from her high-rise apartment in Sheung Wan. Her room was directly above the hole, which was four apartments wide and eight deep. It had been left in the middle of the block for the spirit dragon of the mountain to get to the sea. It was to this spirit that she prayed now. The dragon, she struggled to remember, was the symbol of strength, goodness, courage, and endurance.

Lian felt suddenly uneasy.

As a consequence of grief her mother had never left her bed since the funeral. Each day she slept, in her own dream world, where no doubt she found her missing daughter and her dead husband. Lian brought home dim sum for her every day, which she didn't eat. So Lian would eat it, because she had to or she would get sick too, and there would be no one to look after her mother. The dim sum just tasted like egg custard to her.

"Mother, you need to eat."

Her mother lay still, within the beige silk sheets that her husband had bought for her birthday in November.

"Tomorrow I will go to Mong Kok and buy you more silk and it will make you happy."

Silence. Lian moved her mother's dark hair from her pale face and brushed a tear away.

Lian remembered shouting at the policeman. "Why would my father kill himself? He loved us. He had no reason to do it."

"People do strange things," Detective Shan had replied with a shrug.

Lian was convinced someone had killed her father—but for what reason? Had it something to do with Suki? There was very little crime in Hong Kong, except mafia crime. Did her father owe money to someone?

The phone rang and broke the silence, but for the third time that week there was no one at the end of the line. With a sudden surge of determination, Lian searched for the box of New Year decorations and found them in a hall cupboard. She began to deck Mai Lee's bedroom in gold and red. When Lian was sure her mother was sleeping she left the apartment to make her way to the Wan Chai harbour to watch the celebrations. As she left, she felt a hot wind on the back of her neck and the smell of smoke hung in the air. She thought of the mountain and her prayer.

The streets were packed with hundreds of people shouting, *"Kung Hei Fat Choi—Kung Hei Fat Choi."* But she could not wish them a Happy New Year in return. More than once she thought she saw her father's face in the crowd mouthing the chant, but she could not hear his voice above the rest. She wrestled with the idea of getting the traditional Jiaozi dumplings that they ate every New Year's Eve— perhaps her mother would be tempted by them. Still, Lian could not get *that taste* of egg custard out of her mouth. She ate little these days too, and she noted how thin her pale wrists were getting.

An old woman fell against her and smiled an apology, thrusting a red packet decorated with gold dragons into her hand.

"Leisee," she muttered.

"Not just lucky money," the old woman shouted in her ear. And again she thought she saw her father's smiling face in the crowd and felt the warmth of the mountain wind on her neck. A few paces more and another red and gold packet was placed in her hand, then a third, and yet another until she lost count of how many had been stuffed into her pockets, and thrust into her hands.

"I don't need your money, really I don't. My father is a wealthy man," she said, struggling with her emotions as one more was given to her. She couldn't remember the faces of the people who gave her the envelopes, only the feeling of good intention and wishes that were rapidly dissipated by her own confusion.

Lian ran all the way home, her pockets full of the packets and her heart racing with the effort—and a strange feeling of anticipation, as if something was going to happen imminently. The reflected lights of Hong Kong harbour danced strangely on the water. She put her key in the door of the apartment, her head swimming with the colour red, which brought back terrifying images of her father's death. Her mother was still sleeping. After checking she was still breathing Lian hurried to her room and emptied the contents of her pockets on the blue cover. There were a dozen gold and red packets in total and the gold dragons on each packet glistened under the far-too-bright light of her room.

With shaking hands, she reached out and picked up one of the packets and carefully tore it open. Within it was a business card, that of one Richard Molk of the Pinkerton Detective Agency. Nothing else; no money. Lian reached for a second and opened it. In it was five thousand Hong Kong dollars—a very large sum for lucky money. In the third was a cheque made out to her mother, Mai Lee, for five times that amount. Each envelope either held top dollars or cheques for sums of money made out to her mother. The last one contained something different: a photo of the Man Mo Temple. She recognised it because her father had once taken her there. The temple was very small.

She could taste egg custard again.

That night she had the most wondrous dream that everything was as it should be, with no broken father, no missing sister and a mother who was well and happy with her family. They were having a great feast in an enormous room, with grandmothers bouncing their grandchildren on their knees and singing songs of the old ones, even older than themselves, reaching back into antiquity. In a place of honour lay the dragon, strong and proud and watching over every one of them. The strange group seemed to know one another, as if they had been together for a long, long time.

In the morning Lian remembered the dream and her feeling of pride in her family, the memory quickly becoming a deep sadness. She left for school as usual, but instead of getting the MTR she decided to ring the number of the Pinkerton Agency.

"Good morning, the Pinkerton Detective Agency, how may I help you?" Lian lost her nerve and hung up. She was beginning to feel stupid but she *had* to make the call.

Again the woman's voice with a high pitch tone answered.

"Can I speak to Richard Molk please?"

"Just one moment please." Lian could hear music in the background. It was elegant and yet she found it hard to listen to, for she felt so very, very sick.

"Richard Molk speaking."

"My name is Lian Lee, the daughter of the man who fell from the building in Sheung Wan?"

"Yes, yes I know of the name Victor Lee. How can I help?"

"I need to see you. I have money."

"I really don't know if I can help you—it was suicide—wasn't it?"

"No, no Mr. Molk it decidedly was *not*," said Lian in the most grown up voice she could muster.

Lian tried to coax her mother to eat dim sum, but after taking a little she waved it away. If there was not a glimmer of hope soon she would have to get help for her mother, or there would only be her left to place a candle in the window, with the wish that her sister would find her way home. Before she left, Lian made sure that her mother had plenty of water and snacks, which she placed on the small table by her bed.

Half an hour later Lian was in the smart Pinkerton office looking across the desk at Richard Molk, whom she couldn't help noticing, looked a little like Jackie Chan.

"Well Lian Lee, with very little to go on I don't see how we can proceed. The police have closed the case."

"It's not just about my father. I want you to find out what happened to my sister too."

"I did hear about your sister's disappearance. What happened there?" Molk rubbed the back of his neck with irritation. He had forgotten about how unusual the case was. He had been involved in cases regarding the kidnapping of young girls before, but those cases had been on mainland China.

"This is my sister Suki." Lian handed him a photo of her. Molk couldn't see anything about the girl that made her stand out from any other young teenager.

"How old is she?"

"Sixteen."

Molk sat back in his chair and sighed. "Just sixteen?"

Lian nodded and looked away out of the window down into the busy street, awash with stall traders and shoppers. Perhaps her sister was not really far away, just trapped in a building close by.

"I have something else, Mr. Molk." Lian gave him the photo of Man Mo Temple.

Molk's leather chair squeaked as he leaned forward to take the photo. He looked at it, puzzled.

"I don't see how this can help. Where did you get it from and why do you think it is connected to your father's death?"

"It was given to me in the street. We could go there. I think I need someone to go there with me. I can pay."

"It's not about the money. You are too young to employ a detective." Molk sighed. "Okay, look—I'll go there tomorrow, ask a few questions and look around a little. It's the best I can do."

"One more thing, Mr. Molk."

"Yes."

"When you go to look for Suki, I am coming with you."

Molk shook his head. "I can't take you with me. Give me one good reason why I should."

"Because I'm afraid, Mr. Molk. I think that the men who took Suki will take me too. I need to be looked after as well."

Lian explained that there was no one to take care of her, and that her mother would be all right for the next twenty-four hours or so. Reluctantly, Molk agreed to take her with him and before he could ask, Lian held up her passport for him to see.

Molk rang his friend Remmy, who was steadily climbing his way up the ranks in the police force. With every new promotion it was getting harder to get information out of him.

"Remmy, what do you know about the disappearance of Suki Lee, the girl whose father jumped in Sheung Wan."

"Not much to say, really. I was surprised a Hong Kong girl was taken as that usually happens on the mainland."

"Do you have any leads at all? A note demanding the ransom was left on a seat in a church. You got nothing from that?"

Remmy seemed hesitant to reply but he owed Molk a few favours and perhaps could be useful to him again. "In my opinion the case was closed too quickly and there was some falling out with the police in Macau. There was some reason to think that is where she was taken. Initially."

"Initially?"

"China is a big place. She could have been taken anywhere after that. There are plenty of families that would pay for a bride—but to take a Hong Kong girl, that's unusual. And it would have been easier for them to kidnap a girl from the countryside. Why come to Hong Kong?" Remmy paused, "…there's another thing."

"What?"

"In a similar case, but where the parents were rich, the ransom demanded was one million HK dollars. Why would kidnappers only demand twenty-five thousand? Why not chose a really wealthy family? Was she kidnapped for that little amount or kidnapped to sell elsewhere, or both? It doesn't make sense. Why go to all that trouble?"

"Mmm…I know. Right, thanks anyway, Remmy." Molk put the phone down. "Well, Lian, it looks like we'll be going to Macau. It seems to be as good a place as any to start."

Whilst Lian slept fitfully on the hydrofoil, Molk thought about his own views on life. Evil dwelt in the world, of that Molk was sure. It was all black and white to him though, with no shades of grey. There were those people who would sacrifice life and limb for others: the war heroes, the doctors and nurses whose very lives were threatened giving succour to others. Then there were the thugs who would cut your throat as soon as look you in the eye. There were no grey areas for Molk. His own father had been killed by a vicious psychopath. The psychopaths were all bad. He felt sorry for Lian—he would try harder to find the girl's sister, harder than on any other case he had worked on before.

Molk began to read the book he'd brought with him. *Film Noir* by Andrew Spencer. He flipped through the first few pages. Molk had always wanted to be a policeman or a detective—ever since he had sneaked his father's pulp fiction books and read them in the park on the way home from school. He had sat under the ornamental trees in Victoria Park, when it rained or when the heat was too much for him to bear, and he had worked through his father's collection, one by one. They had taught him about sex (there was always the woman who paid her detective's fee with sexual favours), and he had watched, many times, movies such as *Double Indemnity* and *A Touch of Evil*. He had fallen in love with the melancholia and disenchantment of the characters in the movies. All the women were stereotypical blondes: double-crossing, beautiful, unreliable—and part of him believed in the stereotype. His girlfriend Xue (the name meant snow in Chinese) had left him for another man, who ran an antique centre in Kowloon. Molk had finished the relationship after a somewhat cold encounter one afternoon on the Star Ferry.

The crossing was short and soon they were on the waterfront in Macau; the gaudy casinos with their façades and designs looking as if they had just come out of a Hollywood backlot, or from Disneyland. Molk hailed a taxi and they went to see the contact that Remmy had finally given him, An Nguyen. Molk politely asked if a female police officer would look after Lian for a short while.

Once she was safely in the hands of the female detective, Molk tackled An Nguyen. He had very little to say to Richard Molk.

"Look here, I know you've come a long way but there's very little to tell. The case went cold and we think that the Yakuza have got hold of her. You know the score with them; nobody, and I mean nobody, messes with them. It's bad enough to be harassing the Chinese Mafia. But the Japanese too? No way."

Molk took a deep breath and left the police station. The Yakuza weren't greatly different from the Chinese gangsters, in that they were both into smuggling, gambling, money laundering, corporate extortion, and sex slavery.

Molk couldn't, especially with a child, hang around the streets—and so he booked into a hotel for the night, although he felt uncomfortable sharing a room with Lian. But it was a matter of necessity. He had the couch and she the bed. The child was truly afraid that whomever took her sister would come back for her. Molk was going to ensure that didn't happen.

The next morning came soon enough, with Molk wondering what to do next. It wasn't until they had breakfast, and he a strong, sugared coffee, that his brain began to function properly.

Once out on the street he picked up a newspaper at a corner stall and read the headlines.

"Cop committed suicide." The cop in question was An Nguyen,

whom he had left in good health the day before. He didn't seem the kind of guy who would take his own life; quite the contrary in fact, for he seemed to Molk the kind of person pretty keen on staying alive. Nice suit, no sign of neglecting himself.

Molk returned with Lian to the office where he had met An Nguyen a day earlier. A cop was mooching around and had just cleared the desktop. Molk asked to see Nguyen's superior, with little result, and when the cop left the room to get Lian a cold drink and Molk some coffee, he searched a box that was sitting on top of the empty desk. He found a small notebook amongst some personal possessions and placed it inside his jacket pocket.

The cop returned and handed Lian her drink.

"Thank you," she said.

Molk drank his coffee and both policemen exchanged a few comments about how Macau had changed over the years. Molk and Lian then left the building. She said little, but instead took his hand and clung to it as if she would never let go.

Once back on the street Molk took the notebook out of his pocket and saw that it was, in fact, a new address book made of smooth leather. He thumbed through it, but there was only one entry: 27 Travessa De S. Domingos. Macau was busy enough to get lost in, but Molk was no tourist. He knew how to get about through the streets, where each twist and turn brought you to houses of a Portuguese or Chinese influence. Once at the right address he rang the bell and the door was opened by a pretty young woman in an ice-blue dress.

"Yes, what do you want?"

The Pinkerton detective was tired and in no mood for a long introduction. "Do you know An Nguyen?"

"Who are you? You'd better come in." The woman looked surprised to see the child and hear Nguyen's name mentioned. She seemed anxious to get away from the front door too.

"Why are you here about that person?"

Molk noted the luxurious décor of the apartment whilst Lian made herself comfortable on the couch.

"What's your name?" said Molk.

In her nervousness she spoke too eagerly. "My name is Lin Young. The person you mentioned, he is someone I was seeing. My brother disapproves of him. My brother and I—we don't get on very well—we disagree over many things."

"Have you seen the papers this morning?"

"No. I was up late last night." Lin tilted her head to one side and her black eyes looked puzzled. "Why?"

Molk had never been one to hang around. He threw the newspaper onto the coffee table so that she could see the front page.

For a moment there was a shocked silence as the headlines sunk in. Choking back the tears, she placed her hand over her mouth and whispered. "An Nguyen—suicide? No—never."

"I believe he knew something about the disappearance of Suki Lee—have you ever heard of that name?"

She shook her head. She was shaking uncontrollably.

"Look here, I'm sorry to bring you bad news."

Lin was still shaking a few moments later when he added Suki's photograph to the newspaper on the table.

She stared at the photo. "I have known for a while that my brother was quite capable of harming An, but I never thought he would go through with it—"

"You know the girl, don't you?"

"She is a foolish girl who staged her own kidnapping. She wanted money to go away with some boy somewhere, and then she fell into the hands of my brother. He has no honour. He used to sell drugs, and now he sells anything."

"Including girls?"

Lin nodded and started crying again.

"Do you know where my sister is?" Lian asked her. "Will you help me find her?"

At that moment Molk heard a door open in another room. He placed one hand inside his jacket and frowned at Lin. A girl came into the room, dressed in a kimono covered with gold dragons. She took a few feeble steps and Molk had to rush to steady her.

"Suki!" Lian stood up and ran over to her sister. She threw her arms around Suki and nearly knocked her over.

Suki looked as if she were fighting off the effects of some drug or other. Molk sat her down on a chair and turned to Lin, waiting for an explanation.

"My brother is working with the Yakuza, trading young girls between countries. There is much money to be made. But for some crazy reason Suki has not been passed along. Chen has taken quite a liking to her. I told him he would bring down the police on our heads, and then I met An Nguyen. I was going to tell An about her but I never found the courage."

"He knew who you were though?"

"Even policemen have weaknesses, Mr. Molk."

Black and white; that's how the world had always been for Richard Molk. Until now there had been no shades of grey. A Chinese mafia man who kept a girl in his own home because he was obsessed with her? A policeman in love with a gangster's sister? A gangster's sister in love with a policeman? And, craziest of all—a young sixteen-year-old girl who had paid (out of her own parents' ransom money) for someone to kidnap her, until *that* all went wrong. Molk needed to make some quick decisions.

"Get her dressed, we're leaving. Have you got passports?"

"There was a new passport made for Suki. I'll get it."

It took two hours to get Suki into a reasonable state to travel. Molk had to get her out of Macau and back to Hong Kong using the false passport: any explanations to the police would have to be made once he was on home ground in Hong Kong. The trip back took place without incident; with immigration having some sort of temperature sensor malfunction (the authorities were more afraid of bird flu than checking passports properly). However, instead of waiting for the problem to be fixed, immigration officers waved people through. Suki was well in control of herself by then, for she began to understand that she was on her way home. Lian held tightly onto her sister.

For now, Molk decided to take the girls back to his own place, just around the corner from the Pinkerton office. Suki was constantly exhausted and said very little, giving him just a faint smile when he helped her on and off the ferry. There had been no sighting of Chen Young; his sister had not seen him for a few days, since before her lover's death.

At a quarter past ten in the morning Molk was about to leave the girls sleeping peacefully in his apartment. He had not been able to get the image of the Man Mo Temple out of his head all night. As he was about to go Lian grabbed hold of his hand.

"The Man Mo Temple?"

"I won't be long. You stay with your sister."

"No. I want to come too."

Molk thought about refusing but decided that, as Lian had

suffered so much already, she perhaps was meant to see this through.

They hurried to the temple and once inside were astonished to find a badly burned human corpse. There was no evidence of damage to the temple. Molk felt heat on the back of his head and turned round quickly, putting his hand up to his neck. But he hadn't been burnt and there was no pain. There was no one there but Lian. It was then, as he looked down at the corpse, he realised that he didn't need a positive identification. The body would be that of Chen Young.

Lian smiled.

On returning home with her sister, Lian Lee felt better. When they entered the apartment their mother rose from her bed, put on her best red cheongsam that smelt of jasmine perfume, and whilst her sister slept and recovered in the dreamlands with her ancestors, mother took Lian down to watch the dragon parade. Mai wore a sorrowful yet resolute smile on her face.

The undulating dragon came closer, thrusting its head this way and that, as if seeking out someone in particular. When the dragon men passed Lian and Mai they paused and Lian thought she saw something more than her own reflected image in the dragon's glazed eye. Then the dragon men bowed and held the head of the dragon proud and high. Lian Lee was thankful that she had dedicated the prayer. The coconut candy her mother then bought for Lian, tasted of nothing but coconut candy.

The Critic

The first stage production based upon John Polidori's The Vampyre appears to be Le Vampire by Charles Nodier performed 13th June 1820 in Paris, at the Theatre de la Porte - Saint-Martin.

Anna Wilding nodded to Paula, her associate, who dimmed the lights and joined her on one of the red velvet covered chairs placed in a semicircle around a table; one of six in their small, private cinema. The small theatre was situated down one of Soho's narrow, shabby streets. Hardly anyone noticed the place was there and no one ever prised off the old boards that covered the front entrance. Visitors used an indistinct side door. The drab walls inside the establishment were plastered with faded posters of the vampire greats—those whom Wilding admired. She had chosen Max Shreck as Count Orlock, Bela Lugosi, Christopher Lee and Lon Chaney.

Paula, with her blonde bob cut, was quite a petulant vampire. "It doesn't seem entirely fair that we have to watch Jack Palance in Bram Stoker's Dracula, *again*."

"And you would prefer—?"

"Well, I quite liked Mad Monster Party from 1968."

"Animated vampires Paula—a very poor representation of our kind, as was Draculita in sixty-seven and The Nude Vampire in sixty-nine."

"You really didn't like the sixties films, did you?"

"Oh, I don't know. I had rather a soft spot for The Fearless Vampire Killers in sixty-seven, and then there is nothing comparable to Roger Vadim's Blood and Roses from sixty-one. Beautiful photography, a fine example."

"The Fearless Vampire Killers. Agreed. But did you have to kill the whole cast of Billy the Kid vs. Dracula from sixty-six?"

Wilding gave Paula a cool look. "Think about that for a moment Paula."

Paula settled down into the plush red seat, put her feet up on the table in front of her and sulked a little.

"Cheer up Paula. Tomorrow you can have your choice, so button it down and pass me the popcorn."

They settled down for the afternoon to watch *Nosferatu*, this time with Klaus Kinski in the role, followed by a discussion on the allure of silent film versus talkies.

Meanwhile, Nick Grant, who had been up until dawn the night before, slept fitfully, splayed across his enormous bed in his large mansion on Eel Pie Island:

MAGIC THEATRE
ENTRANCE NOT FOR EVERYBODY

It had happened again; Nick saw the red neon sign above the door and took one step closer. He knew the words came from the novel *Steppenwolf*. Nick's father, Mathew Grant, had been overlooked for the part of Harry Haller in the film. The part had been given to Max Von Sydow. But that is where the book, film, and the nightmare parted company. He had that nightmare for the last seven nights in a row and now, during the day. Each time when he entered the movie theatre it ended in the same way—in his death. The only difference was the way in which Nick Grant met his demise. No matter how hard he tried to resist, he was condemned each time to face the magician, although he could never actually focus on his visage.

As dreary day blended into restless night, Nick was confronted again by the nightmare. In this instance the magician bade Nick lie down on a bed face-upwards to gaze at the already blood-stained edge of a guillotine. The blade lingered, seemed to jar on its descent, and then it hurtled down towards his throat. His murderer was just a blurred image, and as the blade cut through—he awoke with a scream.

Startled from his nightmare, and soaked in sweat, Nick thought he heard the noise of a boat engine refusing to turn over, close to the island on which he lived. His hands were trembling and his step unsure as he staggered to the bathroom and threw cold water over his face. He stared into the mirror. Frustrated, bleary-eyed and angry, Nick went back to bed, praying that he would be able to get some rest. Just as his head hit the pillow his torment returned, and this time he was incarcerated in total darkness. The room smelt like a damp cellar and he could hear a sharp, scratching sound on wood not far away. Someone switched on a light. It was the magician again, and as each other time, the face was just a blur. Nick felt something uncomfortably close by his left shoulder and a gutter-like reek filled his nostrils, just as a rat bit into his neck.

Once more he awoke from the nightmare, shaking.

Nick threw the sheet from his sweating body and sat on the edge of the bed with his head in his hands. Something fell crashing to the floor as he fumbled for the bedside light. He switched on the lamp and looked down at the framed photo that had fallen. It was the picture of his wife and daughter, both wearing identical retro fifties dresses of pale blue with the brown poodle pattern. It usually made him smile, but Nick wasn't smiling now.

He stared at his hands; they were shaking uncontrollably.

Nick put one hand to his throat, pulled it away and then looked down at it. His eyes widened as he rubbed the thin smear of blood from his palm. The blood vanished and he realised that he must still be in part of the nightmare. He stumbled against the bed and rushed into the bathroom to stare into the mirror again. There was no blood, not a speck. Nothing. *No blood—that had to be good, right?* He had never been so terrified in his life. Sitting down on the edge of the bath, Nick tried to think of anything that would break him free from the terror that haunted him.

"Am I going crazy?" he muttered.

He had to ground himself. He thought of Stella and Alison, of who he was and what he had accomplished. He had two homes: one in Hollywood, and one in London. He had a stunning wife, Stella, and a beautiful daughter named Alison.

Nick could feel the tears welling up.

He spent most of his time in Hollywood. He had a golden rule: if his wife was on one continent, he would mess about with women on the other. No mixing continents and women—or cities for that matter. He might be sexually amoral, but he loved his wife.

Still trying to extract himself from the nightmares, he went into the kitchen and poured himself a glass of water.

Could all these nightmares be manifestations of guilt? he thought. *Christ! The women can go to hell if only the nightmares will stop. Keep thinking. Take your mind off the nightmares.*

He liked his London house on Eel Pie Island on the river Thames. He thought of those who used to live on the island, of the artists, boat builders and hippies now long gone, along with the footbridge. The island was only accessible now by boat, and belonged to him—Nick Grant—Film Star.

He dragged himself back to bed and was just beginning to fall into a strange state of half sleep when the phone rang.

"Nick, it's me—Nick?"

He recognised the voice and struggled to wake up.

"Nick, I need you to remind your mother about Ali's birthday. It's Saturday and nothing has arrived. I've tried to ring her but with the time difference and everything; I can never get hold of her. Will you—*Ali stop that. Leave it. Leave it!* Well, Nick, will you find out what's going on?"

He tried to make out the time on the clock. "Stella, do you know what time it is here? It's late."

"Sorry, darling. I know it's late there. Will you phone your mother tomorrow?"

"Stella?" Nick could hear Ali shouting in the background. "Yes—fine, I'll call." He put the phone down. He had told her about his nightmares earlier in the week and she had dismissed them again, suggesting that his imagination was a little too freaky for her to understand.

He turned off the light and stared at the ceiling, afraid of the shadows and terrified of the faceless magician. Unable to sleep, and too frightened to, Nick picked up the bottle of Valium, gulped some down with water and tried again to get back to sleep. He was so very, very tired.

As Nick came round he could make out the smell of stale smoke that sometimes lingered in bars and in places where people crowded together. Bright lights hurt his eyes and he saw that the light was coming from a mirror surrounded by bulbs that dazzled and confused him. His eyes learnt to focus again and he thought he must be in a dressing room. A woman walked in wearing a full length black cloak. She examined his face and his neck closely. As he fully regained consciousness Nick also realised that he was tied to a chair.

"What the hell—how did I get here? What the fuck is going on?"

The woman spoke. "Bringing you here was no problem, no problem at all. I can make you appear and disappear at will. Just like this little fellah."

The woman held a black hat before her, the sort that a magician would draw a white rabbit from. And draw it she did. The rabbit wriggled and squeaked, its legs scratching at her wrist, drawing blood and making her laugh all the more. With a swift movement she bit into its neck and ripped off its head—its blood spraying across the mirror.

Startled, Nick stared at her in disbelief. Reeling from the shock, he failed to recognise her at first. Initially, there was nothing about her body or the way she moved that immediately disclosed anything about her.

It's amazing what runs through your mind when you have just seen a rabbit lose its head, he thought. He noticed that she wore no jewellery; not even a watch.

She sipped from a glass and savoured the taste. "Don't you remember me Nick? You were once rather keen on me, if my memory serves me correctly, before you *acted* in vampire films."

She moved her face closer to his and seemed to sniff his neck. Revulsion flowed through him. Her eyes seemed like black pools within a snow-white face. She was made up in a hideous, geisha style and he still had trouble placing her.

"Let me jog your memory." The woman took off a black wig and tossed it carelessly onto a table. Her hair was red.

"You're kidding me." Nick looked at her incredulously. He had never bothered to remember her name.

"Anna Wilding," she stated plainly.

Nick may not have remembered her name but he remembered his unexpected distaste of her during sex. He had spent the night with her in her hotel room that one time in Rome but made a quick getaway when he had sobered up enough. He didn't really want her then and he certainly didn't want her now.

Wilding continued. "You know, Nick, I didn't think that you would let me down quite so badly." She fingered a rabbit's foot key ring attached to a belt that wound around her slender waist. She took another sip from her glass and licked her red lips. "Your father was pretty piss-poor in the part of Love at First Bite. You seem to have, shall we say, adopted his cinematic presence."

"What do you mean?" Nick braced himself.

"I mean, Nick darling, that I killed your father."

Nick's thoughts went back to his father's accident two years before. Sweat began to form on his forehead and he fought the desire to throw up.

Wilding pulled herself up onto the table. She flung the cloak aside and crossed her long, pale legs that tapered off into killer silver heels. She laughed a little, as if she couldn't wait to share her joke, and pushed the chair round so that Nick faced a computer. He saw himself on the monitor, tied to the chair. Wilding reached for the mouse and clicked. He saw himself in his new film that was doing very well, *The Death Doom of the Double Born*, released in 2007 (the original short story by Bram Stoker hadn't a vampire in it, but the film did now). Many actors that he recognised then came into view on the screen, all meeting their deaths by decapitation in so many, new, horrible and perverse ways.

There was the lead actor from *Dracula Sucks* from 1979, *Mamma Dracula* from eighty, and *Rockula* from ninety. The last one made Nick sick to his stomach; it was a movie still of his father as he appeared in *Love at First Bite*. There was a quick flash of his face in makeup, then the decapitation, some years later in the car crash. His head lay on the blood-splattered floor of the car. Wilding clicked again. Yet another still appeared—again, one of the scenes from the 'accident.' The impact dislodged a steel plate from the truck and it shot through the windscreen. Wilding clicked back to his father. Nick would never forget his face, with his mouth fixed in a terrified grimace and his hair matted with blood.

"My private collection." Wilding smiled. She brought her face close to Nick's neck again and he felt the sharp points of her teeth tease and threaten to puncture his skin. He could feel the heat of her breath and he struggled furiously against the binding.

"You sick fuck!" His stomach wrenched and he fought the desire to throw up once more. She drew away quickly.

"Your father tried to get away from me. He wasn't nearly quick or clever enough. It has always been this way; so many actors to kill, so little time to get round to them all."

Nick heard the door open behind him and another woman entered the room. She had short, blonde hair and the palest of grey eyes. He stared at her, hoping for some fresh explanation of what was happening to him.

"Wow, Paula you look great," Wilding gasped.

Paula turned around so that Wilding could get a better look at her costume, or the one she was *nearly-not* wearing. She looked like some sort of Bunny Girl but instead of being all-black, her tight bodice was covered in crimson sequins.

"Perfect, just perfect. The most glamorous magician's assistant." Wilding grabbed Paula by the waist and gave her a hug.

"I wanted to look my best and this costume won't show the blood. Anyway, this act is a little messier than the last."

Both the women laughed. Paula pulled Nick's chin up and grinned at Wilding. "Everyone who is *anyone* is out there." She looked towards the door and laughed nervously. Before he had time to move at all Wilding was upon him with lightening speed and her teeth pierced his skin. She took great pleasure in his blood. But, suddenly she pulled back.

Paula came closer to him, her eyes coming to life at the sight of his blood.

"No Paula. He is mine." Wilding snarled at her.

Weakened by the ordeal, Nick fell into a half faint, blood still pouring from his neck. Wilding licked her finger and placed it on the wound. A few seconds later the blood stopped flowing.

Still shocked and weakened, he was dragged between the women down a dim corridor and out onto a small, brightly-lit stage with a film screen behind it. On the large screen flickered the photos of all the lead actors that he had seen on the computer screen. The stills included one of his father's head, enlarged to a gigantic size and it towered over the audience. The applause was polite and petered out as quickly as it arose. Nick blinked and wished he could shield himself from the glare of the spotlights. A little steadier now, he could make out the small tables, surrounded by barely-visible forms shifting in the shadows. His throat hurt and he struggled to see clearly.

"I must get out of here." His voice cracked and the words sounded foolish.

This was met with even more polite applause and some laughter. He heard someone cough in the audience. At first the lights had dazzled his eyes, it was just too bright to see—but then *there* it was, ominous and sinister before him—he saw the long black coffin.

Wilding and Paula pulled him over to it. He wavered above it, steadied himself and felt his strength returning slightly before his knees buckled beneath him. With no great difficulty, the women forced him into the coffin. He felt the cool, ivory satin on his cheek, as he struggled—and a sweet rose perfume in the air above him as the lid was closed.

He heard the terrible sound of a saw cutting into wood, felt the coffin vibrate. Horrified, he struggled against the binding, holding his breath. He listened. He waited. Then it came.

"Oh, Christ!"

The saw broke through the wood.

For a moment it stopped and he could see light though the half-sawn lid. A few seconds later he gave out a shrill cry as again he heard the deafening sound of the buzz saw hovering somewhere above him.

"Christ! Let me out—Stop!"

The coffin lid was ripped off and a dark figure stood above him.

"What? What?" cried Nick, the light half-blinding him again as he took in great gasps of air.

A man hauled Nick out of the coffin and onto his feet. There was blood everywhere and something almost tripped him up as he stepped forward. He looked down—into Paula's pale, grey eyes, just before her head rolled over and over, and then off the stage. There was no sign of Wilding.

"It got a little messy, I'm afraid. We only got here with a few seconds to spare. Once *they* agreed that this should be stopped." The stranger helped support Nick and guided him to a small table where he sat him down.

"Are you the police?"

The rope was removed from Nick's wrists and he rubbed the red marks where the flesh had almost been broken.

The stranger sat on the chair next to Nick and smiled. "Well. From now on you just might say we are, since we have to put a stop to all these psychopathic crimes."

"What exactly," said Nick, trying to get his breathing under control, "is going on?"

My name is Goran Decanski and I represent, let us say, the more *traditional* of my kind. Not now to be associated with the diseased filth that lies at your feet. These mad vampires meet here in The Magic Circle with their nasty goings-on and such like." Goran poured himself a glass of red wine from the bottle that stood, already half empty, on the table.

Nick was feeling a little more in control, but he tried not to look at the many blood-splattered body parts around him. He pushed an empty glass towards Goran.

"I am so sorry, where are my manners?" Goran poured another

glass.

Goran was the kind of vampire that looked as if he had just stepped out of the pages of Bram Stoker's *Dracula*. He was Byronic, not at all like the modern looking Wilding, with her red hair and black eyes.

Nick put the glass to his lips and hesitated. "This *is* wine, I take it?"

Goran gulped from his glass and laughed. "Yes, it is wine. Let me ask you my dear friend, have you never licked your own wounds or sucked your own thumb after a pin prick?"

"Well, yes." Nick felt the panic rising again and clenched his hands, ready to run—that is, if he were strong enough.

"Did you like the taste?"

"I can't say I thought about it much."

"Well, blood tastes of birth and life, of a *particular life* if you can imagine such a thing. To me each individual is like wine, some are excellent and some have simply gone off. I accept each life as it comes along; usually the sick and the dying. I don't make a celebration of it and I don't kill actors just because they don't portray vampires in a certain way. Wilding developed a taste for hideous ritual. She began to kill actors, not to survive but to please her aesthetic taste, which to me is abhorrent. I am not proud of being a vampire. I am simply what I am—but I do not make a carnival out of it."

A great sadness struck Nick as he remembered that the mad vamps had killed his father. They had thought it a scream to stage the car accident.

"Wilding got away tonight and I will stop her eventually. But unfortunately she always finishes what she begins. So you must, for the time being, stay out of the limelight."

"My wife and daughter?"

"They must disappear too, until Wilding is stopped."

Goran rose quickly from his chair. "She drank from you?" he said, examining Nick's throat. "Only time will tell if you turn. In the meantime, perhaps you would like to help us?"

Nick took a deep breath. He hesitated for a second.

"Oh yes, I want a piece of that." Nick raised his glass.

Wilding had killed his father, and many times, himself in his nightmares. But it may have taken just the one bite to damn his soul—and he had to work out just how he was going to get revenge. Maybe he would have his own private party next year, especially for Wilding.

Less than a week later, Nick was in the Phoenix café on Hollywood Boulevard looking pretty much as he always did. Still suave, lapping up all the adulation from people in the café who asked for his autograph. Nick had a bodyguard now, a very special one at that, one who had been a vampire for a very, very long time. Goran let a few of Nick's admirers through for the autographs, the last he would ever give.

"One at a time please, ladies. He can only sign one at a time." The impromptu signing over, Nick and Goran retreated to the quiet luxury of a Lamborghini.

"Do you think you can give all this up?" asked Goran, gesturing at the car and the girls.

Nick was more thoughtful than usual, as he considered his wife and child. *Why was it that when you just started to really appreciate everything, it all gets fucked up?*

"I know I can. This life was getting a little out of hand. Do you know how much that birthday of Alison's cost? Five thousand pounds for a performer and Tiffany bracelets in the party bags for God's sake."

"Very expensive." Goran smiled.

"Yeah, but that was my last chance to spoil her. Have you got the documents? Will you see that they get them?"

"I will do that."

Goran showed him the new passports with the new identities for his wife and daughter. Nick knew that today would be the last time he would see his little girl for a while. It would be too dangerous for her to be around him now; and perhaps, if Wilding *had* turned him, that part of his life would be gone forever. He would not have to act the part of a vampire anymore, he might *become* one. The terrible realisation of that then fell upon him like the coffin lid. They would have to disappear and take on new identities, *somewhere*. But not with him.

Wings of Night

The dualitists is a reference to the title of the short story, "The Dualitists" otherwise named, "The Death Doom of the Double Born", written by Bram Stoker. It was first published in *The Theatre Annual* 1887.

It occurred to Elena that perhaps she wasn't living the best possible life; that in fact she was never moved to extremes anymore. She had been afraid to think too deeply or act accordingly. Within her banal activity and thoughtless repetition she barely existed, treading water, hesitant to join the others who called to her from within. Elena was aware of them all; a small army of malcontents who were trying to build a bridge from fresh hewn bones, and bound together with rotting sinews of the dead. Reluctantly Elena stayed away from those darker corners of her mind where the dualitists dwelt and where her former selves waited in quiet expectation.

Every Thursday and Saturday evening Elena worked as an usher at the Royal Exchange Theatre on Cross Street, in the city centre of Manchester. She showed people to their seats, sold programmes and was given a clipboard with a list of stage directions for opening and closing the doors for the actors.

8:22 p.m. Open for entrance of Hamlet, then close door.
8:25 p.m. Open for exit of Hamlet, then close door.
8:26 p.m. Open for entrance of Ophelia, close door.

Those were the kind of duties expected of her, and so forth. At the interval she was required to sell ice cream or coffee and use the antiquated till, which never worked properly and made her look a complete fool when it jammed. A queue would quickly build up with frustrated theatre-goers who simply wanted to be served and take a quick pee before the curtain went up for the second half of the performance.

Still, there were always the perks. Elena had seen *Romeo and Juliet* (in fact, many of Shakespeare's plays), also Tolstoy and Arthur Miller, amongst others. She got to meet actors in the green room and received free tickets for each performance. There was always Thursday night at the Press Club, where the actors and theatre staff would wind down, listen to the singers, laugh at the bawdy, bad jokes of the comedians, and occasionally dance. Some actors would get up, sing and tell jokes too.

Elena met a few famous names there; Vanessa Redgrave for one, who was an excellent actress, if not a little befuddled sometimes. When Elena said hello to her she couldn't help but think about that crazy award speech Vanessa had delivered once; it must have gone on for ten minutes, until the audience slow-clapped her off the stage.

Sure, Elena had slept with one or two of them (the actors, not the playwrights and certainly not Vanessa Redgrave or the audience). Only last Thursday Elena had taken great delight during a performance of *The Moonstone* by Wilkie Collins, in waiting until the last second to open a door for an actor. He had continued to ignore her after a one night stand, she being an usher; she was only the hired help after all. He made it quite clear that a blow job didn't constitute full sex, so he hadn't really been unfaithful to his girlfriend (who was playing Desdemona in *Othello* in York). The ushers were supposed to open the doors for actors, well before they reached the end of the aisle. Elena smiled with pleasure as she watched the beads of sweat roll down her one-night stand's face, when the tip of his golden slipper touched the bottom of the door as he tried to make his exit. She opened the door the instant his nose touched the small round window. When she didn't open the door quickly enough, he swore at her under his breath and glared over his shoulder as he made his way back to the dressing room. He was shaking so much his red satin turban threatened to fall off.

In the green room, she chatted to fellow ushers sometimes but was content to make paper-doll men. She cut them out and held them up, staring intently at the way they held hands and were joined together.

The actors just smiled indulgently at her.

Everything seemed all right for a few months in her attempt to connect with people. She'd only got into trouble the once recently, when she had signed two drunken boys (drunken prawns, drunken boys—same difference) into the Press Club. One of the boys followed her into the ladies, threw her against the wall and tried to get her to have sex with him there and then. The bouncer had sorted that one out.

One evening she left the theatre and was making her way down to the Press Club, just off Deansgate, when she met another two lads in leather jackets who persuaded her that she would have a better time in Rock World; so she went. She dumped them just inside the entrance, when she felt the first rush of excitement as Nirvana pumped through the building.

She had the choice of Jilly's downstairs or the main club above. The glam-rockers mixed with the bikers, the students mixed with the heavy metal gang; everyone was cool. No fights, no arguments, just people hanging around, dancing, boozing and having a great time. Elena had to wear black as an usher so she fitted in just fine there. She even removed her blouse in the club's heat, to reveal a clinging black bodystocking underneath. Many girls were wearing tight, black corsets designed to reveal more than they concealed, so Elena felt suitably dressed. In the ladies she brushed up half her shoulder-length, brown hair in the style of Attila the Hun, and painted her eyes like Cleopatra. She didn't care what others thought. Elena liked what she saw in the mirror and no other opinion mattered.

Now, this behaviour was fine for a while, but then as the weeks passed she became more adventurous. Elena became Marion, played by Solveig Dommartin from the film *Wings of Desire*. She imagined herself high above the sweating dancers, up on the trapeze, wearing a white leotard and the faded wings of a broken angel. Then, jolted from her reverie she would dance and wander the rooms on her own until the final half-hour when she would choose a boy.

No one gave one-night stands a second thought but Elena was looking for more, much more—which she never found. Not with that tall Swede, who looked at her in a funny sort of way and told her repeatedly that she was Irish; nor with the chef who was leaving soon to work his way around the U.S.; and certainly not with the Hell's Angel, Steve, who said he cried when he watched *On the Waterfront* and claimed that he was an immense Brando fan but ironically disliked *The Wild One*. Actually, Steve also blubbed when he talked about *It's a Wonderful Life*, his huge shoulders shook when he described James Stewart's euphoria as he came running back home through the snow. Steve was way too sentimental for Elena. She also drew the line at going home with the kind, hunk of a man called Bob, who smelt like he cleared decayed remains from old houses.

And still she did not find what she was looking for.

The next week she coloured her hair blonde, to be Marilyn with bubble hair, and she drank beer through a straw in the bottle so as not to smudge her red lipstick. These little cameo roles went on for weeks. She became Mia Wallace from *Pulp Fiction* and Kate Fuller in *From Dusk Till Dawn*. But still, nothing really pleased her.

The weeks flew by and she continued to take someone home on Thursday and Saturday nights. She never had them in her large double bed upstairs. The downstairs room had a sofa that converted into a floor bed.

On Fridays Elena was understandably tired and would pick up a baguette, some brie, queen olives, and a bottle of Merlot.

On Saturday afternoon she would go over to her mother's flat and they would curl up with a video that Elena had chosen, perhaps a thriller with Ray Milland in it or a Fred Astaire movie.

She adored her mother but could only spend a few hours at a time in her company because she had heard her mother's memories so many times before, and although she had once enjoyed them, they didn't hold the same resonance anymore. Elena was hungry for adventure and time alone, to wander around the city streets to see what kind of trouble she could get into.

One night she met someone, got very drunk and tried to bounce his phone off an auto showroom window. The man, naturally enough, decided that Elena wasn't his type but had dropped her off in a gentlemanly manner on her own doorstep, at first—he then pushed her face into said doorstep, causing her all manner of confusion the next day about whether she had tripped or was pushed. She decided in the end that she had been pushed.

She went out with a fellow for two weeks once, a social worker. He was older than her, about thirty-five and wore his black hair in a ponytail. He dropped her relatively quickly during an Italian meal, declaring she was *damaged goods*. She had simply commented that perhaps he wasn't cut out to be a social worker, as he was recovering from a nervous breakdown.

Her list of boys and men seemed endless. Sometimes she would chuck them—but mostly they would ditch her. Elena was attractive enough but she always picked the worst of the male species—the ones that were equally fucked-up as she.

She continued her pursuit of pleasure and love, changing her appearance subtly or drastically, to try anything, as long a she didn't have to think about who she was—if she were *anyone*. Sometimes she would lose herself in her old haunt, The Press Club, to go home with Charlie, the singer. He was married but she loved his voice. Charlie, when he saw her enter the club, would stop singing and begin a special song for her, called *Nature Boy*, the one by Nat King Cole. Perhaps the boy in that song was who she was looking for; if he was, Elena never found him either and she suspected that he only existed in the lyrics.

After a few beers—rather a lot actually—the depth of the Press Club, with its blue-green light, began to look like a vast cavern filled up to the ceiling with water, and on more than one occasion she felt herself gasp, and struggled to come up for air. After one late, summer night she walked home in the silent dawn. The rage in her head subsided for a time and she was delighted to actually smell pine trees and the various summer flowers in the gardens, before the cars would come along and leave their trails of smog.

The next Saturday she was out on the pull again. The outfit she chose that evening was a mid-thigh, backless sea-green dress over coal-black leggings. It indeed clung like seaweed on a rock. She changed out of her usher clothes and into her dancing rig after the theatre. As she flew down the stage door steps she knew she could do anything—She was ready again.

The first time she killed a man it was quite accidental.

It was the tall Swede. She had thought it a shame as she quite liked him. They were down by the canal bank and were fooling around. He didn't have a condom, she didn't either. He insisted on going ahead, but she refused. She didn't mean to push him away so hard—she was trying to be coy. He stumbled backward into the canal. She couldn't understand why he wasn't moving and she peered into the darkness. He just seemed to be spread out over the water as if he were floating. Too stiff—too rigid. A cloud shifted from the full moon then she saw a metal rod protruding from his chest and a darker stain spreading upon the oily water. At that point she ran.

In the taxi home the orange glow of the street lights hurt her eyes, and she felt flush with excitement. She realised that, although an accident, she had caused his death, and it gave her a thrill.

Away from the front page morning news of an Uzi machine gun attack on five in Moss Side, the paper had the story way in the middle, under the heading:

FOREIGN STUDENT FOUND DEAD—IMPALED IN CANAL

Elena felt a little pissed off. For some strange reason she wanted it to be front page news—*she* wanted to be front page news. His death was something *she* had been involved in. Men—boys—always let her down. As a teenager she had read all about romance; she kept looking for love, but, always through sex. She always failed. Elena should have learnt something from her past experiences but she was being a dog, really a bitch, chasing her own tail and hadn't learnt anything. Here she was now, after weeks of different identities and still she couldn't find what she was looking for.

Then along came Maurice.

It was her voices who told her about him. They whispered into her ear in the darkest part of the night, rising to the surface of her mind, as if survivors from some underwater wreck. They became bloated corpses—whose skin burst open, revealing an infestation of blind, white worms that slid back into the vacant eye sockets of their hosts. The corpses pinned her by her bleeding wrists to the bed until she promised that she would return with them—to the corners of her mind, where they would continue to corrupt her...and tell her what to do next.

Maurice appeared at Rock World. He was six foot tall, slender, with shoulder-length brown hair and grey eyes. He wore a blue, waist-length military style jacket and looked pretty good to Elena. She would go home with him. He lived on the north side of the city and shared a house with two other students. Naturally, they had formed their own band and shared this hobby, the rent, *and* they shared Elena. He told her that if she really loved him, she would do anything for him

After drinking too much alcohol, but not enough that she didn't know what she was doing, Elena let each one of them have her; a simple and meaningless act. They told her to sit across them and *do* something but she simply shrugged and closed her eyes. All three boys laughed and joked but were slightly nervous about the whole thing. Through alcohol, Elena had numbed herself down so that she didn't feel much of anything. It was as if she could let them do this *to* her but not participate in it. It was enough for them, as they silently slipped in and out of her in turn, like the slugs they were.

She drank more wine with them and pretended that she had

meant it all to happen, which she hadn't. Elena even warmed to one of them when he strummed his guitar and sang of *the lost girl with the grey eyes*.

Lost in time and space—that was her.

One of them took her home later in a taxi but when she refused to give head he pulled out a knife to frighten her into submission. Now she had a cross-stitch of knife wounds on her shoulders from his struggle to force her face into his lap. Elena was learning to hate. What she had done all those times before was of her own volition. This was different.

And learn to hate she did.

The other ushers noticed a change in her. She looked even more distracted than usual and rarely spoke now. She was polite to the theatre-goers, did the door opening and closings quietly with no sense of fun, and never went to the Press Club anymore. She preferred rock music and the dark corners of that club, which felt like the black corpse-ridden places in her mind. In those organic folds lay the creatures she had avoided for most of her life. Now? Elena spent most of her waking and sleeping time *with* them. The terrors of her mind were forming themselves into crimes against mankind. It wasn't just smoke and mirrors anymore, for *it was real to her now*.

It wasn't hard to get hold of the Rohypnol. She knew someone who knew someone…who knew someone…simple. She had the money to pay for it too. At one time it was colourless and tasteless but drug companies now added a blue dye. Still, most street stuff didn't have the dye in. The boys were always eager to get into her, so she would have to work quickly, although she didn't know whether to just drop a tablet in a drink or what; Elena had never used the drug before. She decided that she would grind all the tablets up into a powder with her oversized quartz ring, which she would wash carefully later.

After the theatre on Saturday night Elena went to the rock club. She drank with the boys again, and they were all for taking her back to their flat after the beer and dancing. The music gave her a headache and she didn't want to get too drunk, so she only had three beers.

A few of her old one-night stands saw her leave with the boys. She didn't care that she was seen with them. It didn't matter to her. She was intent only on her plan. They flagged a taxi to the student digs. The rooms were just as untidy as always. It wasn't difficult to get the stuff into their beer bottles; powder in one bottle when a boy was in the toilet; more in another when Maurice was rooting about in the fridge for something to eat; the last of it when the third lad went upstairs to throw all his junk off the bed onto the floor, in preparation for her.

Within ten minutes, and within seconds of one another—just as the boy with the dirty hands was entering her—they passed out. She pushed him out of her. Maurice slumped from the bed to the floor. The last boy tried to stand up, but his knees gave way beneath him, and he crumpled to the floor like a string puppet.

The first part of Elena's plan was complete. The hardest part was trying to drag them all onto the bed in the right position, but she soon managed it. There they were, all in a row, like the paper-doll men she often cut, but the paper men had been all joined together....

One boy was naked from the waist down so she took off his shirt. One was completely naked already and Maurice was still dressed. When she had removed his clothes and they were sleeping like little butcher's dogs—that is how she now saw them—she prepared to carry out the next part of her plan. She removed from her bag a large, black wrap-around pouch and placed it onto an old bedside table. From it she took out the sharper knives. As she withdrew the first, she wondered if it would be sharp enough. It was. With careful precision she cut across the abdomen of the first boy, not too deeply at the first attempt. He groaned a little and shivered on the bed.

Elena sat back on her heels, pursed her lips and shrugged.

She lunged forwards and drove the knife straight through his heart, then quickly through the hearts of the other two. She proceeded with her work carefully cutting and pulling the slippery, pink-grey guts out of each of them, arranging and rearranging them until they looked just right. They would be hers forever.

She stood up, smiled and admired her handiwork again. She used the bed sheets to wipe her red hands. Her new boys were perfect. All lined up in a row, like the paper-doll men she liked to make, and—all joined together.

Medium Strange

Lumbroyd Quaker Meeting and burial ground. Built 1763. Last meeting held 1847. Demolished 1859 Cubley, South Yorkshire.

Four children—missing. No bodies found. Four boys aged between five and seven, lost boys—disappeared without a trace with little hope of finding them again, and a sad trail of weeping relatives left behind.

Who would be next?

It came to me, as I was walking past the old Puritan Graveyard—I stopped to stare at an inscription on the stone plaque embedded in the wall; high up in the trees the rooks clung tentatively to the branches as the cold wind blew in from the moor—

My sister and I would work together again.

Our lives, at times had drifted into periods of no contact or very little. The death of our mother brought us closer now and my sister told me that I had been her rock in our moments of dark despair; I know that she had been mine. I glanced at my watch and worked out how long it would take me to get home. It was normal for me to walk for an hour, four times a week, up and down the lanes around my home, which lay on the edge of the South Yorkshire moorland, not far from the Woodhead Pass. Home was a solitary old farmhouse blasted by the howling wind, with a two-hundred-year-old withering oak for company.

Yes, we would work together again. She would do the medium bit and I, Abbie Marshall, would do the leg work. She would have the visions and I would hit the solid ground running, dragging myself out into the cold to track down the murderer and solve the mystery. *Would she go for this case?* I wondered. I was afraid to be around spirits—ghosts creep me out. I would much rather face-off the real-life criminals, embezzlers and such. The wife-beaters, the phoneys and the frauds; I was fine with them. It was real people I was used to, with their dirty lives, dirty thoughts and wishes. Give me something tactile and I could work with it. The only spirits I was interested in were the whisky and gin I drank to numb my swollen gums.

The Woodhead Pass claimed numerous lives each year as many drivers became impatient behind big trucks, and death by overtaking was common. There was a memorial near an old stone bridge, for a young man who had come to a sticky end in a fast car on that road. A banner was tied to the fence at the spot where he died. It had his name, dates, and plastic flowers tied to it, *even* a racing trophy. Driving down that road one day I had wanted to stop and add to the banner, 'Stupid Fuck,' but my fear of outraged spirits wouldn't let me.

Now, I had my mobile with me and I could walk and talk at the same time, if I could get a signal.

"Hi, Sylvia, I've been thinking. You said you would like to get involved with that boy's disappearance but don't like the limelight. The press don't bother me. You could feed me the clues and I could act upon them—I know you don't want to front it but I could. If you give me what you've got I'll act upon it. It makes sense." For a moment there was silence on the other end of the phone.

"What about the risk to you?" my sister asked.

"Yes I know about the risk. But—what do you think?"

"I don't know."

For another moment there was silence between us.

"Just think about it. If there's something we can do, we should do it—now. Ring me later, Sis."

Sylvia was eighteen years older than me and since our mother died she had been more like a mother to me; I used to imagine that Sylvia had given birth to me and that my mother had lied to hide a family scandal. Although in her late fifties, my sister was still a beautiful woman. Well, she was to me, her little sister. Sylvia's father was an American. I never knew anything about my father (except that I had blonde hair like him), because my mother never talked about our fathers. All I remember is that once, when I was playing cowboys and Indians with my brother's friends, my mother said that Sylvia's father looked like the boy who was shouting more than the others. I looked to find out who was shouting the most and he wasn't a cowboy. Sylvia was of American Indian descent and appropriately enough her spirit guide was of her tribe too. Even as a child she saw spirits and it always scared me when she had conversations with people that I could not see.

The dark clouds followed me over the ridge and it began to pour just as I put my key in the door.

I used web and e-mail and that suited me and my clients just fine, as I preferred to work quietly and without much fuss. The parents, Elizabeth and Steven Patterson, did not want anyone except the police to know that I was involved. I had offered my services as a psychic detective to them before Sylvia had actually agreed. I had all the newspaper clippings with their bizarre guesses at what had happened.

The year was 1999 and Christ's birthday was just round the corner. The Daily Recorder suggested that the boy had been taken for ransom, but no ransom demand had been made. Their son, Jake, had been safely tucked into bed in blue-check pyjamas and with his Snoopy dog. All the doors were locked and no one was staying in the B&B attached to the Victorian tea room. They lived in a small market town at the edge of the moors and the family did not have an enemy in the world—until now.

The wind and rain had not let up all day and it was well into the evening when it stopped, just as the phone rang.

"Hi, Abbie. You know I'll do it, but I'm not happy about it. This isn't just a case involving a lost will or a wife who has walked out on her husband. This is going to get dirty and I have to think about you."

"Sylvia, I will keep my distance. Do you really want me to walk away from this one? The parents...think of what they are going through; think of me when I was little. Could you have lived with yourself, all those years ago, if you hadn't helped?"

"That was different, you are my little sister. I don't want you getting too close to this one. It feels bad, really bad."

"Sylvia, Sylvia, come on now, think of the parents, this is the fifth child. Give me your best shot at it."

There was a long pause; the wind picked up and then dropped again.

"...The boy is still alive but not for much longer. He is getting weaker...," again, a pause, "...We're in the countryside, I see for miles. It is very close to where you live, too close, Abbie. I'm not happy with this. All this is going on very near to you."

"Don't you see, Syl, that's why I have to help."

"...I see a few farmhouses but I'm coming to one that has a fence with moles nailed to it. I go down the track and past the old farmhouse door, past the barn and into the wood beyond. In this wood there is an old cottage, much older than the barn, and the cottage has boards on the windows.... That's all that Sam is giving me. I'm sorry."

"Is that were the boy is?"

"I think so—it isn't at all clear. That's all I get. Are you going to give this information to the police?"

"Yeah, and thanks, Syl. Bye."

It was something at least. Did many farmers hang moles on fences?

The wind let up for a few hours but it was still a cold January day. I rang my contact in the local police force, John. He came round to my house, out of uniform, and I told him what my sister had said.

"Moles you say, not many farmers still nail moles to the fence. I think I know where that farm is."

John telephoned it in and it did not take the police long to act upon it. They found the farm, the barn, and the moles. They took

Jack Moffat, the farmer, in for questioning that night. I went down to the police station although I had promised Sylvia to keep my distance. I had to see him.

Moffat was a man in his mid-forties, dressed in tweed trousers, an old blue jumper, and heavy boots. He did not look like a murderer to me—but what does a murderer look like? Some serial killers look quite innocent, from their photos. Moffat was confused and uncertain, and I felt sure this was not the person who was responsible; they had not found the boy. Without evidence, they couldn't keep him at the police station.

Sylvia rang me again the next day. I told her what I knew. "They've not charged the farmer, Syl. Nothing to hold him with. No evidence in the farmhouse, nor the barn, or anywhere on the property."

"What I said is still right. They didn't mention a cottage? I don't understand it, but it is still right."

It was crazy but I had to go and check it out myself. Sylvia would never forgive me, but I had to go. The farm was exactly as she described; five moles nailed to the fence, then the track, then the farmhouse. An old woman, whom I supposed to be Jack Moffat's mother, let me in.

"You'd better sit down for all the good it will do yer; cos I won't be able to tell yer police anything else."

I kept quiet about who I was and looked around the farmhouse as she made tea. The farmhouse wasn't dirty, but it wasn't exactly clean either. On the mantelpiece there was an old, light brown teapot. Too old for holding tea and was, in fact, a model of a World War One tank, complete with the head of some ruddy-faced Tommy as the handle on top of the lid. On a large oak table set against the wall, sat a huge pottery Alsatian that guarded the doorway to the kitchen, where an assortment of real sheepdogs sat, each keeping a watchful eye on me. An old oil painting of a highland piper hung on one wall, and a selection of hunting traps and guns on another. The old leather sofa had seen better days and had a faded, red throw sprawled across it, reaching out to cover the holes. I wanted to leave but felt that I had to stay until at least after the cup of tea.

The old mother set down the tray, pulled her tatty brown cardigan tighter around herself and fastened a button before she sat down, exhausted from her labour. She gestured at me and the teapot and in the next second I was pouring tea for a supposed murderer's mother. I shook from the fact that the kidnapped boy might still be hidden close by, somewhere out in the cold. I wondered why the police had been unable to find him—as my sister was never wrong.

"I noticed the moles on the fence," I said, taking a sip from the willow pattern cup. My mother had loved the story of the willow pattern and had told me it years ago.

"The moles—there t' keep a reckoning."

For a fleeting moment I remembered that five children had disappeared—

"How do you catch the moles?"

"Jack does it now but his dad used t' use a spring trap—pulled back and placed over a collapsed tunnel. When the mole builds the tunnel up again, the spring gets triggered and *no more Mister Mole!*—goodbye t' the gentleman in velvet." She laughed and the tea dribbled down her chin.

I looked at the gruesome traps that hung on the wall.

"He didn't have any time for traps made with bent hazel and string as they was t' soft for the little buggers, he said. We called him Mowly Jack, or mouldy Jack some days. Got a photo of him somewhere. He moved on then, t' make quite a living at catching the moles with poison rather than traps cos it paid more for the moleskin yer see, t' make waistcoats, and such like."

The old mother pointed at the mantel. "Up there."

Up there was an old photo album with pictures of old dames and young children in below-knee dresses and white pinafores. On one page there was a drab photo of a man with brisk sideburns in a black, wide brimmed hat and he wore a dark, hollow expression.

I showed it to the old mother.

"That's him. Mowly Jack."

"Quite a stern character wasn't he?"

"Stern? He were an *evil* bastard. I could understand anyone suspecting him of murder but me Jack, never."

"Just one more thing. Is there an old cottage close by?"

"...There used t' be, but it were pulled down years ago."

I thanked her for the tea and left the farm, shivering as I passed the five moles nailed to the fence.

The nightmares started that night. First, I dreamt that I was seriously ill in a hospital bed. I couldn't move but was fully aware of the nurses, doctors, and everything else. It is all very well to say that one should die in their sleep, all peaceful. I don't think anyone dies in their sleep peacefully. They might look like it, but that's not the way it is. They go down fighting every inch of the way, terrified of the demons or of serpents coiled around their bodies and that strike each part of their mind again and again. There will be no peace for any one of us. We will see what others cannot see and our minds will twist them into terrifying monsters and there is nothing any of us can do about it.

Then I had a nightmare about Mowly Jack and his moles. He was walking down the lane to Moffat's farm with a sack over his shoulder. When he got to the fence I thought he was going to nail some moles to it, but instead, from out of the bag he took a small child who trembled and cried. I woke up in a cold sweat and rang my sister, before it grew light.

"Moffat will be out of police custody today, they can't keep him any longer and there is no sign of the boy."

"The boy's dead Abbie. Sam told me that he passed over a few hours ago."

"But Moffat is still in police custody, unless the child died where he was imprisoned." My hands trembled. I could hear Sylvia sighing on the other end of the phone.

"A child has disappeared on the spirit side too. Sam won't help us anymore."

"I don't see how you giving me information can have anything to do with a spirit child's disappearance."

"Well it has. Don't you see? There could be killings on both sides now. It has nothing to do with me anymore. Sam won't help if it means losing more spirit children. I have to stop, Abbie—I can't carry on."

"You think that the disappearance is connected to what we are doing. Doesn't the spirit world know who has the child?"

"Spirits can connect to those who want them in our world, and they know some of what we cannot see, but they are just like us in their own world. In their world they live as simply as we do and there is mystery there too."

"Sylvia."

"Yes?"

"How can a spirit child die?"

"I don't know, but spirits can cease to be and that death is every bit as valid as a death in this world. This is the first spirit disappearance that I have come across and the mother is distraught."

"I know Sylvia, I know." I tried to calm my sister down.

A soul is a soul, whether it is here or on the other side. I remembered how I had escaped my own death, with my sister's help. She used Sam, her spirit guide to help her. He had led her to an old, disused steelworks where he had seen the teddybears, six in all. One stood out from the rest, small and made of plastic, beige with a blue bib and a chewed ear. It was mine, but it has never been discovered though I was found.

The next night was the longest I had known in a long time, the weather turned colder, windy, and it began to snow. I usually loved snow, but right now I wished it away and prayed that there would be no more deaths. I lay in a troubled sleep in my bed and it was just after midnight when twigs on the withered oak rattled against the window and woke me. I had been meaning to cut back that branch all winter, but kept forgetting. I decided to get up and go and get some hot milk.

My cat, Orphy, was huddled next to the cooker far away from the kitchen windowsill where he usually slept. "Yes, Orphy, it's very cold."

The wind died and I thought I heard a light knocking on the

door. Not wanting to answer the knock immediately I peeped out the window curtain and switched the porch light on. There, standing on the porch, was the man that the old mother had shown me in the photo. I could see his face clearly by the light. My hand shook as I held the curtain, and I remained rooted to the spot. His eyes were the eyes of a dead man, sunken in and fixed against a bone-white skin. His eyes tried to hold my stare but I could not help but lower mine to look at the small forms that stood on each side of him. I recognised one tiny face immediately—it was the murdered boy, Jake Patterson.

Mowly Jack stared at me in defiance and turned to go up the road in the direction of the Puritan graveyard, his wide-brimmed black hat stuck to his head for all eternity. I could not let him take those spirits. I grabbed my jacket and quickly put on my boots. I had no time to do anything except snatch my phone off the hall table and go after him. What was I thinking? The snow had only been falling for a few hours but it was enough to isolate this part of the world. Anyway, who could I tell...that a dead man had captured the ghosts of two dead children? I was desperate as I followed him up the lane, and I tried to ring Sylvia. *Would there be a signal?* I panicked. I was chilled to the bone but I needed to help.

Finally I got a signal.

"Sylvia, Sylvia. I see the man who has murdered them. He has them with him right now!"

"Keep calm—this is what you do, trust me. Ask the spirit world, ask *them* for help, they have to get the children away or they will never be free of him. Are you still there? Do you understand? This is something you cannot do alone—"

I heard the phone fall from her hands and understood immediately. I closed my eyes against the death-cold snow and begged for help. I begged for a chance to stop him.

Mowly Jack dragged the poor children through the blizzard, nearing the iron gates of the Puritan graveyard. I pleaded as I had never done in my life for some force to come to my aid. I could hear the cries of the small children.

Then—thank God—I saw the graveyard gate open. I saw the Puritans, and Sylvia, reach out and haul Mowly Jack through the gate. He had to let go of the children and they ran to my side for safety. The child spirits kept close to me as I crept towards the open gate and peered through to see what was happening. I had to know. The Puritan spirits dragged Mowly Jack over to an empty grave. He was kicking and screaming and several Puritan spirits pulled a tombstone over him as he tried to scramble out. Mowly Jack was sealed into the holy ground and would walk the earth no more.

I looked down at the children. From each tiny face tears were falling, but their eyes were full of gratitude too. My sister took them by the hand and led them away. She looked back and smiled once more at me, and I watched as they simply melted away in the swirling snow.

When I got home, exhausted and shocked, I saw something lying on the doorstep. It was my teddy bear, small and made of plastic, beige with a blue bib and a chewed ear. I held it close and cried.

The next morning the boy's murder was all over the papers. The police had returned to the farm and investigated the old farmhouse a little more closely. Anyone could have missed the wall. The plaster looked dry. No one had heard the whimpering coming from behind it. It was too late. The poor child had been left to die with the rotting corpses of four others who had already passed over. He was there whilst I had been taking tea with the old mother and admiring the willow pattern on the tea cup.

Author Note: For my sister Sylvia, who passed away 1st March 2008.

The Silk Road

The Decameron by Giovanni Boccaccio, influenced the work of Shakespeare, Keats and Chaucer amongst others. A hundred novellas were written by Boccaccio between 1350—1353.

All the final arrangements were in place and Frieda was to travel to China soon. She was looking forward to the trip and couldn't wait to get away. She looked up from her writing, gazed out the window at the sodden ground and realised that summer was not going to materialise in England at all that year. Global warming had taken its toll and the only decent weather that anyone could enjoy was in May and the rest stayed somewhere around The Azores. It was mid-July, but might as well have been early spring or late autumn for all the sun she'd seen.

Frieda was going to China to do research for a book on the Cherchen mummies. The last book she had written was about how different cultures handled death and bereavement. Frankly, it had made her maudlin and depressed. She had the luxury of being able to write full time which had an effect on the normal, acceptable biorhythms of her life. Affected by insomnia, Frieda would often write until 3 a.m. before finally falling asleep until mid-day. Weeks of that and shopping for more Bolivian Roast at 5 a.m. in the 24-hour Tesco and any writer would get irritable, and depressed.

Depression. Each bout a nightmare, with long days of inactivity caused by disinterest and perhaps biopolarism. At least she experienced the highs on that. During the bad times Frieda would lay flat on her back in bed with quilt tucked tightly under her chin. A prisoner in her own body, her mind locked down with a great big bolt driven through her brain. Trapped. There was no escape, except into morbid thoughts and the feeling that nothing was worth her effort or of any value. Alongside the depression came claustrophobia. To Frieda, hell would be sleeping inside one of those small hostel compartments in Japan.

She couldn't get beyond the trap that human existence was a wasted effort. She could write about life in stories, journals, and facts but why bother, when it was only second hand and others should experience it for themselves?

Frieda had no desire to take her own life. It wasn't that kind of depression. It was the sinking feeling that she could stay so still that she would simply die within minutes: switch everything off in her head just like a light switch, one after the other until her mind was in darkness.

Why write? she must ask. Wouldn't it make it worse?

But writing actually helped Frieda deal with the depression. Sometimes she was a frenzy of activity, putting her horror into words so that her character could feel worse than she did. She furiously thumped her computer keyboard as if punching in a secret code to escape, day after day.

Sometimes Frieda would walk the streets, close to the River Irwell in Salford, where she had lived since graduation. She walked to stave off the bouts of depression, thinking about her writing as she walked. She constantly talked to herself, acting out the dialogue like a madwoman. Some mad people lived their fiction. Were most writers merely rehearsing for the madness and loneliness of later life?

Frieda had never really got on with the opposite sex for more than one or two months, or one or two years in two cases. Habits irritated her and she preferred to sleep alone.

Before she left Salford, Frieda had been on a messageboard and saw a YouTube video, filmed in India. A beggar put down a baby on the street pavement, with a cobra (whose venom had been removed), and onlookers watched eagerly as the baby tried to catch the snake and strangle it. Bets would be on snake or infant and Frieda watched as the cobra, its neck held firmly in the chubby little fist, wound the length of its body around the baby's neck. Frieda shuddered and hoped that China didn't have any horrors like that on offer for her.

The city of Urumchi captivated her. It was located in The Tarim Basin and was one of the ancient cities that once was a hive for traders and the welcome refuge of the nomads on the Silk Road. Huge mounds of melon, tomatoes, and onions were placed in front of the stalls in the bazaar. Normally, Frieda avoided crowds but the hustle of the foreign city was light relief from the dull, wet, streets of Salford. She was excited by the fact that she could escape to another continent for three months, with its new sounds, spice smells, and cheerful activity.

Urumchi had modern changes like skyscrapers, but there was also that wonderful oriental feel to the city. Behind those skyscrapers she could see snow-capped mountains and she felt refreshingly invigorated as the wind whipped down from them in the late afternoons.

Frieda looked at the Indo-European mummies in the glass-topped cases in the Urumchi Museum. They had been preserved by the salt flats in which they had been found. The Loulan Mummy was from Qawrighul (Gumugou, in Chinese). She had a Caucasian face, reddish hair, and amongst her clothes a well-preserved material was found, a sort of Celtic plaid. DNA results of another mummy, Cherchen Man, revealed him to be related to Swedes, Finns, Tuscans, Corsicans, and Sardinians. Here, Frieda had an Indo-European woman, on the Silk Road thousands of years before she should have been there. Some scholars thought that western travellers arrived in China well before Marco Polo, and indeed they did not believe Polo's writings, considering those to be eccentric accounts from a man who did not travel so far to the East.

The female mummy was four thousand years old. What had been her language? Could she write? What had her life been like, and what had killed her? All those questions ran through Frieda's head. Was the woman a sacrifice or had she died of natural causes? Her skin was the colour of rubber bands and she had thick eye lashes and long hair. Her jaw had dropped in death, as the fastening that was meant to secure her mouth shut had rotted. Her cheeks were painted yellow and there were many tattoos on her face. Her ear lobes were pierced with strands of red wool threaded through them.

Frieda continued to take notes in her diary, now focusing on how the strange mummy was dressed. She wore a long, red dress and deerskin boots. Remarkably, she was very tall, six feet and in a good state of preservation. Careful preparation had made sure of that, but she was kept intact for what? An eternal life that was just out of reach?

The mummies had all their belongings buried with them for the journey. Even the little comb found in the female mummy's hands, which some had thought was to comb her hair, could have been the comb she used to card wool for her clothes. Perhaps the mummies could weave their own destiny in the afterlife? Frieda speculated on that, and also that in Salford, as people grew older their houses got smaller too. They swapped them for granny-flats until those were exchanged for the smallest houses of all—and in those they were just given a satin pillow.

Frieda could have stayed hours in the museum but it was going to close soon and she wondered about walking in the strange city, whether it was safe to. She hadn't come all the way from England to lock herself away; if she wanted to write she, needed to see the city.

Frieda looked over at a man. He looked to be Han Chinese. He sensed that she was watching him and looked up. Their eyes met—she looked away. He would not speak English anyway, so what was the point?

He smiled when she glanced back. "Good afternoon, Miss."

Frieda smiled too. "Good afternoon."

"You like our lady, Miss?"

"She fascinates me. I want to write about her and I will be writing about the city too, past and present."

"And the people, will you be writing about the people too?"

Frieda nodded, unsure of how much to say about her intentions.

"My name is Galyma. I look after the Loulan beauty, but not officially."

Frieda thought that, obviously curators, conservationists, and archaeologists looked after mummies—okay perhaps a caretaker—if that was who the man was. Maybe he could tell her more information about the mummies than was in the official records.

"Would you be interested in being my guide around the city?" she asked.

"What would you like to see?"

"Places which tourists don't usually see."

"Are you writing a book?"

"Well, yes, does that matter?"

"What kind of book would it be?"

"Fiction."

Galyma's eyes lit up. "Stories?"

"Yes, stories. Do *you* have any stories about The Loulan Beauty?"

The tall man nodded. "If you meet me I will tell you stories that will interest you."

It occurred to Frieda that she would never find out what she wanted to know if she stayed in her hotel room all the time. They fixed the place for a rendezvous for the next day—Tuesday at 2 p.m.

All her adult life Frieda had been this adventurous, which occasionally helped her escape her depression. When she was at Salford University she had taken her mountain bike and her boyfriend, shoved both on a plane to Salzburg, then on a train to Vienna, and cycled along the Danube to Budapest. It poured with rain some days and they met one fellow cyclist, a German, who had decided to cycle to the Black Sea. He wore only a T-shirt, no waterproofs, and stayed in hotels each night whilst they camped. She asked him why, even though it was summer, why he didn't have any waterproofs? He shrugged. "I didn't think it would rain."

Frieda looked down on the Loulan Mummy. The Chinese had let Frieda come and stay to research her book, but she knew that one or two officials were anxious about the influence of westerners of the present day, let alone those of the past.

Before she left the museum she talked to a curator who was keen to tell her his ideas on the origin of the mummies. "Kazaks, Kyrgyzs, Uighurs who live in central Asia, are all mixed Caucasian and East Asian. DNA tests have concluded that the DNA from thousands of years ago compared with modern DNA of these people is similar. The government has now moved thousands of Chinese from other places, into the area."

"And why do that?" she asked.

The curator smiled and shrugged.

It became obvious to Frieda that the Chinese government wanted to dilute the local population and she supposed that those who moved into the province would benefit from a relaxation of certain laws about how many children they could have.

"Has the tall caretaker been here long?" she asked.

"He's quite harmless but sometimes, how does one say, not quite right in the head. He came from Tian Chi. Left because of some trouble between himself and his family."

Frieda wasn't so sure that the caretaker was harmless; for a start she didn't like the way she caught him looking at her, and she wasn't sure now whether to meet with him or not.

"Actually Tian Chi, The Heavenly Lake would be a good place for you to visit. It's touristy but stay overnight in a yurt higher up away from the lake. It would be an interesting experience for you. You can get there by bus from Urumchi, at Renmin Park, ten minutes walk from the Hongshan Hotel. Get a ticket the day before you want to go."

"Thank you. I might just do that."

Frieda made up her mind to get a ticket for the next day and spend a few days up in Tian Chi. The curator had told her it would take around three hours to get there by bus. The next morning she travelled through lush meadow and pine forest until finally the bus took the ascending route along the river to the lake, which was surrounded by snow–tipped peaks. It was only when she was well on her way that she remembered she had forgotten to keep her appointment with Galyma.

Frieda did as the curator had suggested. She politely declined an offer of accommodation in the lower yurts and made her way up the hiking track to the pastures higher above the lake, where she came across a colourful yurt with a wooden door. A tall woman of indeterminate age sat outside, embroidering a waistcoat with red thread. Frieda caught the woman's interest and used gestures universal to those who need food and somewhere to sleep. The woman cheerfully agreed and bade Frieda sit beside her. The woman managed to convey to her guest that she was called Aianat then disappeared into the yurt and some minutes later she came back with a bowl of something that looked like milk. Frieda knew they drank sheep's milk—quite a lot of it. She gratefully accepted the offer.

Aianat showed her inside the yurt, which was quite spacious. The floor was covered with rich, coloured carpets. The walls were covered with woven strips and Frieda noticed with surprise that some of them were Celtic plaid. Frieda felt quite elated. Aianat smiled at her, sat outside the yurt, indicated that Frieda should sit next to her again and then continued her craft.

Frieda gazed contentedly over the lake beneath below them and to the snow-covered mountains beyond.

Aianat had reddish-brown hair and the Caucasian features that Frieda had hoped to find after studying a book about regional differences within China. Most of the Urumchi peoples were Han Chinese, who were an affable people in themselves but the Kazakhs, the semi-nomadic people, of which Aianat was one and whose features reminded her of the Urumchi mummies, intrigued Frieda more.

In the afternoon they were joined by a young man who led his horse up the grass slope towards the yurt. Frieda supposed it was Aianat's son by the way she greeted him. He was not interesting only because of his height, light brown hair and blue eyes, but because he had the same welcoming smile as his mother. Aianat introduced him as Erken.

After shy introductions they sat on the rug inside the yurt and ate mutton and noodles out of a large bowl.

Frieda pointed to the stew. "It's very good."

Aianat smiled and picked up the ladle to give them more from the cooking pot. Frieda was glad of the food and after they finished the meal she wondered what to do next. It was still daylight and the two Kazakhs chatted quietly about, well, whatever they talked about each evening.

"My mother asks if you would like to see the horses?"

"You speak English?" Frieda was continuously surprised by how many Chinese did.

"I learn from the tourists."

"Why didn't you say earlier?"

"I was too hungry." To that Frieda could only smile.

"Yes, I'd like to see the horses. I can ride too."

"Then, in the morning we ride together."

After talking with Erken about horses and cultural differences until well into the evening, Aianat respectfully hung a bright red blanket across a section of the yurt to give Frieda some privacy. As she settled down under a soft, lamb's wool blanket she could almost believe that she was feeling happy. Still it was a strange experience sharing the yurt with the good looking Kazakh and his mother that night.

The next morning Erken took Frieda to see the horses and with a cheerful smile pointed out her faults as a rider. Before long she mastered her horse and rode alongside him through the lower pastures. They talked little and delighted in the day. Without warning Erken innocently leant across to her and lifted a strand of her hair. A golden glint caught the sunlight.

"Your hair is beautiful Frieda. The women around here like to braid their hair."

Frieda smiled at him and thanked him for the compliment. He suddenly frowned and she noticed his mood change quickly, in the way that he roughly pulled the horse about.

"My mother will be wondering where we are, we should go

back."

They rode back in silence. Frieda tried to renew the conversation, but Erken replied simply a brief yes or no. But, he politely answered more adventurous questions when she asked about how the nomads managed to get all they needed to support their way of life.

As they neared the yurt Frieda could see Aianat talking to a familiar figure and as she drew closer she realised, to her surprise, that it was Galyma, the caretaker at the museum. Aianat didn't look at all happy to see him.

"Galyma, I didn't expect to see you here," said Frieda.

"Hello Miss Frieda, this place is my home, this is my mother and Erken is my brother."

Before she could apologise to him for not keeping their appointment Erken spoke.

"Half-brother Galyma. Different fathers." Erken tethered the horses to a pole at the back of the yurt, entered and banged the wooden door behind him.

Aianat tried to smile at Frieda and bade her follow him. Even inside there was no mistaking the argument that ensued between the mother and Galyma. It might have been a different language but bad blood was bad blood in any tongue. Frieda sat in a corner and wondered whether or not she should leave.

When Aianat and Galyma had calmed down a little they all ate some cheese and flat cake. During his meal Galyma kept mentioning Urumchi to his mother and later kept following her around the yurt, placing his hand on hers whilst she busied herself with the clearing up. She withdrew her hand each time and snapped at him. Erken glowered as Galyma tried to win back his mother's affection. Tired of Galyma, she pushed him away from her and finally he stopped. She took up her embroidery and sat as far away from him as possible. There was no pretence to Frieda that everything was okay; quite clearly it wasn't.

Erken indicated that perhaps he and Frieda should go outside. The mountains and the sapphire lake below were immensely beautiful, but Frieda thought perhaps she should take the bus back to the city the next day. They talked long into the night whilst Galyma peered out at them, through a thin crack in the door of the yurt.

The morning mist clung to the ground the next day. Erken had disappeared; Galyma was nowhere to be seen either. Their mother began to cry and Frieda tried to comfort her. After a while the mother's sobs abated and she moved things from place to place inside the yurt. She fumbled through some old jars in a box, found what she was looking for and carefully poured some powder into a bowl of milk, drank from it, and urged Frieda to do the same. Frieda drank also, partly to calm Aianat. She wasn't entirely sure though about what really happened next.

Aianat tended the fire. Frieda thought she saw mysterious shapes in the blue smoke that circled around the yurt before finding escape through the rough vent hole in the roof. The mother reached for a pot that stood on the ground near her chair. She sat down on the rug, clutched the pot closely to herself and then rocked backwards and forwards, chanting some strange words.

The pot was about the size of the others in the little kitchen area, some contained some chunks of meat, and it was a similar size to one near Frieda that contained wheat. She asked to see inside the pot that Aianat held but Aianat shook her head and cried. Frieda was upset to see her so distressed, for she had grown fond of the woman and one of her sons.

Frieda's eyes began to grow heavy; she felt dizzy and struggled to make sense of what was happening—suddenly she found herself seated outside the yurt. It was daylight and the grass was fresh and damp. In the distance Frieda could see someone on horseback riding towards her at great speed. A short distance from her a woman pulled the horse up abruptly by its gilt harness and swung out of the saddle. Her soft boots scraped the wet grass. She was a tall woman and wore a deep red dress that touched the ground. Frieda noted that she had reddish-brown hair, blue eyes, and wore a tall, woollen headdress, her bare arms covered in strange tattoos of animals and insects. As she turned, Frieda saw that on the woman's left shoulder was the design of an animal whose horns tapered into flowers. She seemed to be in her early thirties, of European appearance and held her head high with an air of importance.

The strange woman smiled. "I am the shamaness, the storyteller of the Loulan."

Frieda was there—with the Loulan woman who had been dead for four thousand years. The shamaness spoke again to Frieda, but this time no sound came from her mouth. As darkness descended around them Frieda could hear two men shouting. She saw the two brothers and then one fell with the other standing over him. Frieda bent over the man on the ground and looked into the eyes of Erken. He then, to her surprise, disappeared. She looked to the shamaness and then at the clay pot at her own feet. Hesitant at first, Frieda lifted the pot lid. She saw the blond hair, covered with dark matted blood and recoiled. Attempting to get to her feet she knocked the pot over and the head spilled out, a dark red sludge following it. It was the head of Erken.

Frieda screamed and placed her hands over her face. The shamaness knelt down beside her, put the head back inside the pot, picked it up and took Frieda gently by the hand to lead her back inside the yurt. As the mother took the pot from the shamaness, Frieda saw the great sadness in Aianat's eyes and a strange look passed between the two.

In the time following her stay with Aianat, Frieda thought about her own future. She decided not to return to the city of her birth—she was done with Salford for a time—but would alternate between staying with Aianat in the yurt above Tian Chi to learn more about her ways and also get occasional work in the museum at Urumchi. She hoped there would be a place for her there.

Some weeks later, in the museum, she was showing English tourists a mummy that was being carefully put back in its case after restoration work.

"Here we have Cherchen Man. You will note the Caucasian features, light brown hair, and his height. Even in death the body is in reasonable condition. Near where we found him in the burial site there were structures that the Chinese archaeologists find puzzling—standing stones, Celtic figures, and odd icons of unusual females. Also, one of the mummies was found wearing a pointed conical hat."

As Frieda spoke she sensed Galyma struggling to wake. He could see little through dried up eyes. She stared down at him and smiled before the curators placed the glass cover over his body.

Galyma could just see out of the corner of his eye the mummified claw of his right hand. He tried to move his limbs, but they were frozen. There was nothing but an eternity of tortured memory ahead of him. Frieda knew this—she wondered how often he'd try to scream.

In A Pig's Ear

*"I have almost achieved perfection you see, of a divine creature that is pure, harmonious, absolutely incapable of any malice. And if in my tinkering I have fallen short of the human form by the snout, claw or hoof, it really is of no great importance. I am closer than you could possibly imagine sir."*From *The Island of Dr Moreau* by kind permission of A. P. Watt, Ltd., on behalf of The Literary Executors of the Estate of H. G. Wells.

Mack looked bad, really bad, but then he was dead. Whoever had done his make-up had never been make-up artist to the stars. Far from it; he didn't suit that shade of lipstick. I had adored Mack but he had never let me get too close. It was odd that since his death the obsession that brought me to biology brought me now to him. I had my eye on Mack's DNA. I was considering the possibilities at his funeral—irreverent or what?—I just couldn't help myself. One minute I was remembering the second biggest wave we rode together and then the big one, that had traded-in his surfboard for a coffin lid.

I considered the second of my two projects. Mack's DNA was too good to let go—far too good. He was much too beautiful, even in death, to go to waste.

There was no one there in front of me except the corpse; the funeral director had let me in for a private viewing. Perhaps he thought I was Mack's girl. I had to get on with it before anyone else could see. I needed hair, fingernail or finger if I could get it. No—someone would notice that. His family was too sharp. DNA from inside his mouth. No—I would probably break his jaw. A few days since his death, surely something would be usable. He had long hair. I would need twenty strands with follicles still attached, or perhaps I could use the flesh from behind the ear lobe. I would have to hurry as someone might come in. I felt like a body snatcher but, after all, Mack wasn't going to need any of himself—anymore.

I opened my white, snowdrop leather bag, took out a scalpel, yanked at a lock of hair to cut into the skin then rearranged his long hair a little. I was anxious about being discovered and in my carelessness I cut my own finger, and sucked at it whilst fumbling with the clasp of my bag. The skin, with hair attached, was in that same hand and I shivered when I realised what I was doing. Blood dripped onto the white leather.

Clutching my bag, which now contained a piece of Mack, I attended the service and sat behind his mother. I felt really bad about what I had done. His mother was crying and her face was puffy and pale. Mack's father fared little better, for it looked as if he was trying to keep his emotions under control and the effort was killing him. I left before the end, before they sang *All Things Bright and Beautiful*. I had always hated that hymn. Christ! I was a scientist but funerals made my flesh crawl.

I was now working on three projects. My main line of research was concerned with residual DNA. I experimented with pig DNA and there was also my little fertility programme. It was old-hat to grow a pig's ear. I was a little more adventurous and wanted to see if I could grow a wing from bone marrow stem cells onto bioabsorbable polymers. I never got tired of trying to grow them into different shapes and coming up with ever more complex designs. Last time they came out like bat's wings and this time I was aiming for a structure of wing like the extinct, gliding reptile, the pterosaur. That would take more time. Some experts said that birds evolved from little feathered dinosaurs but I had always quite liked the hypothesis that birds diverged from reptiles before dinosaurs, and that mammals had evolved from reptiles with the propensity for genetic change that could lead to flight. A whole new take on pigs can fly— perhaps they could, given the right wings, hollow bones and a more developed muscle structure.

My name is Stella Kiefer, B.S.C., Biosciences at Edinburgh University. Alumnus of the year 2025. Commanding cellular structures and messing about with the genome, human and otherwise. Edinburgh. Famous for its medical school, the ghost of

Dirty Mary, and the selling of bodies in Surgeon's Square.

For the next two years I worked hard on all my projects and my obsession with Mack's DNA grew. I never so much as looked at another man. I just wasn't interested in anything but my work. Only on New Year's Eve 2027 did I celebrate with my colleagues.

We went to La Mancha, the Spanish restaurant just off Fifth Avenue, not far from the Rockefeller Plaza and the beautiful statue of Prometheus I had always liked. Prometheus—who gave mankind fire and as a punishment was chained to a crag in the Caucasus Mountains. Every morning an eagle would devour his liver and every night it would grow back again to repeat the cycle the next day. I'm good at growing things too.

And grow things I did, way beyond my guidelines, for I had been playing about with more than pig's wings. I decided I wanted Mack's child, and so combined my DNA with his. I followed an immaculate methodology and the whole process had been fairly easy. I called in a few favours (okay, I had worked outside the law once or twice but I couldn't see the problem with that), and the embryo settled down nicely within my womb.

I had my own midwife for a home delivery. It was just fine. Everything ran according to plan. I had the latest pain blockers and thought how lucky I was to live in the decade I did.

The five-hour labour was easy and I caught up with one film I had been dying to watch for ages, a remake of *The Island of Doctor Moreau*. At the end of the film baby practically shot out of me into the midwife's hands. Her face turned pale when she examined him and she quickly wrapped him in a pretty cerise blanket, handing him to me just before the afterbirth—spilled out.

I passed an hour holding the perfect, delicate pink baby in my arms, trying hard to think of a suitable name. It was then that it struck me that I should examine him myself. I laid him on his back in my lap, counted his fingers and toes and then examined his face closely to see if he had a harelip. No problems there. Carefully I turned him onto his front and then my stomach churned as the realisation hit me that my methodology had not been perfect after all. This beautiful boy, this sum total of my involvement with Mack, had a tail. It was so astonishingly assimilated into his lower back. It was then that the midwife pointed out that he had two tiny lumps, one under each shoulder blade.

Over the next few months my son seemed to grow at the same rate as any other baby. His piggy tail would be sorted out just after his first birthday. Helen, the midwife who delivered him, had become a good friend. In fact she had become his nanny, whilst I brought home the bacon—if you'll forgive the pun. It was Helen who, on numerous occasions, had to be stopped from calling him Piglet and I was rather miffed with her when I found her reading him the story of "The Three Little Pigs"—six times in a row to his human squeals of delight. I let these small annoyances go by with little more than a look and a word aside.

The first five years were great, and Ricky, as I called him, was having a very happy childhood. He had birthday parties and was friends with the other children of the staff at Mount Joy Research Laboratory where I worked. The New England air suited us all fine and we were very content there.

It was just after Ricky's fifth birthday that things started to go wrong. The small lumps under each shoulder blade started to grow larger and all investigations into what they were resulted in a brick wall. There seemed to be some sort of shell just beneath his skin, impervious to X– ray, MRI, or any modern method of examination. I needed time to think and the pressure of everyday work was getting to me. Helen was devoted to Ricky and agreed to my plan. The search was on to find some place to go; I needed to keep my son away from prying eyes in case he began to show any other signs of genetic diversity.

I remembered the film, *The Island of Dr Moreau* and accepted a position as a researcher in a leper colony. Leprosy was one of the diseases that still had not been cured. In the last century breakthroughs in science had even cured the dapsone-resistant strain but the disease had mutated further and now a cure seemed as far away as ever. I applied and received a letter confirming my post on the research into the new strain of leprosy. The leper colony was on Saint Elver's Island on the banks of the Amazon.

The next five years were not so happy; Ricky started asking me all sorts of questions that I could not answer. The humps on his back grew larger. The leper colony was now his home. He did not remember the cool wind of a New England fall where the leaves cascaded into a hundred different shades of red, russet and brown.

The malaria-ridden Amazon was the only home he would remember.

A boy called Neme, who had leprosy, became Ricky's sole playmate. It was hard not to feel sorry for him, a young boy who should have grown up to be very handsome. Even with treatment he would soon go into decline like all the rest. Neme clung on to some hope that a cure might yet be found in time for him. Ricky was ten, Neme sixteen. What sorrow they would face if they had to go into the outside world now.

I spent hours going over the methodology that had brought Ricky into the world. I chastised myself that my protocols had been flawed. Day after day, I experimented with the pig DNA, alongside the procedures on the leprosy virus to try to understand both. Endless experimentation and disappointment, until the day came when Helen came crying into the laboratory bringing the two boys with her.

Ricky was in terrible pain. He stumbled in—collapsed into a heap, grasped at his back and screamed in agony. I had to steady my hand. It was trembling so much as I cut away his clothes and tried to stop the bleeding. The skin began ripping away from his back and the shell—the shell was cracking.

I had been dreading this. As the casing cracked first at one side and then the other, a huge mass of pink skin began to unfold and rise far above his shoulders. In an instant another appeared. Ricky stopped sobbing and tried to see over his shoulder at what had caused him so much pain. His words still echo in my ears.

"Mother, what have you done?"

He knew it was my fault years before I had the courage to explain. He had his father's good looks, my need for science and the wings of a—well, a pig. Or, what a pig's wings would look like if they had any.

Over the next few months he began to forgive me. I even saw a smile on his face as he glided like a flying squirrel from tall tree to tall tree. He would never fly as a bird does because his bones were too heavy and his muscles too weak. I doubted if we would ever leave our remote hiding place.

Everyone adored Ricky and in his late teens he fell in love with a girl called Annais whose leprosy was in remission, then Susie a nurse who did not object when he was attracted to Oli. Ricky rutted on a regular basis and took great pleasure in his conquests. However, I did not oppose the unions. Who was I to stand in the way of such youthful optimism when I had messed about with all that DNA? All the women were content, not a jealous one amongst the first six. Ricky had a natural talent for keeping them all happy. When the babies came along (usually within the first three months of conception), they were born with ready-made brothers and sisters—in litters of six, eight, and more, and all had the lumps that would develop into wings.

Even as I grew older, it never failed to amaze me how resistant to disease my grandchildren were. A snake had gotten into one litter and had bitten three of the babies before a cherubic sibling choked the snake in its chubby little fist. All three babies had a mild fever for a day or two but shrugged off the poison.

The Amazon canopy was Heaven-like, filled with these tiny winged angels that looked like Sistine Chapel cherubs, with their ruddy complexions and winning ways. I adored them all. They were perfect. Each generation developed their wings earlier, and the wing structure became stronger as they glided from branch to branch. It was not me that gave them the name Homo angelus—but it stuck.

In a few years we will be discovered and face extreme prejudice from the rest of the world. I have no doubts that gene dominance can ensure their place at the head of the evolutionary chain, and anyway, the romantic imagery of angels is embedded too firmly into the human psyche to resist. In generations to come—Homo sapiens will have been bred out and the prophetic imagery of the Italian artists will become a reality.

A Poison Tree

"I was angry with my friend:
I told my wrath, my wrath did end,
I was angry with my foe:
I told it not, my wrath did grow."
From *A Poison Tree* in *The Poetical Works*
of William Blake, edited by John Sampson.
1913 Oxford edition.

It was only for a weekend. A short, one hour trip into London, a taxi to the studio, an afternoon of listening to other people getting a little comfort and connection with their loved ones—dead although they were—and then back to a hotel overnight. What was wrong with that?

"But, I don't believe in all that talk about the dead returning. I don't believe in an afterlife. I don't believe it one bit." Jean fidgeted with her blonde hair, stared in the hall mirror and wondered why she looked so pale and thin. She was pleased to see that she had lost a lot of weight. *Perhaps too much,* she mused.

"Do it for me, Jean. I never ask you to do anything for me. I just don't want to go alone. I really want to try and get in touch with Stephen."

"Can't you just go? If you want to so much just get on with it and go."

Jean hadn't liked Brenda's husband, Stephen. She hadn't liked him so much that she stole him away from Brenda and married him. Jean thought him an insipid man and uninspiring. But, it wasn't so long ago that he had died, and amazingly enough, Brenda and Jean remained friends for all those years.

"I helped you when you needed help with your mother, couldn't you just do this one thing?" Brenda implored.

It was true, Brenda had helped her that awful time when her mother died in the nursing home. Jean's mother been left unattended in the day room and wanted to go to the toilet. As she made her way through the fire door she had leant against it. The safety lock released. The door sprang shut and trapped her fingers, almost severing one of them.

Even though Jean's mother had been old and frail she had been given a general anaesthetic in an attempt to save her finger, it had not been amputated. The doctor felt he should try to preserve the old lady as she had lived to her ninety-second year. After the operation, Brenda helped Jean bring her mother back to the nursing home in a taxi. It was a cold day; Jean's mother had only a thin jacket on. Brenda had taken off her own jumper, draped it over the frail old lady's head and wrapped the arms around her neck. It looked like some handless, flat entity was pulling her away to some far off distant place. Of course, it had all been too much for Jean's poor mother and she died a few weeks later after a series of debilitating strokes. Brenda had supported Jean and helped her through those difficult months.

Now Brenda wanted something in return.

Jean's conscience was awakened, just a little. After all, they *had* been friends for over twenty years. Brenda was a very forgiving but needy person and when Jean lashed out Brenda was always the first to make up, *even* though Jean had taken her husband away from her. Brenda was always the first to telephone and always the first to put disputes behind her—which meant she usually had to apologise for something that didn't need an apology.

"All right, I'll go but you can pay for the trip," Jean relented.

Jean knew her friend didn't have much money but it pleased her that Brenda should pay as she wanted to go to London so much. *It is only fair,* Jean thought; someone, other than she, always had to pay.

The studio where Calvin Caldwell played to packed audiences was full of widows and widowers. Like the offspring of a spider, there were dozens of them, mourners of the dead, wearing fixed, pained smiles and hints of jewellery here and there to distinguish them from one another.

Jean was uncharacteristically nervous there. She wore a grey skirt, which seemed a size bigger than when she had dressed that morning, and a low-cut red blouse. For a second, she wished that she hadn't worn the red, for that colour's symbolism wasn't lost on her. Jean had always found it easy to *move on* and when her mother died she had moved on quickly enough. This audience hadn't. Even before the recording some of them had their little initialled handkerchiefs out and were staring her down because she didn't look right. She didn't care too much about that.

"I'd like to come over to the people on this side…somewhere in the middle, about half way up." Calvin waved his right hand in Jean's direction and for a second his glance fell upon her. She quickly looked down at her hands clasped in her lap. She looked up again, and he fixed his puzzled gaze on hers. She was caught before she knew it and she found it easier to let him hold her than to break away.

"Now, I don't mean to scare you but there is a woman by your side with a scowl on her face and I have to say that she isn't happy with you. Can you place her?"

Jean shook her head.

"Well, she says that she is here for you—well not *here* for you but wanting to tell you about her confusion."

Another shake of the head.

"Does the name Jean mean anything to you?"

"My name is Jean."

"I'm sorry. You're Jean? She says that you know her. She's definitely here for you, my love, and she's showing me a picture of a train…not a train…but a train station..but she can't remember why. Another Jean and a train or a train station—do those details mean anything to you?"

Jean shook her head again.

"Would you like to join me on the couch, my love? Perhaps we can help this person remember what happened. She is very distressed."

Calvin addressed the spirit to his left where the audience could see nothing. "All right, my dear, we'll sort it out," and he pointed directly at Jean.

"Yes—you my dear. I have a person here who clearly wants me to talk to you on her behalf, but is holding back."

Jean shifted uncomfortably in her seat.

Calvin turned to talk to the invisible person at his side. "Don't be shy love—I'm here to help you. I'm here in this world to help you communicate from the next. That's it love, come on through—"

Calvin had a small, reverent smile on his face as he stepped back. His expression then changed, it contorted with his effort to speak. The alteration was dramatic: he looked like someone who was in great pain and his features were definitely not his own.

The audience gasped and one or two got up to make their way out of the studio.

"Stop!" he said in a commanding voice.

Everyone trying to leave the studio halted immediately. Some in the audience were quite clearly terrified, others looked on with scepticism, and still others just stared open mouthed.

Calvin began to speak. "She was there at my death. I wish to speak to Jean. My name is Jean."

With that, the Jean in the audience fainted.

The recording of the show stopped briefly, whilst she was attended to in the green room.

Brenda fussed over her, squeezed her hand and apologised yet again.

"I'm sorry, dear. I shouldn't have asked you to come. I had no idea that your mum's passing, and Stephen's...would have this effect. I'm so sorry."

With a wave of a mysteriously thinner hand she pushed Brenda out of her face. "Brenda, stop it. It isn't that. I'll be okay. I just want to get out of this hot studio."

"You're not fine, Jean. There is something obviously wrong."

"Brenda, get a taxi. Once we get to the station I'll be fine."

"But I thought that we would stay over, get a meal and take in a show—you know that you don't get out much. I'll ring for a taxi. Are you sure you can—"

The glare in Jean's eyes was all that Brenda needed to send her scurrying away to find a phone.

Calvin Caldwell had never, in his entire life as a psychic, taken a spirit home with him from the studio—until now. She followed him, the doppelganger spirit of the woman who had fainted on prime time.

"Listen love, you have been sitting on that couch for the last hour. You won't speak to me, you just sit there, and you won't go no matter what I say or do."

He paced the room, working himself up into a sweat. He hoped that the doppelganger would be scared off by his insistence. This proved not to be the case. Her dull, grey eyes followed him up and down the room and around the sheepskin rugs that clung to the floor.

Calvin shook his head. "How can I do anything when you won't tell me what you *want*?"

As he voiced an emphasis on the last word the spirit became more solid, stood up and grasped his arm to pull him towards the front door of his apartment. Once out on the street she pointed to a taxi that was speeding by and finally Calvin hailed one down and they got in. The spirit faded a little as she followed him inside the taxi and sat opposite him.

The taxi driver waited patiently for directions and turned round when nothing was forthcoming.

"Well, Jean?" began Calvin, staring straight at the spirit that faced him. She sat with her back to the driver.

"Well what?" the cabbie asked.

"Sorry, just a minute. I'm trying to find out where to go."

"What? Ain't you that psychic fellah off the telly? Don't you *know* where you're going?"

"Not yet—no. Just hold on a minute please."

"Ere, you ain't doing one of those séance thingies in my cab are you?"

"No, I'm just talking to someone who won't leave me alone."

"Well, don't leave it alone here. I don't want any company on me travels. I like working alone and I don't need no ghost to tell me how to find my way. I did the Bible, I did, and perhaps you would like to take your ghost friend and walk to where you want to go—when you find out."

The spirit sent Calvin the image of the train again.

"Where's the nearest station?"

"St. Pancras."

"I guess that's where we'll start then."

The internationally famous façade of St. Pancras Station came into view. During the Blitz of the Second World War part of the station had been bombed.

The taxi drew up to the curb.

"That'll be ten pounds. No extra charge for the other passenger." The cabbie laughed at his own joke.

In Death's dominion there are no rules of engagement; up until this point Calvin Caldwell had thought that there were, but all indications to the chance that he might regain control of the situation disappeared when an air raid warden, complete with gas mask box over his shoulder, opened the door of the taxi.

The cabbie caught sight of the door opening, but couldn't see who had done it.

"Ere—how did you do that? Come on, don't play any tricks. The fare, please."

Calvin moved closer to the edge of his seat and stared through his phantom companion, who had faded away even more.

"I can assure you, sir, that I didn't open the door and have every intention of paying the fare."

Calvin fumbled in his pockets for a few seconds and mumbled a few choice words under his breath before realising he had left his wallet back at his apartment. He had no loose change either. Jean was still staring at him with her cold, grey eyes and the air raid warden still had his hand on the door handle. The air raid warden beamed at him.

"I—I haven't got any money," said Calvin.

"What? All this palaver and you haven't got the fare?"

"Yes—look. You obviously know who I am. Could you have it on good faith that I will give you the money when we get back from— wherever we'll be getting back from?"

"Faith? *Faith*? I never had any faith in anything but myself. Look—"

Before the cabbie could finish Calvin had bolted through the open door and run off into St. Pancras Station.

"I'm not having that," the cabbie muttered under his breath, "don't care who he is."

Once inside the station Calvin stopped running. The phantoms, Jean and the air raid warden, stood silently on either side of him.

"What now?" he demanded.

St Pancras Station; the location for the Spice Girls first music video, the movies *Batman Begins* and *Harry Potter*. Calvin Caldwell, psychic star of his own programme, felt as if he was well beyond what usually happened to him.

On the telly he was good at using clues, unknowingly given to him by his audience and the vague images that appeared in his mind. But today for the first time images were turning into something a little more solid and as a result he was genuinely afraid that he was going mad, at the worst, or at the very least was stuck with Jean's doppelganger. To add to that, there was the new apparition of the air raid warden who seemed as resolute as the other to stick by his side.

Within seconds Calvin could hear the wail of air raid sirens and suddenly the air raid warden became more substantial—he flung Calvin to the floor, under the feet of the commuters who had just come off the two-forty-five train from Birmingham. The crowd looked on in astonishment as Calvin thrashed about on the floor in an effort to escape the arms of the still beaming, still unseen air raid warden, who was evidently as pleased as punch that he had managed to protect the man.

Only two people stopped to help.

"Hold his arms—he's having a fit," said a man carrying some parcels, who stared down at the medium.

Calvin struggled for breath, "You can't hold my arms, someone is already holding them!"

"Hey—is that, that…Calvin—what he is called?" said the man.

"Calvin Caldwell," answered a thin woman in a grey coat.

"Serves him right—come home to roost and all that," replied the man.

"Look, can't you hear the sirens?" Calvin shouted.

"Sirens? Sirens? Of course we can't hear the sirens. There haven't been any sirens here since the last war," said the woman. "Poor chap, shouldn't we just go along with him to calm him down?"

"Leave well alone I say. Dipsying about with all those spirits has turned him mental," answered the man. "You don't believe in all that rubbish, do you?"

"Of course I don't. My mum does, though," the woman offered.

The sirens, which were causing Calvin an immediate, great headache stopped and the air raid warden (still wearing a silly smile) released his arms. Calvin got to his feet.

"Oh dear, Mr. Caldwell, were you possessed?" said an elderly lady in red who had just joined the two bemused travellers.

"Not exactly," he answered her.

Calvin headed for Europe's longest champagne bar and ordered a bottle. He quaffed two slim glasses of the sparkling stuff before he realised that—he still hadn't got his wallet. Crestfallen he poured another glass and glanced to his left. His taxi driver had hitched himself onto the stool and asked for another glass of his own. The bartender poured the cabbie some of Calvin's champagne. He took a dainty sip and licked his lips.

"So, what now mate? I caught your little performance back there."

"Performance. It wasn't a performance. I was pushed."

"Aren't we all mate? Aren't we all?"

Looking beyond the cabbie (who introduced himself as Quinn), Calvin could still see the beaming air raid warden who looked even more pleased with himself. On his other side stood Doppelganger Jean, but Calvin was even more surprised when he looked over his shoulder and saw the women from the studio; Brenda, and the other Jean, hurrying towards him. It was then when Calvin finally knew that he would never—ever—really have control of the situation.

"What do you all want?"

"I have got what I wanted!" beamed the air raid warden.

"What is that?" asked Calvin.

"To save you from the air raid."

"But I didn't need sav—" Calvin was talking to an empty seat. The bartender wondered if he should pour him another glass of champagne. Calvin noticed, and pushed his empty glass towards him. The bartender obliged. Refreshed for a moment Calvin looked at Quinn, and Doppelganger Jean.

"Don't you think that I'm going anywhere until I get my fare," Quinn warned him.

"I don't think anything. I just want to know what's going on."

Calvin took another gulp of champagne and pushed the empty glass towards the bartender once more. Quinn, with a cheeky smile, did the same.

"You're driving," said Calvin.

"Not now I'm not."

"Well, obviously not now, but in a minute you are."

"Nah, not me I've finished for the night now Ted's got the keys."

"Who's Ted?"

"The night shift driver."

"When, in the name of henbane, hellebores and Hades did you give him them?"

Quinn looked at him thoughtfully for one moment. "Those first two are plants. They don't quite go with Hades. Well…henbane sort of does because it is a plant used to create supernatural phenomena—but not hellebores. Now, if you had said in the name Hecate, Herodiades and Haborym—them being names and all—or Hell, Hades and, say—Hepatoscopy that might be okay…but that last one being divination through the liver or entrails from lizards, black hens, bats, toads and cats, perhaps not—"

"I like cats," interrupted Brenda.

Calvin stared incredulously at them both as Jean, her white cheeks even whiter, stared at her Doppelganger self.

"What, in the name of—" he hesitated and glared at the cabbie, "in the name of—*anything*, do you all want?"

It was Doppelganger Jean who broke the ice. "I want my life back."

"To be done with it all," stated Jean stated blankly as she twisted her wedding ring on her ever-thinning finger. *Funny*, she thought—*it has always been so tight before.*

"Revenge," Brenda shocked them.

Everyone right down the bar, and the bartender, stared at little, mousey Brenda.

"I was happy for you Jean—happy to know that someday you would lose him too. You only wanted him because he was mine, but then you pushed me aside for too long. I knew that you would want me more after his death. I counted on it."

"—to tell the both of you that I don't think that I loved either of you at all," said Stephen.

Amazed and bemused, most of them stared at Stephen. Actually, the bartender looked more bemused than amazed. Stephen then added, "well, perhaps Jean early on in our marriage."

"Who the hell are you?" sputtered Calvin.

At this point the bartender, observing the fact that one of the gentlemen before him seemed to be conversing with the thin air, reached for another bottle of champagne, all the while trying to decide where he had seen this gentleman before. The bartender had been bored and *this* was the best entertainment that he had seen all day. He popped the cork and poured himself a glass whilst staring at Calvin—

"Can't you place him lad? He's that geezer off the telly, that fellah who talks to ghosts," Quinn enlightened him.

"Oh, I knew he was," said the bartender…unconvincingly.

"Look!" said Calvin, flustered and finally now feeling the effects of the champagne, "just what is going on?"

"If *you* don't know, how do you expect us to?" said Quinn, pointing at the bartender and then at himself.

"Shit," muttered Jean as she slowly faded away, to be permanently replaced by her far superior doppelganger, who then walked off arm in arm with Stephen; a Stephen—who, in actual fact, seemed far too solid to be a ghost?

"That wasn't supposed to happen, this wasn't supposed to have any happy endings for anyone except me," Brenda protested as she stared openmouthed at the pair who seemed so happy together.

"What I want to know is—" said the bartender as he poured for himself (smiled at Brenda), and then poured Quinn another glass, "is—just *who* is going to pay the bill?"

Calvin put his head down on the bar and held it tightly in both hands.

Blood in Madness Ran

"Let now your visionary glance look long,
On this your race, these your Romans,
Here Caesar, of Iulus' glorious seed,
Behold ascending to the world of Light!
Behold, at last, that man for it is he,
So often foretold to your listening ears,
Augustus Caesar, kindred of Jupiter.
He brings a golden age."
From *The Aeneid* by Virgil.

It slithered away from her with a tail the colours of gold, green, and blue. Although it was slippery she held it in her hand and looked at the wonder of it, before she placed the eager creature on the mustard green seaweed. It was a tiny version of her, complete with coppery hair that fell to its small waist. Soon there were more of them, a dozen in all, scaled from the tail to the neck, with arms and upper bodies that bore the traces of their affiliation with human beings. Their pale faces looked human but *human* they were not.

How could she keep them safe this time? They were so small but not entirely helpless. They were wildly curious and indifferent to the many dangers of the sea. Her cavern would be their sanctuary for a while but keeping them contained had always been a problem. Her last brood had fallen prey to sea-hunters and also her tiny creatures had fed upon one another to survive.

Lamia would bring them food for a while but then the lure of the open sea, with a thousand different enticements, would be too much for them and they would be gone.

A snowstorm reared its head, unusual for any time of year in that part of the world, and headed towards the island where lay her cave. A ship was heading her way too, and that meant food for the Lamiae; her children would not go hungry as they writhed and explored the swells of water that threatened to send them crashing against the cavern walls.

"Eleven, only eleven now," hissed Lamia to her offspring. Small, sly faces with eyes the colour of green ice laughed back at her as she offered her breast to each in turn. She would have to get food for them before the storm, as they grew too quickly to be only fed by her, and besides they latched on to her too savagely with their sharp needlepoint teeth. She would not leave them in the cavern with the threat of being pummelled against the rocks. In her lair she had a fisherman's net that she gently lay and bound the baby Lamiae within, placing them above the water in a niche far from the cavern's entrance. In a flash of coppery green Lamia swam deep under water, out of the cavern, leaving her infants screaming behind her.

The ship had anchored in the natural harbour and seemed to be safe from the rising storm.

It was a dark night with no visible moon and young Jack, a young man so very far away from home, was on watch. Young-Jack-Slack-Jack. Without a brain-in-his-head-Jack. Jack who stared open mouthed at the siren vision of green who licked the salt from his neck, pressed her writhing hips against his and drew him closer to the waves as they crashed over the deck. Her mouth held his as they rolled in the black depth of the sea, until Jack was dead.

Lamia took Jack to feed to her children. She feared that they would be all dead by the time she returned but only one more had been lost leaving ten to take part in the meal. Jack's body floated face down in the water and the offspring fought over him, plucking the eyes from their sockets then sinking their needlepoint teeth into his flesh; Lamiae with the faces of angels and the tiny teeth of piranha fish. The offspring who, in their feeding frenzy, ripped some of their own siblings apart until their mother put a halt to the bloody banquet and wrapped the little darlings back in their net.

Skylla and Cethos were the worst. They fought all the time and both were strong. Skylla had the advantage, for circled around her waist were six long-necked dog-fish heads. Each with a mouth and triple row of sharp teeth.

The snowstorm subsided and the ship left the harbour, sadly lacking Jack, and a week went by.

The six Lamiae that were left grew quickly and were soon the size of yearling seals. How they loved their underwater world, playing tag in the giant kelp and tormenting their mother.

Lamia never slept and was too afraid to do so in case the remainder of her brood became victims to the sea, or worse.

They took on all manner of creatures in their feeding frenzies. The six of them were growing very strong and ventured further each day. No creature was safe from them. They attacked dolphins, sea turtles, and even sharks. Soon their appetites turned, to take on a more bizarre nature. They had a distinct desire to mate with mankind. They swam up towards the fishermen's boats and openly taunted the men as they hauled their catch on board.

They were the sirens of the sea and called humankind to the rocks on which they perished, and Lamia was proud of her children.

Then came a night when Lamia saw the ghost of her sister Dido, Queen of Carthage, amidst flames that melted into the green-grey depths, and she knew her sister was dead. In her madness Lamia thrashed her serpent's tail and her screams could be heard on the decks of ships above as men put down anchor for the night.

Lamia craved revenge, and upon one ship in particular. It was the ship that sailed on proudly, guided by Jupiter. This ship did not put down its anchor. It was the ship that belonged to Aeneus, he who had deserted Dido and been the cause of her death. Lamia swam beneath the bow of his ship and shuddered her green scales with excitement and loathing.

Iulus heard an unearthly cry from the sea and joined his father on deck. The air grew cold and Iulus did not see a column of green sea mist rising from the sea, a phantom of shimmering green that swept across the surface and to the side of the boat, behind the bow.

"Father, what was that cry?" asked Iulus.

"Nothing, just some creature of the sea or the howling wind, no more," replied his father Aeneas. "Get some sleep, Iulus. I will take this watch myself."

"There is something out there, Father."

"There is nothing, Iulus—get some rest!" Aeneus was irritable and exhausted, and yet they were only at the beginning of the long, sea voyage to Italy. Iulus, annoyed by his father's tone, went to check on the crew.

As Aeneus peered through the silent mist out to sea he was not aware of the shadowy form of Lamia creeping up behind him. Something touched his arm and he turned to stare into a pair of piercing green eyes.

"Why did you desert my sister?" Lamia hissed. "She showed you devotion and pledged herself to no other man—why did you do this to Dido?"

Aeneus took one step back, horrified by her scaly body but was transfixed by the beauty of her face and the sound of her sweet voice.

"Out of obedience to Jupiter," he proclaimed.

"You should die for leaving her."

Lamia swayed from side to side and her slime-green tail ventured closer to Aeneus. He felt powerless to move. Lamia held out her arms to him and he took one step towards her.

Over Aeneus' shoulder Lamia could see Iulus brandishing a sword in his hand and a look of astonishment on his face. With a shudder and a scream she threw herself back into the water.

"Father, Father—are you all right?" Iulus cried out.

Aeneus struggled to regain his senses and sadly nodded his head. He pushed Iulus to one side and headed below deck. Both the son and the father had little sleep that night as Lamia told her daughters of the great Phoenician Queen who once ruled Carthage and was dead because she had loved Aeneus.

The eldest of Lamia's brood, Skylla had seen the handsome Iulus, son of Aeneus and she knew that she wanted him. The next day the Lamiae followed the wake, called to the crew and haunted the dreams of the young men until they no longer knew who they were, and yearned to throw themselves down to the strange women of the sea. By night their songs had become too much for them and five sailors threw themselves into the cold, dark depths and into the waiting arms, and needlepoint teeth of the Lamiae.

When their appetites were partially sated, Lamia called her children to her. She made a vow that angered them, especially Cethos.

"You did well my daughters—but we will leave them now. I forbid you take any more lives."

Cethos railed the most. "But what of your sister, Dido? Why

should Aeneus live?"

Lamia coiled her tale around her daughter's waist and gently tightened her grip. "Jupiter has given Aeneus a mission to complete and if we stop him Jupiter will destroy us."

The offspring convulsed as one, hissed and argued against their mother who insisted that they stop their slaughter. Lamia reared and spat words of caution and rebuke at her children. Her six daughters, now bolder in their bravery and drunk with the taste of human blood, cornered their mother, until their teeth were within an inch of her neck.

Skylla broke away before her siblings fell upon their mother. She did not see, nor did she care to look back over her shoulder as she headed to the ship which bore her prize, her Iulus. He would be hers and hers alone.

Skylla did not see her sisters drag their mother beyond the pink-stained coral and into the cold chasm, to the bitter depths where amongst the dead things they drank her blood until she lay half dead, a pale serpent woman who had once been the daughter of King Belus. At the point of her death they came to their senses, and were ashamed of what they had done. They carried her back to the cavern where they were spawned.

Skylla heard their cries, her sisters wailing and lamenting what they had done. She hesitated and considered whether or not she should go after them.

Skylla hissed through her teeth. "But why stop now?"

"Why indeed?" a voice echoed through the ocean. Skylla turned to seek out its source. The voice belonged to Juno, wife of Jupiter and protector of the city of Carthage.

"I have a mission for you alone. Kill Iulus, for one day his descendants will destroy my beloved Carthage. I will have no Roman General, no Scipius Aemilianus to scatter salt over the ruins of my levelled city."

"And what then for me?"

"Your race shall forever feed upon the flesh of men, for it is what you desire most."

"Not enough. Will you rid me of these?" Skylla revealed the savage dog-fish heads around her waist.

"I will."

"And what for my mother?" Skylla was surprised she had even

thought of her mother but she did not sanction the actions of her sisters.

"She will be restored to you."

"Then I will take Iulus."

As Juno melted into the depths of the sea Skylla smiled and the points of her teeth shone like needled pearls. Had she not wanted him anyway? She slithered in pleasure and then darted through the sea towards her prize. Through the mist that hung low over the ship she could see him and she sang to him in the siren-sweet voice that did not betray the writhing of worms in her mouth and the dark glaze of death on her skin.

Iulus heard only the song of an angel and saw the body of a beautiful mermaid in the water. He leaned over the side of the ship to see more of the divine stranger whose hair was the colour of gold, green, and blue. Skylla took him quickly, making little sound. As she pulled him into the depths of the ocean he tried to fight her, but only briefly. Soon his struggles ceased and Skylla kissed him hungrily on his mouth until it bled.

She found her sisters skulking in the birthing cave. They slithered and wrapped their tails around one another and Cethos hissed a warning to Skylla as she approached. Skylla took no heed and dragged Iulus closer to Lamia, his limp body already bitten and ragged from the bites of the dog-fish around her waist. The dog-fish then began to wither one by one.

Without hesitation Skylla fed the heart of Iulus to Lamia. Little by little she fed her, until Lamia's eyes opened and then she fed herself.

Iulus was dead. His descendants would never rule. There would be no Procas, no Numitor, no Amulius, no daughter of Numitor to couple with the God Mars, and no twins to be suckled by the she-wolf. No Rome, no Julius Caesar. Only Carthage for Juno, who hid in the shadows and feared her husband's wrath.

Lamia was restored as Juno promised. The others recoiled as Skylla drank from her mother's breast and the salt sea washed a trail of blood from her lips. Skylla, whose mind was losing the knowledge of the sea, then swam to the shores below the lighthouse at Carthage. She slithered out of the water and took her first footsteps on land.

And thus the first vampire to walk the earth was born out of the blood of Rome.

Dissolution

"So, in the secret of the shrine,
Night keeps them nestled, so the gloom
Laps them in waves as smooth as wine,
As glowing as the fiery womb
Of some young tigress, dark as doom,
And swift as sunrise. Love's content
Builds its own monument,
And carves above its vaulted tomb
The Phoenix on her fiery plume,
To their own souls to testify
Their kisses' immortality."
From *The Altar of Artemis* by Aleister Crowley.
Copyright Ordo Templi Orientis. Used by kind
permission.

There was a strange, half-light that emanated from the church. It was so far away but the mother, trying not to stumble as she went. By the moonlight everything could be seen with great clarity but there was no one to see her as she made her way towards the church. A crow flew high over the hillside and low over the fence towards the great gables of the church roof. It followed the struggling woman, swooping low, never veering from a straight path, never in danger of encountering any obstacle. On a gargoyle it landed and waited, eye bent, looking down at the young woman who trailed against the icy blast.

The gate was locked so she squeezed through the crooked bars of the iron railings. She tightly held her babe in her arms, and she slipped on the grey, batched cobbled path that led to the church entrance.

It was there on the coldest Sunday morning in the month of December, that they found her and the babe. Incredibly, the child was found alive in the arms of her dead mother. The child was only one day old. The mother's face was frozen to the old oak door and the weight of her body had begun to rip the skin away from the bone.

Everyone vowed it was a miracle that the child had survived, but survive it did. Pinned to an old, blue and red striped blanket was a note and on the note were written the words: "Treat her kindly. Her name is Mary."

The *Chronicle* reported that the woman was well dressed but had no personal belongings with her, except for her infant. It was not unusual to find a foundling on the steps of a church in Wisconsin. It was unusual, however, to find a baby that never cried from that first day. Who was this child? Who was her poor mother and why had no one come forwards to claim her body? No one seemed to have any inkling of the mother's origin. The following, which is very little, I learnt about my grandmother, Mary:

The baby Mary was adopted by a lawyer's family who had been unable to have children of their own. They wondered at the black-eyed, pallid child and in years to come they would regret their decision to adopt her. They were more confused and horrified when, at the age of ten, they found her naked in the frosty meadow below the house. Transfixed by the moon she stood there. A holly wreath encircled her head and her arms were held high, as if to the goddess of the night. Beads of blood ran down her forehead.

A few years passed and the child grew up to be an even more precocious and demanding girl. When she was fourteen she ran off to St. Joseph, Missouri and came back with a husband twelve years older than herself. As years went by it seemed that perhaps

Mary would conform after all.

She gave birth to one child but soon after decided that she was bored with motherhood and she took to throwing wild parties. Deep into the night hideous laughter could be heard by the indignant neighbours across the parkland. Her husband was said to have finally had enough of his domineering child-bride. He left his wife and fled, leaving her to find a new husband which she did, to reside in the large dark mansion in Midland town.

When my family moved to Chicago I asked again about my grandmother, and why we didn't see her anymore. Their silence greeted my questions. Not one was answered again. I railed against my parents and demanded answers to my enquiries. I asked why we didn't go to see her at Christmas like normal families do.

One evening I said I wanted to know more about the family history.

"Don't interrupt, Harlan, can't you see I'm in my pace here— for what it is,"

"But, Father, I just want to say—"

"Well, say it somewhere else. Better still—*to* someone else."

Comments could be heard around the dinner table. Then the conversation slowly faded away, time turning its weary hands backwards, and I was there at my grandfather's funeral. Winter 1891.

My mind flashed back to the private service for him in the manse. The vicar could barely be heard. An elderly aunt looked flustered as my grandma overlapped his verse with her darker words, nay, almost incantations of her own. The vicar then uttered obscure Latin verses that had never been heard from a vicar's mouth before.

But, now I will tell you a little of *my* formative years. I was a child genius, so everyone said; I am not hesitant to blow my own trumpet. From a very young age I acted on impulse (not unlike my grandmother when she was young), and was taught to converse as an adult and join in eloquent conversation with my elders…unless the topic under discussion was the family. It was of no surprise to anyone when I left on my fourteenth birthday. I decided to board a train from Chicago and go to see for myself who this mysterious woman was, and why no one would even speak of her.

Within two hours I was in Kenosha. The parkland of the great houses stood before me. Behind the sprawling elm, walnut, and beech I could sense every illicit rendevouz, every dark family secret except my own. Standing before that dreadful house I felt a piercing of my heart and I did not relish the encounter. No turning back now, and besides, my curiosity had got the better of me as it always had, and always would. I did not enter the abode of some doting grandmother who knitted by the cosy fire in the depth of winter. I was Hans Christian Andersen's Kay, in the Snow Queen's fortress; I was St. George before that dreadful dragon; I was Moses taking on the great wrath of Egypt. I would battle my grandmother and no good would come out of this, I believed...no good at all.

The towers of the great manse loomed above me. I imagined them threatening to hurl their gothic stones down upon me (like so many imaginary castles of my childhood had done before), and I envisaged dark servants with boiling pots of oil pouring the bubbling, black Beelzebub brew upon my head.

I shuddered, but quickly rang the doorbell. A servant of no notable feature opened the giant worm-ridden door. I was inside the house before I knew what I was doing and around me I could smell its rancour and decay.

The scale of the old hall was impressive and it ached my neck to look up at the lurid bacchanal on the ceiling, with its mythical beasts that ate and caroused their way through a banquet fit for the devil himself. In her time, I had heard that grandmother had thrown a few wild parties.

I was shown into the circular library and everything in that room seemed larger than it should have been. Even the giant tomes in the circular bookcases appeared to have been made for a race of beings that had the physiques of some huge carnival freaks, rather than those of simple men and women. Nothing about this house was simple. The velvet armchairs were enormous and ostentatious. A vase containing a huge display of withered flowers overran with silver spiders. I would not put my hand in that vase for anything.

I walked over to the empty fireplace, bowed my head and stared up into the dark, vast chimney which, if reversed, would have found its way down to hell itself.

My attention was broken at that very moment by the creaking of a door. Here, was my grandmother, entering the great library in a floor-length red velvet ball gown, complete with walking stick, looking dwarfed by the grandeur of the hall.

"What do you want from me? Your father left as soon as he was able. Why do you come here? Why now?"

"Grandmother, I came out of respect for you. I came to see you, why else?"

"Liar," she spat. "However, as you are here, you can speak with me for a short while. But you are not to expect to stay the night, even if the weather worsens. Understood?"

"I would not expect otherwise from you grandmother and I certainly do not want to stay the night."

I dreaded entering the dining room and it did not let me down. There was dirt and dust everywhere, covering the rich brocades and materials of a long lost era. And there amid the lost grandeur of another age my grandmother took her seat at the immense, oak dining room table.

"I suppose you are hungry. Well, are you?" I jumped at the sound of her cracked voice. For a small woman she certainly could carry an effect some distance. I was at the farthest end of her grand table, keeping away from the rank smell of her at the other end of the room.

"Er—yes," I replied, looking around forlornly.

She pulled the bell cord and an old servant appeared who was almost as old as her. I withheld a nervous smile, yet the meat and potato soup was surprisingly palatable. I doubted that it warmed the stiff old bones of my grandmother's.

I had no tactics to speak of so I came right out with it. Like Daniel before me I braved the wrath of the lion—or rather this lioness.

"What happened to grandfather?"

Her silence was intense. Still, the ceiling did not come crashing down and I was not turned to stone. Grandmother said nothing to my question and there followed a stare which chilled me to my very core and made me once again think of Kay and the Snow Queen.

"And how is your poor father?"

I thought about the word *poor*. Poor covered all the facts. Poor, as in lacking in money, therefore poor in stature, poor in spirit, poor in everything. All the men of her family had been a disappointment to her and I was assured of my rightful place by their side as they prepared for judgement day.

"He manages."

My father had told me of the harsh measures she had metered out to him in his childhood. It made me almost sick to my stomach to broach my subject again but I would not rest until I knew more of the matter.

"What happened to grandfather?"

"Nothing — *happened* to your grandfather."

I felt a cold squeeze as if her hand on my heart and the curses from hell fall on my shoulders.

I sat back in my chair and thought very carefully about my next words. "How did he die?"

"You know how he died. A heart attack — weak heart. The Mortimer men always have weak hearts."

We were interrupted by a flash of lightening across the window and my next words were drowned out by a clap of thunder that would have prided Zeus himself. At this point my grandmother raised her stick in defiance as so many fearful witches had done before her and would do for all eternity. I saw her reflection in opposing mirrors, more of her than I would ever want to see in my worst nightmares. My words echoed to enhance the effect.

"How did he die — how did he die?" I could hear the words spreading through the large house like a canker on a wasting rose.

Grandmother rang a bell that was within easy reach. "I'm tired now — I will retire. You can stay the night after all."

From out of nowhere the elderly servant reappeared to escort Grandmother to her bedroom. I sat back in my armchair and dozed before the servant returned to show me to my room.

Later, in my canopied bed, I lay awake as the rain railed against the windows like some great sea creature lashing its tail, and I pondered why I was there. My efforts to find out more about my grandfather had proved fruitless and I was failing dismally to discover any truth surrounding the mystery of his demise. I put on the lamp and stared at the clock on my bedside table. It was well past midnight. I stared at the huge doorway beyond which loomed irregular and I thought of escape.

I heard a floor creak in the room above, imagining all sorts of terrible things there. I was startled by the sound of something crashing to the floor and wondered if grandmother had an intruder in the manse. I hurriedly put on my clothes and peered around in the half-light for a weapon with which I could creep up upon whatever scoundrel was at that moment rifling through the family heirlooms and daring to injure the dubious matriarch of my family. I was surprised that I cared.

My steps were silent as I ascended the stairs; like Theseus in the labyrinth of the Minotaur; I was Heracles after the Nemean lion; Odysseus against the Cyclops. I was all these and more rolled into one and there was no one more heroic than I.

On the landing I looked upward, my gaze following the twisting stair that ascended to—only God or the Devil knew where, and then I stared into the great shadowy hall below. My mind was filled with shapes of grotesque creatures and of things half formed but not fully defined.

My racing thoughts began to slow as I looked out through the window at the rain that vanished into the darkness of the parkland below.

I put my first foot on the next stair. They seemed to go on forever. The creaking I heard came from directly above my bed but these stairs seemed to climb much higher. The banisters were carved with entwined vines and branches. As the moonlight struck the staircase I thought I saw the face of Bacchus himself, with his half-mad eyes staring at me from beneath a banister.

Then he was gone.

Once at the top and on the landing I stood opposite a door. My mind flashed back and I was four years old again. I had the most horrible of nightmares. I saw myself outside this very door in fact, and had heard the scream of a bird in pain. The door had been partially open, enough to see the flash of a blade in the moonlight, and then a silence, strange and final.

A spilt second later and I was back in this new, more terrifying, situation. It was a moonlit night once again. As I slowly entered the room I could hear the ruffle of feathers and could just make out the structure of what appeared to be a wooden altar. Determined to be as brave as ever I could be, I continued but stumbled over something on the floor, falling backwards as the deep, dark scarlet wings of a bird brushed my face. Recovering myself, I took a deep breath and stepped forwards towards the wooden altar. It was inscribed with a Latin text, adorned with a pentagram and had a stained glass window in its centre. As the moonlight reflected off the coloured glass more dark shapes lurked in the corners of the room and I was even more afraid of my grandmother's house with all its dark secrets.

The house echoed then with the sound of thunder and a bright white beam of light lit the room frantically for a second. What I saw then was enough to terrify me for the remainder of my life: there before me, lying in a shroud and as withered as the great pharaohs of Egypt, was a body. Over it stood my grandmother like some high priestess of ancient Egypt with a knife in one hand, holding a sacrificial bird by its feet in the other.

With the next flash of lightening I could see that the bird had ceased its fight for life and its blood poured over the musty shroud. The servant woman by her side fumbled in the dark and lit a lantern. She held it low and my grandmother peered at the shroud. My eyes reluctantly left the shrouded body and searched for more horrors in the room—I saw the dozens of dead birds scattered on the floor.

"Not enough—never enough," she cried bitterly.

It was then, with a look of madness in her eyes, she turned to me. I ran. Once outside the mad wings of crows beat, as if in slow motion, as they settled on the rooftops in silent mourning for their fallen brethren.

I did return to the manse for my grandmother's funeral and saw her shrouded body laid out in its black coffin. I felt that even in death she mocked me and the male line of my family. I was the only person besides the servants to attend the funeral and I was surprised that she had not been buried in the backwoods with others of her ilk. I had only the servants' word for it that it was my grandmother who lay in that coffin and not secreted in some evil corner of that house. But the old witch had not finished with me yet.

Many years later I was performing some magic tricks in a rather modest theatre in New York. In the middle of a rather famous little trick of mine I looked up with a smile on my face and stared into the audience, anticipating the look of wonder from them. To my horror I saw my grandmother's burning eyes looking back at me. It had not been the first time that she had appeared to me. A few weeks earlier, during the interval of a play, she had appeared in the quiet cloister of my dressing room and crept close to me, breathing blasphemies in my ear. It was more in fear than rage that night when my voice trembled as I suffocated the desolate Desdemona. I wished I was strangling my grandmother's ghost. My grandmother had whispered to me of my tragic flaw and how all the men in the family would never achieve their potential because, ultimately, we are too weak.

In her will she bequeathed the manse to me and any children that I might have but I refused to go back. She taunted me in her ghostly form and I found I could not concentrate upon anything. All I could think about was the house. It became an obsession, an obsession that would consume me, and of that I was more afraid.

Eventually I did take up residence in the house. I had kept on the last, old faithful retainer. I did not, however, ever venture into that room that I had entered twice before. It was kept firmly locked and for a time my grandmother left me alone. That was until one Christmas Eve when her spirit stirred and came once more to visit.

I was sitting by the fire in the library. I felt her vile breath in my ear until I was driven to a sudden madness and hurled myself into a rage, tearing books from the shelves and scattering them across the tattered carpet. It did not stop there. More books found themselves onto the fire and soon I was looking for a bigger bonfire in which to burn her books of sorcery and witchcraft.

I dragged the decrepit manservant from his bed and threw him outside into the snow, cursing him a thousand fold for aiding my grandmother in her evil ceremonies, for I knew now that she had doomed me and bound me to the house.

"Cursed!" I screamed and heard it echo through the house to the graveyards beyond. And within that one word, in that final moment, all the horror was concentrated.

I bolted the door and ran back to the library. The books made a large fire but it wasn't enough. I knew what I needed to do next. Pulling one burning book of necromancy (an evil testament to an evil life) from the fire I tossed it onto the middle of the rug.

I threw more books on top of it, and more still, until the flames leapt at the large armchair, and the curtains beyond. I could see through the flames to the window and fancied that I saw my grandmother's face, larger than in life, once more mocking and laughing at me.

There was nothing I wanted more now than to destroy the manse. It was a shrine to the unholy, to the folly of an old woman who only ever loved my grandfather with an intensity that she wanted to preserve forever. In my madness I thought I saw her body go up in flames and I ran once more from that house.

As I looked back that final time, I saw the crows billowing out from under the eaves like some threatening cloud, followed by the tortured remnants of evil. I watched the house from the safety of the parkland; I watched it burn to the ground, knowing that within those dark corners burnt the remains of my grandfather and grandmother.

Dedicated to Orson Welles.

Silence is Golden

"It is easy to go down to hell; night and day, the gates of dark Death stand wide; but to climb back again, retrace one's steps to the upper air — there's the rub, the task." From *The Aeneid* by Virgil.

Vince Taylor was soon to bury his wife, but not before he had kept her in the house for seven days, awaiting her funeral.

Mary Taylor had been a very rich woman and some naïve folks said that they couldn't understand why Vince had married plain Mary, while others said they would have married her for the money too. Whatever the truth of the matter was, it didn't matter now. All that *mattered* was that she had stipulated in her will, that for seven days and seven nights she was to lie in an open casket in the front parlour. She was to be surrounded by four ivory pillar candles which must never go out, and four bouquets of white roses which must never die before her funeral — or Vince would be out on his elbow without a penny.

Vince considered himself to be a smart guy, ten years younger than Mary. He had gotten to know Mary when he delivered meat from Naylor's shop to her house once a week. She had fallen for his long brown hair and lost-boy looks. That was over two years ago when he first came to Madison County. She had just turned thirty-eight when she disappeared on a Tuesday afternoon in December and was found dead on a Wednesday morning in the Crown Hill Cemetery Creek by the graveside of her friend Miriam Newbury. Why would someone stay so long at a graveside that they froze to death?

The coroner, Geoff Newbury, examined her body that same day.

"No evidence of anything unusual. The condition of the body is consistent with what you would expect in finding it out in the cold. She died of exposure."

"Why would anyone visit a grave in that weather—crazy?"

The coroner peeled off his gloves. "Now that, Sheriff, is for you to find out."

"And I'm sure I will. This town is too small for unanswered questions. There *will* be a reason, I tell you. There always is. Anyway, we finished here? Can her husband take her home?"

"Home?"

"Got a phone call from him this morning, said that if it was all right with you and me, then the undertaker would do what she had to do to bring Mary over to him, as per the instructions in the will."

"Her will?"

"The one Mary wrote that stipulated she was to be taken home for seven days until her burial?"

"That's—er—a little unusual wouldn't you say?" asked Geoff.

"Geoff, I've been the sheriff here for thirty-two years. There is nothing under the sun and moon that is unusual to me. If you think that being taken home before burial these days is unusual, they used to do it all the time in the old days. You know that. Finding a body all bricked up in a cellar, now that is unusual, or dead and sitting up for seven years in a rocking chair—now *that* is unusual."

"But this is 2008."

"Wow, beejesus, we're modern and the dearly departed aren't allowed home before they're shoved in the ground or burnt to buggery—"

"Easy, Jake, I was only saying—"

Geoff stared at the wedding ring on Mary's hand, wondering if there was any point trying to get it off for her husband.

Perhaps the undertaker would do that.

At that moment Jake remembered that Geoff had lost his wife only a year earlier, and at the same time of year too.

"Sorry, Geoff. I'd plain forgotten about Miriam."

"That's okay, Jake."

Feeling embarrassed, the sheriff zipped up his jacket, put on his hat and left.

Vince wrung his hands and wondered what condition his wife's body was in. Dead and buried she should be, not unburied and coming home to him. He was not a man to be messed around with and he had waited two whole years for his freedom; Vince was eager to do what the hell he wanted with her money.

There was a knock at the door and he opened it. Two individuals of equal height, a man and a woman, stood before him. The woman looked slightly younger than the man but they could have been related, they looked so alike with pale, grey eyes and blonde hair.

"Mr. Taylor?"

"Yes."

"My name is Frances St. Germaine and this is my brother, Gerald."

The three shook hands and Vince couldn't help but notice that Frances St. Germaine looked far too good looking and young to be a funeral director. He was a little disturbed by seeing her in a black suit, white shirt and black tie. She didn't look right and yet, *somehow*, she did.

"Mrs. Taylor is ready for you now."

That shook him. Vince felt his hands turn clammy and he rubbed them on his trousers in an attempt to remove his anxiety.

"Shall we bring her in?"

"Er—yes." There was no way of avoiding it—if he wanted that money.

There were four funeral directors altogether who brought the casket containing his deceased wife into the parlour. It was the ugliest coffin he had ever seen, gold and white.

She never did have any taste, thought Vince. Once the coffin was settled on the trestle, Vince spoke out:

"Is that what Mary chose?" he pointed at the casket.

"Oh yes, it is exactly what Mrs. Taylor stipulated." Frances brought a catalogue out of her briefcase, opened it and pointed to the page. His eyes followed her finger.

Devotion
20 gauge steel, hermetically sealed. White enamel finish with gold shading. Cream Madeira crepe interior, with church window/praying hands lid panel.
Swing bar handles and adjustable bed.
$4692 including traditional funeral.

He saw the dollar sign before the hideous picture of the casket. "Jesus, how much?"

"Your wife was very particular. She wanted that casket and was very insistent upon it."

"Do people usually plan their funeral down to the last detail before they die? Isn't that what the relatives are for?" He flipped the pages of the catalogue, astounded at the funereal detail.

"A lot of people plan their own funerals as they don't trust the choices their relatives might make when they are grieving." Frances smiled at Vince and he couldn't help noticing her peach perfume as she bent closer to him.

"I see, well, I suppose that sort of wraps that up then." Vince gave her back the catalogue.

"Not quite, Mr. Taylor. We have the candles and the roses to bring in and then we will be back in seven days for the funeral." Frances gestured to the nameless funeral directors and they all left the room.

Vince shuffled around uncomfortably and thought how much he hated the William Morris wallpaper on the parlour wall and the matching William Morris curtains. The Brother Rabbit pattern was inspired, according to his wife and May Morris, by the 'Uncle Remus' stories. Vince hated the green patterned, rabbit filled wallpaper and Mary had insisted that the curtains be made of the same pattern; it seemed to Vince that his wife had never heard of the word contrast. And, they had cost a *fortune*. She knew how to spend her inheritance and Vince was always worried that she was going to spend it all. But apart from a few favourite furnishings, and now a bloody awful casket and the roses (he didn't know how he was going to keep them alive for seven days), she had been reasonably frugal. Still, she knew that he never kept anything alive; his dog Doody had pegged it, along with a cat, two gerbils, and a baby croc that had gotten into the plumbing somehow.

It did not take long to arrange the white roses and light the four candles. Two of the four funeral directors left, leaving Frances and Gerald. Vince swallowed and almost wished that Frances would stick around a little longer. He was not looking forward to spending seven days with a corpse, even if it was mild mannered Mary.

Gerald stepped forwards and took a screwdriver from his pocket. Puzzled, Vince looked across at Frances. She simply shrugged. Gerald started unscrewing the casket lid.

"Whoa, what's going on here?"

"Another little stipulation, Mr. Taylor," she replied.

"What stipulation?"

"An open casket for the next seven days."

"Christ, you have to be kidding, right?"

Gerald spoke for the first time. "We don't usually joke about these things, sir."

Well, not in front of the customer, thought Vince. *Lord knows what they get up to behind closed doors.*

It didn't take long to get the lid off. Vince crept closer; after all he was an educated man and knew they put make-up on bodies — right?

Wrong.

Mary looked terrible. He saw her face briefly as the casket lid was removed but then a froth of white burst forth, like an airbag in a very bad accident. Mary was wearing the horrible wedding dress that she wore on their wedding day, the one that meringued and then settled into a stiff bell shape. Now, it threatened to show all underneath. She looked *very* undignified.

It was the undertakers turn to look uncomfortable. Gerald glowered at his sister. "I thought you had sorted that?"

Frances stifled a giggle. "I have some tape in the hearse. I'll have it sorted in a jiffy." She ran out of the room and Vince thought he could hear her suppressed laughter in the hall and all the way down the icy path. She returned in a few moments with some white tape, having managed to composed herself. Gerald held the stiff taffeta down whist Frances went to work with the tape. Vince looked on in disbelief as they tried to tape the dress around Mary's ankles, with very little success.

Astounded at what he saw Vince shook his head. "Just a suggestion, but wouldn't be an idea to remove the hoop underskirt?"

"Ah, well—I think we might have to." Both of the funeral directors were growing more flustered as the dress kept bouncing up and slapping them in the face. Frances finally removed the hoop underskirt as Gerald held up Mary's grey legs. Vince tried not to notice the creaking of limbs. With the aplomb of a magician's assistant Frances presented the hoop skirt.

"Right, now we can go."

"Just like that?" Vince stared at the body of his dead wife. Mary looked like she had been dead for several weeks and the cold weather hadn't done her any favours either.

"I have to spend *seven days and seven nights* in the house with— with that?"

No answer.

"I need a drink."

Vince helped himself to the bourbon as Frances moved to the front door.

"Mr. Taylor, I'll leave you with my phone number in case the flowers die. See you in a week."

"Is—is she going to be all right like, like that? For a week?"

Frances smiled. "Keep the heating turned off in that room and she'll be just fine. It's going to be five-below tonight."

Vince was anything but fine. He was exhausted and found himself wandering around with a full glass all afternoon. He turned the heating down in the parlour and lowered the temperature in the rest of the house as well. It grew dark early and as darkness descended he grew more and more uncomfortable. He couldn't eat...but what he could do was drink—and he did—until he collapsed in a heap on the bed.

At precisely 3 a.m. Vince awakened with a start and his head felt as though it was going to crack open like an egg into a frying pan. He stumbled downstairs to check on Mary; the candles had gone out.

"Aw, what the fuck," he mumbled as he lit them again.

"They w-went out w-whilst you were a-a-sleep."

Vince froze. It was Mary's voice.

"Sweet Jesus, I'm going mad," he said.

He crept up to the casket and peered at his wife.

"I s-said you—"

Vince jumped at the sight of her mouth creaking open and nearly shat himself.

"You let th-th-them go out," she said, obviously having great difficulty speaking (he supposed, crazily, what with her being dead and all).

It took a few seconds for Vince to register what was happening.

"You bitch. You're not going to get the better of me. You're supposed to be dead!"

"D-dead?" said Mary. Her filmed eyes tried to focus upon him.

"Yes, dead. Dead so you don't embarrass me anymore, dead so I don't have to go to bed with a fucking corpse."

Mary's tight grin became wider and Vince fled the room.

"I'll teach you to mock me. You just watch, I'll get through this week and I'll get your money."

Vince knew exactly where to look. He fumbled through her dresser until he found Mary's sewing basket. He needed a stout needle and thick cotton thread; his hands were shaking as he threaded the needle.

"Right. I'll soon sort *this* out," he said as she tried to speak again.

He was clumsy with the first few stitches but the rest went in just fine. Vince took a swig from the bourbon bottle, stood back and admired his handiwork. The horror of what he had done struck him at that moment. He had used black cotton. Mary now looked like some patchwork doll that had misbehaved and then some peevish child had put some gigantic oversized stitches on her. Vince then ran back to her dresser and found a piece of cloth left over from the Brother Rabbit curtains. He rushed back and placed it over her face, like some naughty child covering up his trouble, and then threw himself into an armchair. It was at this point that Vince got very, very drunk and became oblivious to everything until the morning.

With a head that pounded like a thousand Hiroshima bombs all exploding at once, Vince woke up. It was well into the morning. Tuesday. It was *only Tuesday* and he had the whole week to go. He was still in his nightmare situation—and Mary was still there in her nightmare situation too. She still had the remnant of the Brother Rabbit patterned cloth on her face, which Vince was most definitely *not* going to remove. He might have the biggest hangover in all creation but he was still well aware of what he had done.

He rubbed the stubble on his chin, lit the pillar candles (which had gone out, again), checked that the white roses were still fine, left and locked the room. Frances had given him a copy of the instructions that his wife had written before her death. He took them upstairs, placed them on the dressing table, and then had a shower.

As the day grew shorter he began to feel a little better. No matter what happened next, he was not going to leave the house and lose his fortune. He had enough supplies in the freezer and what he didn't have, he could always ring out for. In fact, if he wanted, he could have one of those Chinese takeaways that his wife would not have in the house when she was alive.

By the time it got really dark he was feeling much, much better. He had eaten his Chinese, and not bothered to clear up after himself either. *Mary would not have liked that,* he thought, and grinned. Just before midnight he was ready for bed and he definitely was not going to unlock the parlour and check on the candles. Who would know if he let them go out anyway?

Vince was woken from a heavy sleep by the slamming of a

door. He was sure that he had made certain both the front and the back door were locked. He could see that the moon was full. He was about to close the curtains when he saw Mary, in her white wedding dress, with her mouth all sewn shut—hanging out the washing.

This was all too much for Vince. He staggered down the stairs to the back door and flung it open. He did not shout. He said in a low voice. "Mary! Mary!" He tried to attract her attention—the attention of a corpse.

Mary carried on hanging out her washing, standing in the snow, as if the sun was shining brightly. She had found one of her pink, floor-length nightgowns and was stiffly hanging it on the line. In the light of the doorway Vince imagined his silhouette could be clearly seen. Mary turned her head and as the light from the kitchen behind him fell upon her face he could see that she had been trying to unpick the stitches on her mouth.

Vince checked out the neighbourhood, looking across at the nearest neighbour's house. *Shit!* How could he forget who lived there?! The house belonged to Geoff Newbury, the coroner—what would he say if he saw the corpse he had pronounced dead a few days earlier, hanging the washing out on her line? How was he to get her to come in? In fact, the answer came straight away as Mary pegged out the last of his socks on the line, picked up the basket with an awful snapping of...something...and made her way back to the house.

Now what should I do? he thought. Then it came to him: *if she has no hands, she can't do anything.*

For some reason, known only to the dead Mary, she preferred the comfort of her casket to sitting on her sofa and it was there that she headed. As she passed Vince, who pulled away from the smell of embalming fluid, she whispered in his ear, through the side of her mouth where she had worked the stitches loose.

"C-Candles, Vince. C-Candles."

"Shit! Fuck the candles. Get inside quick, before anyone sees you."

It took a long time for Mary to get back to her casket, appearing happy to have finished one task. She found the matches and attempted to light her candles.

"Aw, for fuck's sake Mary—leave the damn things alone."

Vince grabbed the matches and lit the candles. Addled, Mary managed to get back inside the casket, unaided.

She didn't even wince when Vince found his old butcher tools in the cellar and cut her hands off. Before he went to bed that next night he placed her hands next to her feet at the bottom of the coffin.

"There, that'll stop you fiddling with things tonight," he said smugly.

Vince had ordered in a whole case of bourbon to get him through the week. He had opened another bottle before his little operation, to steady his nerves. As he got into bed a blizzard blew in and the snow began piling up in a drift at the back door, as if it didn't want Mary to get out again either.

At precisely 3 a.m. he felt the bedclothes moving and could feel something cold fumbling against his skin. He sat up and in a drunken stupor and reached for the lamp. As light flooded the room he saw Mary clutching the covers of his bed in the stumps where her hands should have been.

Vince nearly hit the ceiling as he jumped out of bed. "Ah, man—that's gross," he said. "Shit—you can't have been trying to get into bed with me, that's just *wrong!*"

With all the charm of a partially preserved corpse Mary gave him that half-stitched smile again.

"Now listen, Mary, get back to your casket—or I'll give up on the money and leave you here on your own—got it—all alone?"

His threat seemed to do the trick, for Mary stopped smiling, manoeuvred her way to the stairs and descended them with great difficulty. At one point Vince had to catch hold of her wedding gown to stop her falling. Once she was in her casket he turned to the bottle again and spent much of the next day drunk, and cursing his luck.

"She *ain't* going to get the better of me, she just *ain't.*"

Vince looked her up and down where she lay, still and quiet in her casket. He checked her hands were still there, next to her feet. He rubbed his chin, thinking about what to do next. "You can't walk if you don't have feet, right?" Out came his old butcher tools again.

Nothing happened that night. But Vince was so out of it with the alcohol he had necked that night, that a noise loud enough to wake the dead would not have awakened him. At daybreak he stumbled down the stairs, unlocked the parlour door and entered the room. Mary was quiet. He had found another pair of William Morris curtains (Mary had changed the pattern every two years when she had the parlour decorated), and placed one of them over her, up to her neck where she lay in the casket. This pattern was called African Marigold and she had been quite proud of the imitation Prussian blue dye that had been used in the making of it.

"Right, no mouth to talk with, no hands to mess with, and no feet to walk away with, well—guess that just about wraps it up, Mary—just a few more days to go and you'll be in the ground and I'll be the richer for it."

The days were turning into one, long, drunken nightmare for Vince. He was at a bottle day and night and he had no trouble getting through them now that Mary couldn't move. But something was bugging Vince—he just couldn't put his finger on it. It was in the late afternoon of no particular day (he'd lost count), that the door bell rang.

Vince answered it and was greeted by a young woman with an enormous bunch of white roses. The girl silently handed him a card. On it, in Mary's own handwriting, were the words:

By now it will be the sixth day since I was laid out and the day before the funeral. You will need the fresh roses now because the bouquet of the first day will be a bit faded and I want everything to look great for tomorrow.

Your devoted wife, Mary.

And by the way I want one rose to be placed in my hands for when the family comes round to pay their respects before the funeral.

"Shit," was all Vince was capable of saying to that as he slammed the door, put his back against it and slipped down to the floor with the enormous bunch of roses still in his hands. He only hoped he could come up with a solution to the problem that bits of Mary were in the four corners of the casket. He was thinking hard on how he could get away with keeping the casket open and still get the money.

"Christ, how can I place a rose in her hands? They're at the bottom of her feet?"

Vince had to admit it wasn't going well at all; only twenty-four hours to go and he had messed up, big style. How on earth was he going to get his money now? He struggled to his feet and made himself exchange the faded roses for the fresh ones, making sure they had enough water to get through the next twenty-four hours. Then Vince turned to the bourbon that was going to get *him* through the next twenty-four hours.

He looked across at Mary's face, covered with the Brother Rabbit cloth, and at her body with the African Marigold curtain— *Now what?* he thought.

Before he had time to think much more about the mess he was in there came another knock at the door. He hesitated, thought *'Fuck it!'* and opened the door. Before him was Frances St. Germaine, dressed in her smart business suit, white shirt and black tie.

"Good morning Mr. Taylor. I thought I would drop by and see if you are ready for tomorrow?" she didn't fail to notice the bourbon bottle in his hand. "May I come in?"

Vince started to sob but he let her in. He pointed at the parlour door.

"You might as well see. I ain't going to get the money now anyway."

Frances entered the parlour, noticed that the candles had gone out but was pleased how beautiful the white roses looked. Then she looked into the casket.

"Why is your wife covered with—?" She took away the Brother Rabbit cloth and saw Mary's black cotton mouth, with the stitches slightly unravelled at one side.

Frances turned to look at Vince, who shrugged through his blubbering.

"Did you do this?"

Vince nodded, and sniffed. "She just wouldn't shut up. I *had* to do it—she was walking and talking, and driving me mad." Vince flopped into the armchair. "What's the use—who would believe me?"

The Brother Rabbit cloth was placed back over Mary's face. "I believe you," Francis admitted, shivering nevertheless.

"What? You do—why?"

"Because I saw someone do all that once before."

"Who?"

"Miriam Newbury. When I was preparing her body for the funeral, she sat right up and talked to me."

"She did?" Vince stopped snivelling.

"She told me who killed her."

"Who?"

"The same man that killed Mary. Both women rose before their burial. They were killed by the same man, but I wouldn't know how to go about proving that."

Frances uncovered Mary. She was horrified when she saw where Vince had placed his wife's feet and hands.

Just then there was a knock at the door.

"What am I going to do?" Vince clawed at his hair.

"I'm not going to cover up what you have done," said Frances.

Frances opened the door and let the sheriff in. As he walked down the hall, Vince practically blocked him.

"Tell him Frances. Tell him what you told me about the dead women talking."

"Now Vince, calm down," said Jake, "What's with *who* talking?"

Frances took Jake into the parlour and showed him poor Mary. He looked Frances straight in the eye and shook his head.

"Will you do what you can for Mary?"

"I will. I'll try to put it right but it will be a closed casket before the funeral."

That just set Vince to wailing one more time. Within seconds the sheriff was marching Vince out the door, into the car and off through the melting snow to the Madison County Law Enforcement Centre. Jake took Vince away and left Frances to make all the arrangements. She looked down at poor Mary. "Who would believe me if I told, Mary? Who would believe me?"

The funeral was a strange affair, as lavish as Mary had planned, and those who had paid their respects at the house marvelled at the gold and white casket with the lid firmly closed. They loved the tall pillar candles and the beautiful white roses, and even Mary's William Morris Brother Rabbit curtains. Frances thought that they were hideous and in very bad taste, but, what did her opinion matter?

The snow had almost disappeared, much to the relief of the gravedigger though not because the ground would have been hard but because he hated the cold. After the brief graveside service the few mourners drifted away. Frances stayed until they left. She stood a little away from the sheriff and Coroner Newbury.

"That was no way to treat a good woman, Jake, no way at all," Geoff said, shaking his head and looking down at his own wedding ring. As he left, Geoff felt that he was being watched with rather more interest than was respectful at a funeral. He looked up and saw that Frances St. Germaine was looking at him in a funny sort of way, with a quizzical look. He repeated his words to the sheriff as he left the graveyard, and he glanced back at Frances.

"That would be no way to treat a good woman Jake, no way at all."

No sooner was Vince locked up for cutting off his dead wife's hands and feet (*and* sewing up her mouth), but he was thrust into yet another set of bizarre circumstances. Vince met Nurse Gladeye. (He had named her that as soon as he had set foot in the asylum property, on account of the fact that her pretty brown eyes seemed to look east then west, but not at the same time.) Here he was in Mount Sinai Asylum, given to the grateful people of Madison County with the capacity to keep over five hundred raving lunatics in varying degrees of lunacy. To be honest, most were in the state pen because of cost cutting measures: the doctors were expensive, so Mount Sinai only had about fifty inmates.

Nurse Gladeye (her real name was Penelope Maple), called for vast amounts of drugs just in case Vince gave her any problems. A portable case was handed to her containing almost every sedative known to man, and more besides. Penelope had her own reasons for wanting Vince Taylor malleable and quiet that night and it didn't involve cocoa and sleeping.

She had her own set of special inmates that lived on Mallet Ward (*lived* being too generous a word to use as they barely survived), and she didn't want them disturbed. On Sanderson Ward, soon-to-be-comatose-Vince—when Nurse Gladeye got round to him—thought he could hear the baying of a dog.

He stared at her; well—he tried to look her in one of her eyes, and then down at the case.

"What's that?" He looked apprehensive.

"Nothing to worry your head about, young man." Gladeye put an arm around his shoulder and gently guided him down the white corridor to a set of very shiny metal gates. The howling started again and Gladeye nodded sternly at an attendant by her side. The attendant went off to see what all the commotion was about.

"Now, young man, let's get you settled and get you your supper."

She licked her ruby red lips and Vince swore he saw her salivate at the same time. She wiped her mouth, smearing her red lipstick, then put the case down for a moment. She never let go of Vince once, and held him like he was some sort of prize rather than a mad appendage-cutter. How she found the door lock Vince didn't know, considering she was holding him so tightly, but she managed to put the key in the small hole with great dexterity and then she turned it.

Vince felt a cold chill run down his spine and bile rose up in his throat, as if he had just taken a mouthful of Tennessee swampland. All the decay of the black, swamp bottom stuck to his tongue and came up through his clenched teeth. With the hissing sound of a coil of cottonmouths he threw up all over Gladeye who, from shock and repulsion, kicked him sharply—and effectively—in the crotch.

Between spitting out the vile, black bile and holding his balls—
and between the ineffective groans of a man caught in a gator's
grip—he tried to fight off two attendants who appeared on the
scene like screaming white banshees from the swamp.

"You can't get away with that, aren't there rules about that sort
of thing?" he spluttered.

Gladeye's gaze roved over the ceiling. "There are no rules that
protect you in here, Vince Taylor, after what you did to your
wife—no rules at all."

That was all he needed. Of course there would be no rules for
him. They would all have it out for him after what he did to Mary.

At least he had a cell to himself; it was a dirty cell, the only
concession to cleanliness being new sheets and a new slop
bucket—and a sink—no mirror though. Locked up and the key
thrown away and all Vince could think about was whether the
sheets really were clean or not. He sat down on the grey-and-
darker-grey striped blanket and was at least thankful that they
had put him in a cell on his own.

Within a minute he was a quivering wreck in the corner of the
cell for there, on the corner of the bed, sat Mary. As real as if she
had never been buried. All the stitches had been picked from her
mouth:

"I was just about to say before you sewed my mouth shut, that
I know who my killer is."

"Jeez—*Jesus*, Mary, you just can't be back again."

"I can and I am," Mary said, looking around the room with
disdain. "No mirrors in here, Vince and I wanted to see how I was
turning out...being dead and all."

He could see how she *was* turning out and it wasn't good at all.
Her skin had taken on an even-more-marbled grey look, and he
thought he could see the squirming of *something* moving under
the skin near her mouth. It didn't bear thinking about. And what
came next made his recent bout of sickness look like baby puke on
an angel's bib. He thought *he* had been vilely sick; what Mary did
now, was the most disgusting, the most hideous, heinous, downright hostile thing he had ever seen her do in her life. (And on top
of that he remembered she was dead.) She vomited on him—*all*

over him. He wasn't bathed in swamp slime here. (Well, if grave slime was swamp slime, he was.) There Vince was, sitting in the corner, covered with every fat maggot from Mary's grave, every meat-eating worm, every insect that had ever chewed down to the bone. Mary was laughing and that was not all: Gladeye was standing at the doorway with a big smile.

Vince pulled the blanket off the bed as Mary stood up with only the smallest crack of the bones in her spine. Vince tried to wipe the slime from his face.

"Did you see that—did you see what she *did*?"

Nurse Gladeye turned her head at an odd angle to look at Mary.

"Come on Mary, let's put you away for now, don't want you scaring the rest of our family."

Mary obeyed with a look of confusion as Gladeye stepped back and made way for her to pass from the room. Vince heard the key turn in the door and turned to the wash basin, placing his hands on the sides. He began to weep.

They left him there all night, and at daybreak the cell door opened and a fresh, young attendant stepped inside. He stared at the filth and beckoned for Vince to follow him. Vince rose wearily from his filthy sheets and was led to the shower block. He had heard all about shower blocks in prisons and loony bins. *What now?* he thought.

The hot water revived him, a little, and the strong-smelling soap washed the stench from his nose. Thankfully the shower block was empty and only the young attendant was there, who faintly reminded Vince of a distant cousin. The attendant looked like a young John Malkovich (before he got inside his own head).

Vince Taylor had no notion of just how Mary had risen from the dead again, or how she had got into Mount Sinai Asylum. What had *Gladeye* to do with anything? *That crazy-assed woman should be locked up, but not with me*, he thought. Why did Mary leave when she told her to? Mary had been the good wife, but she had never done anything *he* had wanted her to do for him; well, not below the waist anyhow. Why did she go when *Gladeye* told her to?

Once out of the shower and into clean inmates clothes Vince was escorted back to a different cell down the row. He could see a cleaning squad enter room 133 and he was relieved he wasn't going back *there*. Vince was still shaking; he felt cleaner now, but it didn't stop him from putting his hands through his hair and feeling in his ears again, just in case. He had checked all the other orifices at least twice in the shower. He sat down on the bed to contemplate his dire situation.

Milo was the young attendant's name. Considering the asylum could hold so many inmates Vince was surprised to learn, from Milo, that there were only six other inmates in his wing. They were all there for crimes beyond comprehension.

Milo's calm and apparently docile nature lolled Vince into a state of passivity that bordered on sleep. Milo sat down on the bed next to Vince. His deadpan pale face, short black hair, and shy nature made Vince wonder if the orderly had ever heard of sunbathing, surfing, and watching scantily clad girls in tweenie-bikinis—Vince studied the serious face again—perhaps not. He looked like he should join Frances St. Germaine and become an undertaker, or maybe a corpse.

"Who else is banged up in this wing then?"

Milo took sudden, great delight in the revelation.

"There's Slouch, he killed his father after his dad wouldn't let him borrow his Buick. Slink, who did for every dog in Ferry Creek and ate them. I'm a cat lover myself. There's Adler—got to killing people who could play jazz better than him. Then Winster, Whaler, and now you."

"What about Winster and Whaler?"

"Winster set about his business copying the Boston Strangler but he was from Cleveland, and Whaler put poison in cans of beer and killed sixty people."

Vince sat back on the grey blanket. "So they're all killers then?"

"And have you got a problem with that, Vince?"

"One fucking big problem—I'm locked up with a load of mutt-murdering, poisoning-bastard, copy-cat-killing psychos and I hate jazz too."

"Well, I can say I've had many conversations with these gentlemen, and they have all been pretty civil to me."

"You're not female?"

"No, I most definitely am not."

"You're not related to any of them?"

"No."

"Do you like jazz?"

"Er—no."

"Obviously you're not a dog, and you look like you don't drink beer. What've *you* got to worry about?"

"And you're point is, Vince? I thought you'd probably get on with Winster with what he did to the fairer sex."

"Jesus—Milo! Do you think I *wanted* to do what I did to my wife? After all—she was already dead."

"Would you like to talk about that, Vince?"

"Who suddenly turned you into a psychiatrist then?"

"I just thought—I just thought...." replied Milo.

"You do too much thinking."

Milo fiddled with the keys in his hand. "You know, I think it took a great deal of courage to do what you did."

"Get out Milo. I ain't proud of what I did to Mary and I don't need no hero worship, and by the way what nickname have you given me?"

"I haven't as yet but was thinking of Franken—"

Before he could finish Vince dragged him off the bed, opened the unlocked door, and stuck his boot up Milo's ass. Vince pointed at the door, at Milo, then at the lock, indicating what Milo should do, before he did any more damage.

The six inmates on Sanderson Ward were kept away from one another, especially at shower time. Milo would accompany Vince to the cubicle and step aside to give him some privacy. In fact he usually waited for him quite patiently, holding Vince's towel; Vince took his time. He let the hot water pour over his shoulders and down his back. The steam rose to the ceiling, trying to escape, just as he should be doing. In the three days he had been there he had hardly heard a sound from the other inmates. Perhaps they were all too drugged, which made him wonder what Gladeye had in mind for him and why it had not happened yet.

Sometimes he heard the occasional drift of jazz music down the corridor, or a soft knocking on the door. At other times he thought he heard Mary's voice and yet he still had not been seen by any doctor to say he was mad. Well—he *must* be—to do what he did to Mary.

Frankenstein.

Milo was going to call him Frankenstein, but Vince knew that he was no doctor who had made a monster from dug-up body parts. He was Vince Taylor, a man just trying to get a little peace and quiet.

Milo was quiet again too, today. Yesterday, Vince had turned around to find Milo unusually close to his shoulder, as if he was trying to sniff him. Today Milo kept to a reasonable arm's length and looked a little timid.

"I've left you some books on the bed," said Milo in a hushed tone. He backed out of the cell as if he had already disturbed Vince's reading. The door clunked shut.

Milo had put three books on the grey blanket. Vince picked the first one up, Mary Shelley's *Frankenstein*.

"Piss—taker," he muttered.

The next was *The Green River Murders*, still in the dust jacket but well thumbed. "Thinks I'm starting an apprenticeship now." The last book was small and dainty, with a dull red cover and gold edging. He read the title. *The Divine Comedy* by Dante. Good. He had no idea who the fellow Dante was, but he liked the sound of the title and settled down to read with the faint strains of Elvis coming from down the corridor. An hour later he began to nod off and fell into a troubled sleep.

It seemed to Vince that he had only been asleep for a fraction of a second, but the dream was real enough. He dreamt of a dark, dismal wood. He was struggling up a hill. Before him lay three terrible beasts—a leopard, a lion, and a wolf. The wolf was coming down the path towards him, saliva dripping from its mouth in that hungry kind of way that dogs do. But this was no dog, just the biggest fucking thing Vince had ever seen, twice as tall as himself and twice...no, make that a *thousand* times uglier. As it drew closer Vince backed up: not too much, mind, because he didn't want the wolf, the leopard *or* the blasted lion to think he was afraid. No, not Vince Taylor. He wasn't fucking afraid of anything (except dead Mary and Nurse Gladeye.)

The wolf crept closer. Vince backed up some more. The wolf came even closer. Again, Vince backed up, and then he could see amid the dark shadows that the wolf had something in its mouth. Vince froze; the wolf dropped something at his feet—a hand—and what's more, it was Mary's left hand. Vince recognised it from the gold and silver wedding ring, third finger. The wolf merely sat there on its haunches and smiled. Next thing Vince knew, there was Milo with this huge wolf-thing, stroking it and the leopard and lion were strolling round and jumping up at him like two fairground puppies (the leopard and lion were much smaller than the colossal wolf, so *that* was all right then).

Milo picked up the grisly remains of his wife's hand and walked off with all animals in tow up the hill, into the dark woods. *Now, what was that all about?* Vince turned on his heel and scooted down the pathway away from those dark woods. He stumbled in his nightmare and woke himself up.

He struggled to open his eyes. The book had fallen to the floor. Vince sat up and as he did so his hand slipped under the pillow. He felt something cold and pulled it out. The object was not in his hand long enough to leave a smear of blood or anything. He was horrified and began bouncing the thing from hand to hand—then he finally threw it against the wall. It wasn't in his hand long enough, no—but *just* long enough to leave scratches on his skin— five *deep* scratch marks.

The door creaked and Milo stepped over Mary's hand, gold and silver wedding ring and all, but turned his nose up in disgust, and deposited a tray of porridge on Vince's lap.

"You put that there, Milo. You—wormtail shit, didn't you?" The tray was shaking on Vince's lap.

"I don't think so, not my style you see. More Gladeye's thing, if you ask me."

"Well. I'm not asking I'm telling. It was you Milo, you shit."

"Would the person who is considerate enough to bring you breakfast in bed be putting *that* under your pillow?"

Vince threw the tray aside, jumped up and pinned Milo against the wall. "If you didn't put it there how did you know it was under my pillow? Crud. How?"

Milo spluttered, indicating he needed to speak. Vince relented, a little.

"Things are always found under the pillow; roses, love letters, teeth. For glory's sake the tooth fairy puts stuff there!"

Vince slammed him again. "Admit it, you're a liar—a damned liar!" Then he let go.

Milo choked and spluttered again. "D-Damned?... I think the only one who is *damned* is you, Vince Taylor. After all, I'm not the man who sewed his own wife's mouth up, not to mention what happened to her hands—and feet. If anyone is going to Hell—" Milo pointed at the book, "it's you—you're suffering, in fact if you don't repent you'll *stay* here. No little side trips for you, no roundabout course of retribution, straight in and no—will he go to purgatory first? Straight in—no toll charge, no forgiveness, no nothing! Except burning in the eternal fires of Hell. No Elysian field, no rejoicing with your loved ones (because of what you did to her), just the eternal damnation in the eternal fires of—"

"You said that already." Vince kicked him hard in the mouth— it seemed the only good way to shut up his ranting.

Vince heard a noise behind him: just before the lights went out for the second time in the last twelve hours.

On wakening, he felt drowsy and was loathe to open his eyes. Perhaps nurse Gladeye had given himself something from her magic bag? He had a crashing headache. He saw Milo sitting on the end of his bed, nursing a buggered lip, with his eyes full of reproach and yes, pity.

"You can still make it out one day—if you would only embrace the possibility that what you did was very, very wrong."

"I know I did wrong," replied Vince.

"Do you really mean that, Vincent?"

Vince couldn't work this guy out. One minute, for God's sake, he seemed to admire what Vince had done to his wife, the next, Milo condemned him.

"No one ever calls me Vincent, except Mary and my mother. D'you hear that, Milo?"

"Yes, Vincent. I mean *Vince*. Did you read any of the books?" Milo asked.

"Yes, that *Divine Comedy*, but it didn't make me laugh. I just fell asleep and had the worst goddamn nightmare."

"Really, Vince, what sort of nightmare?"

"One about a blasted wolf, twice the size of me or more."

"And was there a lion and a leopard there too, Vince?"

"What?"

"*The Divine Comedy* is an allegorical tale, it isn't meant to be funny."

"You're right about that, it ain't funny at all. What's with you? Yesterday you said it took a lot of courage to do what I did."

"What's with me Vince? With me? I don't recall me doing any such thing. Let's get back that allegory. Do you know what allegory is, Vince?" he said without taking much of a breath, "a story or description in which the characters and events symbolise some deeper underlying meaning."

"Jesus, Milo, I can't even think straight let alone think about God. How much hell does a man have to go through until he gets some peace?"

"An infinite amount, Vince. An infinite amount."

"Will you damn-well stop repeating yourself man."

"Repeating myself, Vince, repeating myself? Well I suppose I do sometimes when I'm agitated—yes." Milo smoothed down the front of his white, buttoned jacket. The kind that dentist's wear but never gets splashed with patient's blood.

"Milo, do you have to hang around me? Couldn't you just leave me alone to my own thoughts? I'd kinda like to make my way through this mess without any distractions."

"Just as you wish. Would you like me to remove the hand?"

Vince took a deep breath and his eyes, before his mouth, answered everything.

"Of course I'd like you to remove the hand."

Milo picked it up, held it as if making an introduction, and with a sheepish smile on his face turned to leave.

"Wait!" Vince snapped, sharper than a starving croc at an eat--as-much-as-you-want diner.

"I want her wedding ring."

Milo put the hand on Vince's tray and without too much disruption of the skin, managed to prise the ring off the finger.

Vince snatched the ring and put it on his wedding finger, in place of the ring he had removed after Mary's funeral.

"I don't know if I should let you keep that. I could put it in the safe—"

"This ring is staying on my finger until I prove I didn't kill my wife—got that?"

"But you did dismember her?"

"Dismembering ain't killing—got that too?"

"Yes, I have that too, Vince, but you really don't have to shout. Now—are you going to eat your porridge?"

Vince looked at Mary's grey hand (that was beginning to ooze something that didn't look like blood this time.)

"No thank you, Milo. I don't think I'm hungry enough."

Frances St. Germaine took it upon herself to visit Vince and was granted permission quickly, as was always the case when a funeral director came to call.

After they briefly discussed the last of the details concerning his wife's grave, Vince whispered to Frances all about Mary's visit. Frances didn't look surprised.

"I know. It wasn't Mary that I buried in the casket. I just weighted it down with sand."

"Why would you do that?"

"I wanted to keep her around and get her to tell someone else what was going on."

"Did she?"

"No. She played dead for my brother. Wouldn't talk. He thought I was crazy for not burying her and wanted to tell the coroner."

"Did you stop him?"

"Yes—for now."

"I'm telling you, Mary is here, right in this piss-poor place, and what's more, Milo has seen her too. Well, part of her. Gladeye— Penelope Maple—is part of it." Vince swept the hair out of his eyes. "Hey—wait a minute who *did* kill Mary?"

"Geoff Newbury."

"The coroner?"

"Yes—the coroner."

"You mean that so-called, respectable coroner?"

"Yes, Vince—the coroner. We have to stop Newbury from killing again," Frances said.

"And just how do you stop a county coroner from doing that? Who would believe us? You never spoke out when I was arrested."

"Would you have?"

Vince shook his head.

"Times up." said an attendant.

"I'll think of something, Vince."

When Vince woke up he found himself in some sort of cellar. The hospital had many of them but not one decked out like the laboratory that belonged to Doctor Frankenstein.

The light was bright enough for him to see a morgue table, and on that table was obviously a body covered in a sheet. Geoff Newbury was hovering over the table. He didn't look as composed as he usually did and he was wearing a smeared, rubber apron.

"You bastard—you didn't kill her too, did you?" Vince groaned.

The door opened and Gladeye entered pulling Frances (who looked like she had been given something from the magic bag) in with her.

"Thank God," said Vince.

"Ah, Miss Germaine. I need to explain. I hope you are not going to be too distressed by what I had to do?"

Frances looked him straight in the eye. "You'll get caught. I know all about it. Others know too!" she threatened. "My brother, my brother will tell."

"You mean this brother, Frances?"

The coroner pulled the sheet off the body, or what was left of the limbless body. Frances could still recognise her brother's face and the blonde hair. She started to weep.

"Why do this — *why*?"

"You are asking that — in a mental institution? It's all about you, Frances, always will be, from now on. Mary is back where she should be now. I'll see that she doesn't get out again."

The door slowly opened and Milo stepped into the room. He pointed a gun at Newbury and Galadeye — mild mannered Milo smiled at Vince.

Frances walked unsteadily over to her brother. She touched him gently on the cheek and Vince pulled her away.

"There's nothing to be done for him now, Frances."

In shock, though still partly sedated, Frances held on tightly to Vince. He moved slowly towards the door.

"We'll get some help Milo and we'll come back for you."

"I can't leave here, Vincent. I can never leave here."

Vince looked down at the ring on his finger, took it off and gave it to Milo. "I think that I need to move on now."

Milo smiled at him. "I rather think that you do, Vincent. I rather think you do."

Vince was about to catch Milo about the name again but he thought better of it. "See you around, Milo."

"Oh, you will, Vincent — you will."

As he helped Frances down the corridor Vince could hear Milo's soft voice.

"What shall we do whilst we wait? I know, let's talk about Dante's *Divine Comedy*. Now — in which circle of Hell do you think you both belong? Any suggestions?"

Pompeii

"For several days before (the eruption,) the earth had been shaken, but this fact did not cause fear because it was a commonly observed feature in Campagnia." Quote from Pliny the Younger: Eyewitness to the Vesuvius Eruption, 24-25 August, 79 A.D.

The women fought by torchlight in the hot, dusty amphitheatre in Pompeii. Stripped to the waist, heads bowed with the weight of their helmets, they faced each other warily. Each armed with a short sword, and shield made of birch and lined with felt. Achillia circled her opponent, and although she could not see the other woman's face, she knew her by her diminutive stature and black hair, cropped to reach just below the helmet. This was the first time Achillia had fought a woman, as she was used to fighting male dwarves who were easy to finish off, and whom she usually dispatched within a few minutes. This was the last woman Achillia wanted to kill, for this was her friend, Amazon.

The crowds urged the female gladiators on, for one of them to strike the first blow. Her friend lunged first and Achillia blocked it with her shield. It was followed by a second fierce thrust from Amazon and Achillia jumped back, almost losing her balance. Steadying herself, she sprang forwards and was forced backwards once more by the blow of a shield upon her arm protector. Achillia didn't want to fight her friend—didn't want to kill her. Amazon recovered and moved forwards again, with renewed vigour, and Achillia had no option but to muster up the aggression she needed to enter the fight with a determination to win.

Both were sweating now, with the weight of their armour and the night continued to descend over the arena like a shroud over the dead. Both women lunged and blocked blows, sidestepping as the thrusts came faster at each other. Amazon moved more quickly, but Achillia was stronger, and her louder clashes with her opponent's armour echoed ominously in the amphitheatre. Suddenly, Amazon stumbled backward and Achillia saw her chance. With all her strength she jabbed her short sword into the stomach of her friend, upwards towards the heart.

Achillia flung her helmet aside and looked down upon the covered face of the dead female gladiator. Wiping the sweat from her brow, she threw her sword aside and made her way out of the amphitheatre, over the bodies of the dead and dying who blocked her exit.

The heat of the day had corrupted the corpses. Slaves, dressed as Mercury, pulled at the rank and bloody pile of defeated gladiators. The slaves moved gracefully as if conducting the souls of the dead to the next world: heads bowed in reverence as they dragged the bodies towards the perimeter of the arena. The crowd watched as Achillia climbed over the mutilated bodies, slipping in their blood as she went. When she had reached as high as was possible, she held up her bloodied hands, to the cheers of the crowd who screamed her name.

In 2007 the summit of Mount Vesuvius, above the excavated ruins of Pompeii, looked fairly innocuous but the mayors of San Sebastiano al Vesuvio and Torre del Greco had, time and time again, pressed the government for a sensible evacuation plan. In 1984 the government evacuated forty thousand people from Campi Flegrei. Chaos had ensued to such a degree that the government turned its back on any future plans—and the conclusion was that seven-hundred thousand people on the north side of Vesuvius could become the new Pompeians when the mountain blew. It *would* erupt again, that was a certainty, but whether it would be within two, twenty or forty years, no one knew. Generations of Neapolitans had lived and died in the shadow of the volcano.

Neapolitans: scooter-mad and crazy to go anywhere so long as they looked good doing it. They rode their scooters and drove their cars, as if each day was their last, and presumably, if the crater did collapse they would die with a smile on their face in remembrance of things past. *La Dolce Vita* then, and the next minute one mad whirlwind of smoke and ashes.

Mia had her own evacuation plan. It wasn't a great one but it was the only one she had, and she had formulated it after a visit to Pompeii a few months earlier. In the countryside there were still the preserved footprints of those who had walked away from the volcano almost two thousand years before. She could see Vesuvius through the window of her classroom where she taught history to 4C. They would be going on a school trip to Pompeii the next day.

"Remember children—those of you who are coming tomorrow. Bring a packed lunch and plenty of water. It will be very hot. Bring sun hats as we will be in the open for most of the day and there will be little shade."

A hand shot up at the back of the class.

"Amadeo?"

"Will it be safe, Miss?"

"Of course. Would I take you anywhere that wasn't?"

Another hand went up.

"Ciana?"

"My dad says that when that mountain goes we will all go with it."

There was a giggle from a few in the class.

"I'm sure that won't happen in our lifetime, Ciana. If it does we will have plenty of warning and will be able to put into operation the evacuation plan."

Mia had little confidence in that plan, but she didn't want to alarm the children. Also, she still wasn't sure how they were going to react to seeing the plaster casts of the inhabitants of Pompeii and especially the dog. She knew how young children were.

"Right—be here at nine a.m. for the bus and don't forget to bring everything with you—lunches, drinks, and hats."

At that moment the bell rang and her class hurried to get their books away and get through the classroom door. Some flung themselves into the arms of parents, others tentatively took hold of their childminder's hands and some children hung back with their friends for a last minute chat before they all went their way, either across the hillside to farms or down to little white houses by the sea.

A few of the parents had objected to the Pompeii trip, saying it was better that the children didn't know about the death and chaos that had happened so long ago. It was all in the past and would probably not happen again for a very long time; after all, they had the evacuation plan. Mia recalled the conversation with one family in particular.

"We don't want to think about the risk, and besides, there isn't any risk as far as we are concerned. We have farms to think about and our families have lived here for generations without anything happening. Children should not think it will happen to us."

Mia was cautious but spoke her mind, sweeping her long red hair out of her face. "It *will* erupt again. Scientists have said so. Perhaps not now, but certainly your children or your grandchildren will know about it."

"Our people will worry about it then. Until that time we prefer not to think about it."

With a shrug on both sides the discussion ended and that parent had stormed off. Mia was confident she could look after the children and they would learn from the trip. What was the point of another generation living in the shadow of Vesuvius, not knowing what it was capable of?

Only ten children, all around nine years old, would be going on the trip to Pompeii. Fabrio, a fellow teacher, would accompany them.

The night before the visit Mia decided to make a simple pasta. She chopped some herbs and washed some tomatoes. She felt a little nauseous but carried on, beginning to chop the tomatoes, until a shaft of sunlight hit the blade of the knife—for an instant she didn't quite know where she was. Then her vision cleared. *She was in the amphitheatre in Pompeii—fighting for her life. She could hear the roar of the crowd and sweat was pouring from her brow.* Another flash of light and she was back in the kitchen, sitting on the floor with the knife in her hand. Had she, almost two thousand years ago, been a female gladiator?

When she began to feel better (which took several minutes), she got up from the floor, poured a glass of wine, and steadied herself against the wooden table.

The next morning Mia felt better and she convinced herself that she had been out in the sun too long. She left her small apartment in San Sebastan and walked to school. She was, embarrassingly, a little late. Another teacher had taken the children to the bus, ready for their departure, and put the rest of Mia's class in with her own for the remainder of the day. Aria, a dour looking teacher, had taken them from Fabrio who now sat on the steps of the bus, hat in hand, patiently waiting for Mia, his constant smile hiding many insecurities. They had been lovers a year before, but split up because—well, Mia hadn't been quite sure why. He always seemed too close to his mother and been too immature for Mia. She still liked him, to some degree, but thought it best to keep some distance between them. Fabrio helped her onto the bus and let his hand linger on her arm, longer than was necessary and she turned to shoot him a warning glance.

Aria was not happy to have a larger class for the day and didn't disguise that fact when she waved them off.

The bus journey was hot and uncomfortable, but the children were excited and Mia was happy to take them. The site itself was enormous, with many buildings restored or left as the archaeologists found them, complete with colourful frescoes. She had a guidebook to the excavations with transparent overlays of the archaeological sites so that the children could see the difference in what each place looked like then, and now. She sat next to Ciana and showed her a few of the pictures. Mia didn't show her one of the frescoes of the house of Vetti, with its lewd subject matter, skipping instead to the forum, the temple of Apollo and The House of the Tragic Poet. Mia had planned their route around Pompeii: they would not be able to see everything, the site was vast, and so she had drawn up a sort of treasure hunt, where each child could tick the things she wanted them to see, off a list. They would see the black and white mosaic of the guard dog with the words, *cave canem* underneath, and the statue of the Faun in the garden of Casa Del Fauno. The theatre too, the bakery (complete with millstones), and of course the plaster casts of the tragic victims of the seventy-nine A.D. volcanic eruption. The parents of the children on the trip had given permission for them to see the casts and Mia had recently shown postcards to them, so they would be prepared when they actually saw them.

Ciana pointed at one picture of the bakery. "They found loaves of bread here, didn't they Miss?"

"That's right, Ciana, but you would break your teeth on them now if you tried to eat them," Mia smiled and turned the page. Paolo knelt on his seat, eager to see too.

"Hey, why is Ciana sitting next to you, Miss? It isn't fair—I want to look at the book too."

"Paolo, sit down. You will be seeing it for real soon. Better to see it close up. You can find the mosaic of the dog."

The children had already made mosaic pictures of the dog in art class, using black and white gummed paper cut into little squares. They were all quite excited to see the real thing.

"Woof," began Paolo and all the children joined in until the noise echoed all over the bus.

The bus driver gave Mia an annoyed look.

"Stop that!" She scolded Paolo, who backed down into his seat quickly, surprised at the harsh quality of her voice. Mia had stood up to reprimand him and she towered threateningly over him. The rest of the children whispered quietly to one another for a few minutes after that until they eventually returned to their good humour.

The bus driver dropped the small party off at the Piazza Marina and would pick them up four hours later at the Piazza Anfiteatro further down the road. The plan was to start at the Temple of Apollo first, and then roughly follow the suggested tour for the four hour trip. However, Mia thought that might be too long for them. She had made red sashes for the children, set against white shirts and blue check dresses so that she could spot them if one lagged behind.

"I'll take Paolo, Ciana, Santino, Gia, and Luciano. Fabrio, you will please look after the rest. Now children, listen, at all times those who I have called out will stay close to me, the rest will stay close to Fabio, understood? Otherwise there will be no treats at the end of the day, right?"

"Yes, Miss," came the chorus, all eager to be on their way; there was the dog to see and name.

It was already getting hot as they climbed up the causeway to the Temple of Apollo. Mia looked up at Vesuvius. She had seen it before but it looked like a brooding mass today, a giant of a thing that festered and would awake eventually with the rage of the forgotten gods. Once inside the temple she let the children look at the sundial and explained to them how it worked. Two bronze statues stood near the portico. One was Apollo shooting arrows, and the other Diana. Paolo was disappointed that Apollo's bow was missing.

"Not everything could survive being buried in ashes."

"I bet I could," replied Paolo beating his chest and stamping about like a little Apollo. "I'd fight my way out of the ash."

As the children trundled around the statues and looked at the sundial Mia could feel the sun beating down on her head. She had left her own hat behind—after making sure that every child had a sun hat on. She started to feel dizzy again, like the night before. For an instant Mia thought she could hear a familiar voice, and indeed it sounded much like her own:

They will slow you down, you will need to leave them.

Recovering, and believing it to be mild heatstroke, Mia wiped the perspiration from her forehead and started to gather the children together again.

"Are you okay, Mia? Here, take my cap. I'm used to the sun more than you."

"Thank you, Fabrio."

In the next few hours they found the mosaic dog, named it Fabrio (the children seemed amused by that), and saw The House of the Faun, complete with bronze statue of the latter, and had a picnic in the Teatro Grande. Behind the theatre was the Quadriportico which had also been used as the gladiator's barracks—which wasn't exactly close to the amphitheatre. The guidebook said weapons and parade costumes had been found there. There were frescoes depicting the Loves of Mars and Venus. Mia hurried the children on.

On the Via dell'Abbondanza, Mia felt unwell again, just like before. One minute she was walking down the long dusty road and then she seemed displaced in time again. Once more she heard the cheers of a crowd and could see quite clearly gladiators in procession returning from the Anfiteatro. Some limping along, leaning on the shoulders of comrades, whilst others who could walk unaided were clearly wounded, holding dirty rags to the multitude of cuts that crossed their bodies. It was the first gladiator that most shocked Mia, for leading the weary men was a female gladiator, head held high, with a bloody sword in her hand. There was no mistaking the woman: she looked just like Mia, had long red hair just like her, although the woman was burnt by long days of prolonged exposure to the sun and her body was stockier, more toned. The woman looked Mia straight in the eye and spoke directly to her. *You will endure, but you will survive.* As quickly as the vision appeared it was gone and Fabrio was holding Mia by the shoulders, talking to her urgently.

"Mia, Mia, are you all right?"

For a moment she didn't recognise him. Then slowly his features became familiar once more and she stared at him.

"I don't know. I feel strange. Did you see?"

"Come on, Mia. Let's make our way to the bus. Not far now."

Some of the children looked worried as they were not used to her being so distant. The heat of the day was getting to them too. They had finished all the drinks they brought and were looking listless in the afternoon heat.

"Can we go home now, Miss? I want to go home," Gia implored. Also—Ciana, a child not prone to tears, began to cry.

Fabrio herded the children together and led them further down the street.

As they walked on down the long Via dell'Abbondanza they felt the first tremors underfoot. Mia put a hand on Fabrio's arm. The street was becoming more crowded with tourists now and a woman close by cried out in alarm.

Fabrio looked concerned and the children started to move closer to the two adults.

"It has done this before, Mia, you know that. Nothing ever comes of it." He shrugged and smiled at the children. "Do you think the authorities would not have seen the warnings? After all, they monitor it."

Mia looked back at Vesuvius and saw a thin vapour trail spiralling upwards which had been seen many times before.

"Right, children, we are almost at the Anfiteatro where our bus will meet us," Fabrio said.

No sooner had he finished speaking when the ground shook with even greater vigour, followed shortly by the sounds of an explosion behind them. A huge force had projected pumice and rock high up into the air and over the children's heads. In the distance, Fabrio could see a small red flow appearing near the top of the crater.

"Children, here—into this building!" called Mia.

The children started to cry as they sought shelter under the roof of the nearby villa. Just then pumice pounded down upon the building like hail and the children huddled instinctively into a corner, walls protecting them on two sides.

Mia looked at the children's anxious faces and tried to think about what to do next.

"It isn't far Mia," said Fabrio. "Perhaps we could get them

through to the bus?"

"Do you really think that it will still be there?"

"Well—it might be."

"Even if we found the bus the roads will be chaos. No bus could get through on the road now. There will be too many people."

"What else can we do?"

Mia thought about the preserved footprints she had once seen and that some of the city's occupants, instead of fleeing to the harbour, had tried to escape through the countryside. It wasn't a great evacuation plan but there weren't many options.

"We'll stay here. Not every time the volcano explodes does it bury the city," Mia tried to put on a brave face but inside she was thinking that this was *the* dreaded eruption that no one had wanted to believe was coming.

The eruption did not cease its violence and as Mia, Fabrio and the children took refuge in the villa the pumice and ash piled up against the doors, almost sealing them in. More than once Mia heard the crack of beams as the roof began to buckle under the weight of the burden. The smell began to make the children sick and the ash began filtering through cracks in the ceiling. They made the decision to leave.

Thankfully, there did come a time when the pounding on the roof subsided and Fabrio just managed to get the main door open. They all tried once more to get down the Via dell'Abbondanza to the edge of the city. As they tried, with great difficulty, to move even a few metres down the cobbled street the ground shook and a crack appeared in the wall of one of the restored Pompeian houses. The two teachers hurried the children along to where the bus should be waiting for them.

When they were almost at the end of road, close to the entrance of the Anfiteatro, the volcano erupted again and roared to the heavens. It was a deafening sound. The crowd panicked as the top part of the volcano collapsed. Darkness closed in immediately as hot ash fell from the sky. Mia and Fabrio grabbed the children closest to them.

"Santino, Ciana, come quickly!" The two adults tried to remain calm but the urgency in Mia's voice made the children even more afraid, if that were possible. Mia and Fabrio dragged the ten children into a tunnel that lead to the Anfiteatro and they began to cry and call out for their parents. Mia tried to dust the hot ash off little Gia's shoulders.

"It is hot, Miss. It hurts so," the child wailed.

They were pushed deeper into the tunnel as other frantic tourists barged in from behind. In the distance Mia could see the dim light of the Anfiteatro. The children clung to her as they were swept along, until she almost tripped. Dozens of the tourists were now seeking safety in the small stone tunnel too, pushing them deeper into the darkness. Fabrio was shouting for the people to stop but his voice was drowned by the cries of the crowd. There was hardly any room to move as more tourists poured in and shoved the children underfoot. Mia thought that she heard the crack of a child's back, as she screamed at the crowd to stop.

"The children — watch out for the children!"

She saw their red sashes disappear one by one as she lost track of them. She screamed again and shouted their names. She had three of the children, and one of them was Paolo. She was too blinded by her own panic and the darkness to see who the other two were. She hoped that Fabrio had some of them. Mia reached down and could feel the head of one boy as he dropped to his knees and clung to her legs. She hauled him back up. Then — before her, she could see a little more light. Mia stifled a sob. *No!* The crowd was pushing them into the open again, into the arena where the hot ash was falling like winter snow and people were clasping their hands over their mouths to try and block out the heat that was searing their lungs.

Most of the children were lost to her now, many were trampled underfoot by a hysterical crowd that didn't realise what it was doing. Once in the open Mia felt the hot ash on her skin and burning pain as she tried to breath. Gia was dead already in her arms and Mia looked back at the tunnel, at the people lying on the ground, charred by the ash. They coughed, choked and reached out blindly with hands that could only capture the dead. Mia could hear what sounded like a hurricane rushing through the streets.

As she fell to her knees tears made a trail through the ash that blistered her face. She looked at the pile of bodies that partially blocked the entrance. She saw a flash of red. For a brief moment she saw herself standing astride the dead with a bloody sword in one hand. Then she heard the words in her head.

For once — I'd rather die with some dignity than climb over the bodies of others.

Deathside

"And I shall have some peace there,
for peace comes dropping slow,
Dropping from the veils of morning
to where the cricket sings."
By kind permission of A.P. Watt Ltd,
on behalf of Grainne Yeats, from
The Lake of Innisfree, Poems of W. B. Yeats,
the MacMillan edition 1962.

"When men and women die, other people summon priests, their loved ones, or the doctor. Lorne Delaware wanted me. He said that no one else would be able to see that his wife, Darla, got there safely to the other side. You see, Captain; I know that it is at the moment of death that the dying *are* at their most vulnerable, for they slip into some dreamlike state. At that moment *It* could snatch them. Take them, to that no man's land as their soul leaves the body, seconds before they can muster the strength to pass over."

"Are you shitting me?" was the captain's response. "What off-world notion is that? You're that crazy goon I read about, the one who says that there is something that grabs us when we die."

I shrugged my shoulders. "I can't help it if you don't believe me, Captain. I'm telling the truth as I see it."

"You're damned right I don't believe you."

"But even if you don't believe it, no one should die alone, right?" It was more of a suggestion than a statement.

The captain thought for a while. "I don't believe a word of what you have said, John Valen, but on the other hand if you want to sacrifice yourself to this virus, then hey—that's your problem. I don't think much of our chances, after what the doctor told me. But once you go into the isolation unit on this ship, you stay there—understand?"

"I understand."

"No one will come out to us from Althea, they are too afraid. Even with stringent quarantine regulations, they won't come. I've asked them." The captain began to cough. As I left the room he slammed his fist down on the table and his coughing became more persistent.

Looking back now, it was just like the time Darla passed over, but Lorne had more faith in me then. I began to save so many. After that I could have had anything I wanted, status and wealth, but I only wanted one thing, and that was to get away from what I'd seen. That's why I booked passage on this voyage; to get away from the dark entity that was hungry for souls and haunted the dying. The dying knew real terror and now I knew it too. I was running scared and my fear had caught up with me.

We had been stricken by some alien virus and it was picking us off, one by one. I had told the captain who I was, because I was afraid for the entire ship, full of families with children. They thought they were on an easy run to Althea, a planet which was in the Poseidon galaxy, *"A Water World Beyond Your Wildest Dreams,"* the promo declared. In reality, if they all died, they would be facing the greatest journey they had ever taken. Just how was I going to see that they all made it to the Luminary safely?

In these last few weeks, some families complained of a mild sickness but it seemed nothing much to worry about, that is until half the crew became very ill and the travellers started to panic. We were only five days away from our destination.

I had done everything I could for Darla and Lorne had known that. I had been very close to her, in those last moments as I held her in my arms. I kept a cool head, not panicked, and never let my guard down once. I had been Darla's bodyguard, or rather the guardian of her soul, and delivered her to the Luminary. The Luminary are from another world, for indeed there is one—in fact, there are many. I had ensured that Freya Banks had gotten there safely, and I saw her shimmering form dance and smile as they led her away. With John Ryan it was another story. The evil thing (for I had never found a name that could encompass the horror), descended upon him like a huge black shroud, stifling his soul. When my concentration lapsed and I became weaker, *It* blighted and withered him away. *That* is what has haunted me since. I wish I could save every soul on Earth, but I knew that was an impossible task.

I was running away again. Lorne was running too now, and had left Earth a bitter man, mourning the death of his wife. It was to be some sort of new beginning for him and his daughter, Celina, but now they were facing the deadly virus and the other unseen enemy.

That's where I came in. If the worst came to the worst and they died, I would try and ensure their safe delivery. I have seen, with my own eyes a soul snatched from the arms of the Luminary and dragged screaming away. I couldn't stand the thought of that happening to Celina. Then there was me. I was not afraid of dying but what really scared the shit out of me was—just who would ensure *my* safe delivery to the other side?

I had been allowed, once suited up, to sit with the dying. In the last seven days I had won every battle but one. For how long could I carry on? I never left the confines of the isolation unit. Even the Luminary looked worried and that was saying something. If anyone had told me a year ago it was possible there would be this death-side struggle…I would have laughed in their face. The entity would surely want me more than anyone else, as I had cheated it so very often.

I did what I could for the dying and then the captain became really sick. With only an isolation suit between us, we communicated. The captain was sweating profusely and his hands looked marble-veined. He was only in his mid-thirties but he looked much older at that moment. He struggled to find the words:

"Look—look, John, I have never seen anything like this before. It will pick us off one by one, all of us dead within the next week, unless we do something about it." The captain coughed and looked like he was going to throw up.

"I don't know what to do," I admitted.

He could hardly sit up in his bed. "I have no idea how the virus got on board. All I know is that it is highly contagious...and if *we can't* work out what is going on, we either all die on board...or we can try again to get help and risk spreading the virus."

I stared out of the window into deep space. "If we all die and someone comes to salvage the ship, won't this spread?"

"I don't know," he said with a sorry shake of his head.

It wasn't the thought of dying that scared me. There are deaths and there are Deaths, and once in a while there comes along a Death that is oh, so special, different in so many certain and profound ways—and that would be mine. There are no other guardians like me, as far as I know. There would be no one there to free me from *Its* cold grasp. I didn't know why *It* couldn't come near me when I was alive, but when I was dead I feared that would be a different matter.

Three days before we reached our destination, more and more of the passengers succumbed to the sickness and panic began to spread. Whole families lay huddled together in corridors and in their quarters, either too sick to move or too terrified to leave for fear of contamination. Three days before—what?

I went to intercede for the captain. He was unconscious now, oblivious to the coming onslaught. I sat down on his bed and waited. I did not have to wait long. Through the visor in my suit I could see the entity moving closer to the captain. His death-rattle became more pronounced and the black shroud crept closer, threatening to envelope us both. This terror was final: nothing could have made me shake more as *It* tried to become more manifest. I could see the white-balled eyes fix on us both. The terrible eyes were the only thing that remained constant in *Its* shifting shape and shroud. I could smell the foulness of it, even inside the suit, as I cradled the dying man in my arms and hoped against hope that the Luminary would come in time. The captain took his last, rattling breath and I could see his body shimmer. There were only seconds remaining before his soul would leave his body and the thing would take him away.

I felt myself slipping into unconsciousness as fear filled my mind. I felt the entity try to take me as well as its prey. *I must fight it. I must.* I felt myself giving up, succumbing to the will of something that should not live, that should be dead itself. Then I felt the terror cease and I saw them—the Luminary surrounded us, caressed and reassured us. I saw them take the captain. The entity retreated before their incredible presence.

After the captain died and the disease became rampant I saw no reason to stay in the isolation unit. The virus was spreading too fast. After all, there was no one to bring the dying to me, so I went to them. I could not get to everyone in their last moments. Whilst attending one family, all dying at the same time, I was deserting another—but at least in my desperation I never turned to God. I didn't know who the Luminary were, but I felt that no manmade religion could readily explain them away. They did not seem to need divine intervention to help them. They seemed like good Samaritans to me, who themselves took a risk to intercede. I believe they are the loved ones of the dead, who are drawn back from who knows where? Possibly, they are souls who have had an actual physical connection with the deceased whilst they were alive. I may be wrong. I was an orphan and spent my formative years in a home where I was careful never to get close to anyone— usually because they went away.

No one would be waiting for me.

I deposited the dead in an airlock and ejected them into space. Their marbled faces a parody of the beautiful Greek statues that were still to be found in the museums on Earth. I hoped that the virus would die with them. I felt defeated when Lorne died. His body was dumped into space and floated slowly away with a look of terror fixed firmly on his face. The Luminary hadn't come to him in time and I hadn't been there for him either. *It* had interceded.

The last day before the ship reached our destination, I attended the death of the only other person left alive on board. Lorne had died two days earlier and his little girl now lay in my arms, with her marble–veined hands trying to find someway through my isolation suit to get to me. It was at that point I gave up. Who was I kidding? No one would come board the ship so long as there was anyone else alive. Even the salvage crews had left us alone. I took off my gloves and held her little hands in mine. I may have been tired—but there was no way *It* was going to get at her. There was no sign of the entity. It was not long before the Luminary came to take her away. Amongst them was Darla, for it was her little daughter, Celina, who had just died.

Soon it would be my turn. I was the last man standing. I felt what it was like to be truly alone. Althea was only a day away but I might as well have been on the other side of the universe. I started to cough and tasted blood in my mouth. I looked down at my hands and saw that they had taken on a blue-white hue and felt myself weakening. I could make out the dark shape of the entity starting to form. There would be no Luminary for me, to light my way to some other world. I had been alone in life and I would be alone in death, except for *It…* that waited, biding its time now for my life to slip away. At least Celina was safe.

My breathing became more laboured and my dying breath was upon me. It left in three long, drawn-out gasps and gently I set myself free of my earthly body, and faced my nemesis. Too weak after this rebirth to move; I felt as thin as air and helpless to do anything as *It* came closer. The impenetrable blackness crept forwards towards me. *It* hesitated as a great, new light began to fill the room. I felt some of my energy return and I managed to drift round towards the light.

It was such a beautiful sight, for there before me was every soul I had ever saved, old and young alike. Amongst the hundreds I could see those of Darla and little Celina. It was Celina who then held out her tiny hands to me.

Author note: This story was written for my mother shortly after her death. I read "The Isle of Innisfree" by Yeats, at her funeral. 13th May 2005.

CPSIA information can be obtained at www.ICGtesting.com
Printed in the USA
LVOW05s0818051213

363844LV00002B/256/P